# A Heart Held Captive

By Katy Eeten

A HEART HELD CAPTIVE by Katy Eeten

ANAIAH ROMANCE
An imprint of ANAIAH PRESS, LLC.
7780 49th ST N. #129
Pinellas Park, FL 33781

First Anaiah Romance eBook edition March 2019
First Anaiah Romance Print edition March 2019

Edited by Candee Fick
Book Design by Laura Heritage
Cover Design by Laura Heritage

For my kids, Lincoln and Jackson.
You light up my life.

# ACKNOWLEDGEMENTS

THANK YOU TO MY PUBLISHER, Anaiah Press, for all they've done to help me grow as a writer. I'm thankful for my editor, Candee Fick, who painstakingly combed through my manuscript to make it come alive in a way I couldn't have done on my own. I'm beyond grateful for my husband, Jason, for allowing me to rejoice and worry and vent and stress about this book and all the labor it entailed. A big thank you to my sweet kids who have put up with many nights of Mom typing away in her bedroom. And thank you, Lord, for your unending love and grace. I'd be lost without it.

# CHAPTER 1

W*HEN A GUY GOES OUT OF his way to make his girlfriend happy, he should get bonus points.*

Cole Pearson glanced outside his car window. It was too beautiful a spring day to not be tailgating at a baseball game or hiking the nature trail near his house. Instead, his girlfriend had sent him halfway across town for her favorite frozen coffee drink while she basked in the sun on his patio with her toy poodle. Snowy was lucky he was so cute, as he had a knack for peeing everywhere he wasn't supposed to, including inside Cole's shoes and on his favorite overstuffed chair.

Heather insisted he go to the coffee shop on Hickory and Main Street, which was six miles and several stoplights further than the exact same coffee shop a mere three blocks from his house. *"They don't make my drink the same at that one,"* she'd said. He'd learned from past experience that it wasn't worth the argument, so instead, he'd clenched his jaw and grabbed his keys.

Trying to make the best of his situation, he turned the radio dial to the broadcast of the local baseball game, then rested his elbow outside the wide-open window for the duration of the drive. After grabbing his Americano and Heather's frozen drink from the barista at the drive-thru window, Cole headed back home. Hopefully, she'd be grateful that he'd gone out of his way instead of finding something else to complain about. Was it bad that he was more excited to quell her nagging for a frappe than he was to actually spend time with her?

On the up side, things with Heather were comfortable, and he was certain that was the reason he'd stayed with her as long as he had. Call it selfish, but he didn't relish the thought of going back to the phase of a relationship where he had to care about whether his socks had holes or pretend that he enjoyed watching chick flicks. But was comfortability worth sacrificing a true connection with someone? Did they even have that special spark?

He turned the radio up to distract himself from the knot that had formed in his stomach. He'd been wondering for a while now if they should call it quits, but actually saying the words was another story. Most of his relationships in the past had ended out of necessity—his high school romance because of the distance caused by their separate college selections; his main college squeeze deciding to move three states away for her job after he'd landed the perfect position at a physical therapy clinic right in town; catching his previous girlfriend in the act of cheating four years ago.

Those relationships had had clear and necessary—if not pain-free—endings.

But Heather... well, she was different. Nothing had really changed, nothing bad had happened. He just wasn't sure he loved her. In fact, he *knew* he didn't. So, what was he doing? Why was he complacent being in such a loveless relationship? He ran a hand through his hair. What was he waiting for before he would decide to stop this charade?

When he pulled into his driveway, Heather was now reclined on a chaise lounge chair, staring down at a fashion magazine on her lap while Snowy licked the cement slab nearby. Cole grabbed her drink, the condensation on the outside of the plastic cup soaking his hand, and forced a smile as he approached. As usual, not a single hair of Heather's was out of place, and her makeup was fresh and flawless despite the fact that they had zero plans this lazy Saturday afternoon. No one could deny Heather's outward beauty. The jealous glances from other guys when they were out in public made him feel like she was a catch, but they had no idea what he had to put up with. Besides, he was more of a jeans-and-T-shirt kind of guy.

She didn't look up from her magazine as he handed her the cup but muttered an obligatory, "Thanks," before taking her first sip. A moment later, her face twisted in disgust. "This is *melted.*"

He forced himself not to roll his eyes. "Sorry. It was a bit of a drive, and it's warm today."

The expression on Heather's face told him she didn't want his excuses. "Great. I've been waiting for the last half hour for a frozen drink, and now it's basically water."

Cole studied her. Hadn't he spent the last half hour playing errand boy? It was the last straw. While he enjoyed the arm candy, he could no longer stay with someone so narcissistic. He had far too many years ahead of him to settle for someone who only thought of herself. Comfortability was great, but enough was enough. "I can't do this anymore. This relationship isn't working, and I think we should see other people."

His bold words surprised even himself, but the fact that they had been so easy to say was further proof that this was the right decision. The relief was instant, but he scanned Heather's face for her reaction. Hopefully, he hadn't completely blindsided her. Comforting a bawling woman was not on the list of things he wanted to do today.

"Are you serious?" Heather shoved her sunglasses on her forehead, revealing her bewildered eyes.

Cole sat down on the other lounge chair so they were at the same level. How could he make her understand? "I am. I've been thinking about it for a while, and I just feel like we're on two different paths. I mean, we've shared a lot of good times, but I..."

Before he could finish his sentiment, he was silenced by the shock of freezing liquid all over his face. It took a moment to realize that his now ex-girlfriend had thrown her drink at him. *Well, that was mature.* But despite the awkwardness of being covered in cold coffee, he was relieved to see Heather stand and pick up Snowy.

As she stomped away to her car, she called over her

shoulder, "You're making a big mistake."

Cole shook his head, almost laughing at her words. The only mistake he'd made was staying with her so long in the first place. In fact, for the first time in nearly two years, he felt *free*. Like he had his life back again. He wasn't quite sure what to do next with his newfound independence, but the obvious first step was to go inside and wash off the mess. He chuckled at how that wretched drink had actually ended up being the best cup of coffee he'd ever bought. Worth every penny to have secured his freedom.

As he leaned over the sink and splashed water on his face, he shook his head at his own foolishness. At how long it had taken him to realize that a one-sided relationship was far worse than having to find someone new. And why did he think that was the only alternative, anyway? Wasn't it perfectly acceptable to live the bachelor life for a while? No women, no relationships. Maybe that's what he needed—a break from the opposite sex, a clear head, a little change in perspective. *A little "me" time.*

Turning off the faucet and reaching for a towel, a plan formed in his head. He was sick of relationships, sick of dating altogether. Today was the day he would press the Reset button on his life—no more dating for at least six months. Maybe longer. He couldn't hide the smile on his face at the thought of what the next six months would hold.

# CHAPTER 2

L IKE THE HEATHER BREAK-UP DAY a year before, it was
a beautiful Saturday in early May. Except on this
particular morning, Cole was stuck at work. A glance at
his watch told him he was already over halfway through
his shift; less than three hours to go.

The state-of-the art physical therapy clinic where he
worked was hosting its monthly open house, trying to
appeal to those who might not have a compelling
medical need for physical therapy, but that could benefit
from elective services if their insurance agreed to pay or
if their budgets allowed.

A couple of teenage girls glanced his way from the
lobby, but when he nodded at them, they turned away
and giggled. It was a good thing his coworker, Patty,
had been the one to greet them and their dad moments
ago. He wasn't sure the blushing teens would make it
through the tour if he were their guide. Patty led them

down the hall to show them the facility, but not before she gave him a smirk.

Cole knew what that was about. There was a rumor floating around the clinic that during the open houses he worked, their sign-on numbers were significantly higher than others, due to not only his sandy brown hair and flawless smile, but also his easy-going, friendly disposition. He shook his head at the baseless rumor. He hadn't been opposed to harmless flirtations in the past, but it would be unethical to fraternize with a patient. And besides, it had been a full year since his dating ban began. The first month had been a breath of fresh air— he was on no one's schedule. He ate what, where, and when *he* wanted. Watched only what *he* wanted on TV.

The second month of his social experiment, he'd started to yearn for female companionship. But instead of caving, he'd let his sister-in-law, Maria, talk him into attending her church—reluctantly at first, maybe even out of obligation to his brother, who often worked Sunday mornings. But it had soon become more than that for him. Not only had the truths revealed there lead him to an earnest relationship with God, it had also convinced him to extend his dating strike for another six months, opting for spiritual enrichment over the potential of relationship bliss. Oddly enough, during the entire past year, no one had crossed his path that sparked his interest or made him wish he could renege on his self-imposed ban.

As he shuffled papers at the front counter, he noticed a flyer for the Pediatric Medicine Awards banquet. This was the first year he'd been nominated for an award. While he was proud of that accomplishment, the recognition he would receive did not answer the quiet want in his heart. He'd recently become aware of the fact that he was finally ready to settle down with a person, not a plaque. More than ever, he wanted his next relationship to be for the long haul.

Just then, a boy wearing a leg brace on his right leg limped through the door, followed by a slender woman with a pale complexion and light-blond hair pulled into a pony-tail. The boy appeared to be eight or nine years old. He wore a dirty shirt and ripped jeans, and Cole instantly wondered what the cause of his injury was. What was his range of motion? Open houses were hard, because he always wanted to jump right in and start addressing the issues. But he had to remind himself these weren't his patients yet.

"Good afternoon! Welcome to PT Possibilities." Cole was somehow able to make the scripted greeting sound perfectly natural. "My name is Cole. How can I help you?"

The woman smiled politely, though her lips were pressed firmly together. "Well, I guess I'd... I mean *we'd*," she corrected herself, smiling at the boy, "like a tour of the facility. Do you do that? Are we here on the right day?"

Cole couldn't help but notice the sweet, gentle quality in her voice. "Absolutely. We just ask that you fill out the basic contact info on the top of this form." He handed her a clipboard with a pen attached to it by a thin grey chain. As she took it from him, he noticed the absence of a wedding ring on her finger—not that it mattered, given the clinic's rule about fraternization. But still, she was cute. "You can skip everything below that first dotted line, and if you like what you see or want to sign up for treatments or more info, we can take care of the rest after the tour. How does that sound?"

Shifting her narrow frame, the woman nodded. "Sure. I mean, good. Thank you, uh… Doctor—"

Doctor. He liked the sound of that. He could have been one, too, based on the amount of student loans he'd finally paid off. "Not a doctor. You can call me Cole."

The woman smiled with relief, small dimples forming on each of her cheeks. "Thank you, Cole."

Holding the clipboard in one hand, she guided the limping boy to a nearby seat with the other. He watched out of the corner of his eye as she filled out the paperwork. Was the boy her son? Did that make her a single mom? She was attractive, but not in a showy way—not like Heather had been. There was an air of inexplicable innocence about her, and one of those faces that could get away without wearing any makeup, which he suspected she wasn't wearing that day. She seemed young, but something in her face revealed a maturity that might go unnoticed with a casual glance. It was possible she was even close to his thirty-three years.

*Dial it back, Cole. You can't date clients anyway.* He grabbed his own clipboard with the literature he would be using to try to sell their services for the woman's son, and moments later, she returned the form to the front desk with the boy by her side.

Cole glanced at it briefly in order to find out his potential patient's name. "You must be Tyler?" He smiled, focusing his attention on the boy who frowned and stared at his feet. Cole then scanned the form again, but the line for parents was blank. Instead of searching the rest of the fields for more information, he held his hand out to the woman. "And you are?"

"Oh, I'm Emily." She reached out to shake his hand. "Sorry, this is all a bit new to me."

"No worries." Cole turned his attention back to the boy, wondering what his story was. "It's nice to meet you, Tyler. I think you're going to like what you see here. Have you visited any other physical therapists?"

The boy nodded but seemed unwilling, if not unable, to offer anything further. Cole frowned. He'd seen his share of questionable accidents, even outright abuse. The vibe he was getting from this boy made his stomach uneasy. But Emily hardly seemed the type to allow something to happen to her son.

The woman cleared her throat. "We toured another facility the other day, but it seemed like they barely had time for us. And it looks like insurance isn't going to cover this, so… I want to know it's a good fit, especially if I'm going to be paying out of pocket. You know what I mean?"

Cole nodded. "I completely understand. We know this type of service can be a drain on the checkbook, but rest assured we take our patients' well-being as our number one priority. And we can check with the insurance company just to be sure. But honestly, you can't put a price on excellent care for a loved one."

It was a cheesy line, but the manager of the practice insisted they recite it to potential clients, so over the years it had become routine for him. He asked a few more questions of Tyler, receiving only minimal responses from the quiet boy, whom he found out was nine years old and recovering from a broken leg and a dislocated shoulder—the result of two separate incidents. That was either really bad luck, or he had an abused boy on his hands. He shot a few darted glances toward Emily to see if she might be the reason for the boy's shyness. Or maybe she was covering for an abusive ex? He wasn't sure, but he would definitely try to get to the bottom of his injuries by the end of the tour.

As they walked around the facility, Cole explained what a therapy session would entail and all the opportunities available to their patients.

"PT Possibilities specializes in pediatric rehabilitation, so you've come to the right place." He primarily addressed Emily as they walked and talked, knowing that the decision of whether to commit ultimately rested with her. "We use more up-and-coming methods and procedures than most standard physical therapy practices. I've seen firsthand the radical transformations that traditional methods can take months to bring about, if at all. And I know not everyone can afford it, but I strongly believe everyone should be given a chance to thrive. We can provide that possibility."

The rote speech took on a new meaning as he studied the bashful boy before him. He often saw his work as just that—work. But every now and then, someone like Tyler came along who made him remember the difference he could make in a kid's life.

Physically, no doubt. But in other ways, too. If Tyler was in a bad situation, he wanted nothing more than to swoop in and save him from it all.

They entered a closed hallway with three upholstered chairs facing a large glass window, just as Patty and her small tour exited the adjoining therapy room. He smiled at the girls out of instinct, which led to another chorus of giggling. Cole suppressed a groan, thankful that his current audience included no teenagers.

As the exit door closed behind Patty's group, he gestured through the glass window. "This is where the magic happens." The facility resembled a weight room, with blue foam mats on the floor, a small set of wooden steps in the corner, large inflatable exercise balls, parallel bars, and other fun gadgets used during a typical physical therapy session. This clinic far surpassed the other one he'd worked at his first few years out of college. Their budget had been minimal, and it had shown in the quality of their equipment. He felt blessed to have worked at PT Possibilities for the past six years instead.

He led Emily and Tyler through a steel door and into the expansive room, showing off some of the more high-tech contraptions in an attempt to convince them to stay. Tyler scanned the room in silence, but his quirked lips showed he was impressed.

At the end of the tour, they walked back to the front of the office, and Cole turned to his audience of two. "Do you have any questions?"

Disinterested in the details, the boy limped over to

the waiting area where he began watching TV. Meanwhile, by the look of Emily's glazed-over eyes, Cole wondered if he'd overloaded her. Hopefully, she could at least tell how much he enjoyed what he did and how sincerely he believed in what took place within these walls.

"Do you have anything that shows me how much all of this costs? I mean, when insurance isn't in the picture?" She bit her lip and glanced over at Tyler.

Cole rifled through the paperwork on his clipboard before handing her a pamphlet. He watched her study the numbers, wishing it didn't always have to come down to price. "The back page explains our payment plans, so please know we'll do whatever we can to make this financially possible if it's what you want."

Tyler needed therapy to get back to being fully mobile after the nasty break he had suffered. But based on his ragged clothes and Emily's pointed questions, he sensed that cost was the only thing preventing them from being all in.

Just as he was about to remind her that one couldn't put a price on caring for a loved one, she opened her mouth to speak. "I'd like to commit to two months of therapy for Tyler. If you end up needing to see him for that long, that is. And we can see how it goes after that."

Cole smiled. "I'm so happy to hear that! Your son will be really well taken care of here."

Emily's body stiffened, her eyes wide. "Oh, he's not my son."

Cole pressed his lips together, hoping he hadn't offended her. How had he misread the situation? He glanced at the form she'd filled out. "I'm sorry. I guess I didn't catch what your relationship is then. Sister? Aunt?"

Emily's face grew red. "Um, no relation. I guess I should have explained up front. I'm a nurse at Kansas City Med. I met Tyler this past week when he came in for his shoulder. I saw that his leg wasn't healing as quickly as it should, based on the history I read in his charts." Emily lowered her voice as she continued. "And since he's in foster care, I knew it was unlikely he would be given the treatment he truly needed."

Foster care. That explained it. At least that meant someone had intervened, even if a little too late. But did Emily even have the legal right to bring him here, or would they get in trouble with the authorities? He didn't like the sound of this, although he longed for the boy to get the help he needed.

Emily glanced over at Tyler watching television and paused before refocusing her attention on Cole. "He's a good kid. He just needs a chance to get back on track. Thankfully, his social worker agreed to let me pursue this."

Cole blinked and shook his head as he tried to absorb what he was hearing. He swallowed hard. "Wow. What made you decide to fork over this kind of cash for a stranger?"

"Well, it's like you said. You can't put a price on caring for a loved one, right?" She smiled softly.

Cole tilted his head, confused. "But... you said you don't even *know* him."

Emily gave a nonchalant shrug. "*I* don't, no. But he

has to be a loved one to *somebody.*"

# CHAPTER 3

A LOVED ONE TO SOMEBODY. COLE frowned. From where he sat, that supposed loved one had done more harm than good. After discussing the logistics of what the next few weeks would entail, he scanned the area to ensure confidentiality before asking for more information on Tyler. "You don't have to betray any confidences that will get you in trouble, but I'd like to understand the situation better, if that's at all possible."

Emily peeked over at Tyler, who was watching cartoons, completely oblivious to the two of them talking at the counter nearby. Then she glanced around at the empty lobby before facing Cole and responding, her voice nearly a whisper. "His story breaks my heart. His biological dad is out of the picture, and from what his social worker told me when I asked for permission to help, his mom has been on and off drugs for the past few years, which left her boyfriend with the run of the house. The broken leg was from the boyfriend pushing him down the stairs a while ago. Tyler somehow kept that under wraps until a few weeks later, when his teacher noticed bruises—completely unrelated to the stairs incident—on his arms and cheeks. Tyler's mom and her boyfriend were questioned after the teacher reported her suspicions, and the full story came out. And then, Tyler was placed into foster care."

Cole furrowed his brow. A boy that age should be riding his bike around the neighborhood, not worrying about his mom's abusive boyfriend. Accidents were one thing, but this broke his heart. "Poor kid. That's... that's terrible."

Emily shifted her feet and sighed. "I know. A few more weeks passed by the time I met him. He came to the ER with a dislocated shoulder from a school bully. Tyler had supposedly instigated the fight, but it was clear the other boy had the upper hand. I read his charts and medical history, and my heart just ached for him. Despite the fight that brought him to the ER in the first place, he is just a super sweet kid who's gotten the short end of the stick in life. So, I felt like I had to intervene."

Cole nodded, in awe at Emily's compassion. Would he have done the same in her situation? He wasn't so sure. "That's heart-breaking. But what you're doing is amazing. I'm really impressed."

"Oh, don't be." Emily waved her hand in the air, dismissing his praise. "Anyone would have taken action of some sort. He just needs love."

Her words tugged at his heart. *We all just need love.* And this generous woman was giving the boy the same gift God gave them all.

Emily glanced over at Tyler, and a smile lit up her face. The joy she had in helping this boy she barely knew was endearing. Contagious, even. He had never known such selfless generosity, and for a second, he wondered if he should offer Tyler's therapy pro bono. Not that he had a say in that. Okay, now he was getting carried away.

"Tyler, we have to get going." Emily returned her attention toward Cole once the boy stood to join them. "I'll wait for the call to set up our first appointment this coming week."

"Sounds good." Cole shook her hand, then smiled and held out a closed fist to Tyler as he did with all his young patients. Tyler stared wide-eyed at Cole's fist for a moment, then a small smile crept to his face as he curled his fingers together and fist-bumped Cole's hand. Considering their only interaction until now had been a few mumbled words, Cole was pleased with this bit of progress and hopeful he'd be able to help the boy open up even more over time.

He watched them leave, then promptly walked to his office to be by himself. He needed a moment to make sense of what had just transpired. This sweet young woman was spending not only her Saturday but also a good chunk of her paycheck on a boy she barely knew— and his company's services weren't exactly cheap. The whole concept stunned him a bit, and for some reason, Heather's image came to mind. No, he wasn't used to people being so kind, especially to perfect strangers.

To have someone like Emily—someone who would

go out of her way to pay for a stranger's physical therapy—walk unassumingly through the doors of his clinic was refreshing. And challenging, in a good way. He knew without a doubt he wanted to know this woman better. To find out what made her tick. Once he got over the shock of her sheer generosity, he reviewed his schedule for his next opening and headed to the front desk.

Like he'd told Emily, the receptionist would call on Monday to set up the initial consultation, so Cole attached a detailed note to Tyler's paperwork. He wanted to be sure Tyler's case would be assigned to him, and Friday was the first opening where their schedules aligned. He also put a reminder on his own desk to follow up on this case on Monday. This one was special, and he wanted to be sure nothing slipped through the cracks.

EMILY WAS UPDATING A chart at the nurse's station Monday morning when her cell phone vibrated in her pocket. She glanced at the unfamiliar number. Since she was expecting a call about Tyler, she walked toward the staff break room before answering.

"Hi, Emily. This is Shannon calling from PT Possibilities," the professional but friendly voice on the other end said. "I'm calling to set up a consultation for Tyler. It says here you met with Cole on Saturday, is that right?"

"Yes, yes it is." Emily was unable to hide the smile that came to her face knowing Tyler was going to get the therapy he needed. Although, deep down, she knew he needed more than just physical therapy. Would he ever be able to get on his feet in this lifetime? Would someone take him in and love on him the way every nine-year-old needed to be loved? The way she'd longed to be loved at that age?

"Okay, well he asked me to set you guys up for an hour session on Friday afternoon. Does 4:00 work for you?"

Emily had off work Friday, and the last time she had talked to Tyler's foster parents, Fridays were good for them as well. "I believe so. Can I call you back if there's a problem after talking with Tyler?"

"Of course. I'll put you down for Friday at 4:00. Just be sure to give us a twenty-four-hour notice if you have to cancel or reschedule, okay?"

Emily's smile grew wider. "Will do. Thank you so much! Do I need to bring anything?"

"Yes, you'll need to contact Tyler's social worker and fax over the authorization to release his medical records. Also, I see you're marked as out-of-pocket, but we can always retro insurance coverage if it turns out it's available."

Emily had already made a number of unsuccessful calls to request government assistance, but after praying about it, she didn't mind footing the bill herself. After all, she would spare no expense for her own child's well-being if she had one—it wasn't Tyler's fault his parents weren't in the position to do the same.

"Oh, and we'll want to schedule Tyler's next several appointments depending on how often Cole decides he needs to be seen. So, you may want to bring your calendar as well," Shannon added.

"Thank you. See you then!" After hanging up, Emily walked back to the nurse's station, opting to call Tyler's foster mom after work to share the good news. The choice to go with PT Possibilities felt like a wise one, and she was glad Cole would be the therapist working with Tyler. He had been so nice and knowledgeable, and Tyler seemed to respect him—he had been shy at first, but he'd warmed up throughout the duration of the tour. Clearly, Tyler needed positive male influences in his life, and from the very little she knew about Cole, he seemed to at least be a step in the right direction. In fact, her gut told her he would fit the bill quite nicely.

Of course, Cole was attractive as well, but truth be told, that wasn't something that mattered much to Emily anymore. In another life, she may have gotten tongue tied around him or looked forward to seeing him again, flirting with him like a high school girl, fantasizing about where their encounters might lead.

But Emily hadn't been interested in a romantic relationship in years. Not since the accident, when her world was turned upside down and her priorities drastically changed. Now, she preferred being single, as it allowed her to focus on things that really mattered— like ensuring a neglected and abused nine-year-old boy's broken leg healed the way it should.

# CHAPTER 4

EMILY PARKED IN FRONT OF TYLER'S foster home on Friday afternoon and walked past the beautifully landscaped yard to the front door. At least the boy now lived in this quaint suburb of Oak Pines. If only *she* could leave her own rough neighborhood behind.

A few seconds after knocking, Tyler's foster mom, Barb, appeared in the doorway. For a moment, a knot formed in Emily's stomach. What if Barb had changed her mind about letting Tyler go? But thankfully, Tyler approached from behind his foster mom a moment later.

"You ready?" Emily asked him through the screen door.

"Actually..." The middle-aged woman patted her short, tight curls. "I was wondering if you wouldn't mind me tagging along on this first visit? It might be good to see what this is all about, in case I can help him at home and stuff."

"That would be wonderful. I'm happy to drive, if that's okay."

Barb nodded, then grabbed her purse and closed the door behind them.

The clinic was only a few miles away, and they arrived five minutes early. Cole stood at the front counter wearing khaki pants and a navy-blue polo shirt monogrammed in yellow with the words *PT Possibilities*. He was filling out paperwork, but he glanced up a moment later and smiled.

Walking over to greet them, Cole held out his closed fist to Tyler first, who smiled and bumped it with his own. He then shook Emily's hand. "Nice to see you again." He extended his hand to Barb as well. "Hi. My name is Cole. And you are?"

"I'm Barb, Tyler's foster mom."

"Ah," Cole replied, as if putting the pieces together in his mind. "Nice to meet you. Why don't you all follow me?"

He led them down a hall and into a private patient room. "It's good you could all be here. Today will primarily act as a consultation so I can assess where Tyler is at and what he needs most to get him on the path to full recovery. I've also reviewed his medical records, so we'll get started on some exercises today along with a few strategies you can practice at home, depending on what we find. All this will help determine how often I'll need to see him these next two months. Sound good?" He looked each of them in the eye one by one. Emily may have been imagining things, but it seemed that his gaze lingered on her the longest. An unexpected flutter rippled through her stomach.

They all agreed to Cole's plan, and he proceeded to reference Tyler's file as he talked to him about his leg, his pain, and the areas where he struggled most. Then Cole brought Tyler into the large room Emily had seen on the tour. There were two other therapists in the room, each working with a child on various exercises.

For the next half hour, Cole assessed Tyler's current agility and strength, while Emily and Barb watched through the observation window. At times, Tyler grimaced in pain, which tugged at Emily's heartstrings. But Cole was a professional, and she trusted he knew how far to push his patients. And seeing someone else serve a troubled kid was inspiring. She loved watching how Cole's job energized him.

A few minutes before the end of their appointment, Cole brought them all back to the private room and explained what he had done with Tyler that day. "I'd like to see him twice a week for the next few weeks, and then hopefully taper down to once a week for the next month or so, if it's okay with you both."

"Sounds good." That was about what Emily had factored into her budget, so she was pleased with the plan and impressed with their experience so far. Barb agreed, and they walked to the front to schedule the next several sessions with Cole. Emily had off on Tuesdays and Fridays, so she would pick Tyler up after school and drive him to the clinic—with or without Barb.

While Barb and Tyler made their way to the water cooler in the far corner of the waiting room, Emily recorded the upcoming appointments on her phone as

Cole organized his client files. "Thank you so much for what you're doing with Tyler. I can tell you're really good at what you do, and Tyler already looks up to you. It's neat to see the instant connection, so thank you."

"No, thank *you*. I'm not sure I've ever seen someone invest so much in someone they barely know."

His gaze swept over her, causing her face to grow warm. She handed compliments out freely, but she wasn't the best at accepting them. Barb and Tyler were headed out the door, so she politely said goodbye to Cole and hurried to catch up with them.

"Wait!" Cole called out.

Emily stopped in her tracks and turned around. "What is it? Did I forget something?"

"Uh, yeah." He reached for a stack of papers, then came around the counter so he was by her side. "Here are some extra exercises for Tyler. Hopefully, he can do these every day so when I see him again, he'll be a pro." He handed over the papers with a heart-stopping grin.

She scanned the handouts and gave him a friendly smile in return. "I'll give these to Barb. Thanks again." Her heart pounded a little faster as she walked away. Tyler would soon be progressing toward complete healing—physical and hopefully emotional as well. And although she wasn't interested in dating, it sure didn't hurt to have someone as handsome as Cole in charge of the task.

AFTER WORK, COLE DROVE to his parents' place an hour north. He tried to visit them at least once a month, and tonight he'd been invited over for his mom's famous meatloaf. He and his brother didn't have the heart to tell her it wasn't famous for the right reasons, but out of respect, he would suck it up and eat the dry mound of meat without complaint.

On the drive up, he couldn't get Emily out of his head. Sure, Tyler was a cute kid. And he was happy to play a role in helping the boy get back on his feet. But what made this woman so generous toward a stranger? If the roles were reversed, he would have let the system take care of the kid. And what did that say about him? Did he even deserve someone as kind and selfless as Emily? He squirmed in the driver's seat, then lifted his thoughts above. *God, why am I obsessing about this woman? Please give me patience and clarity. Guide me in how I act toward her, and toward whoever You might have for me in the future. And be with poor Tyler. Help him to get the love and guidance he needs.*

As he walked to the front door of his parents' house, he was grateful for the distraction of family to clear his head.

"Cole!" His grey-haired mom answered the door dressed in a long jean skirt, a white blouse, and a red checkered apron.

He greeted her with a hug, then walked down the hall to use the bathroom. The hallway was lined with the usual family photos. He scanned them for a moment until his gaze landed on one in particular. He touched his fingers to the glass and swallowed over the lump in his throat. This image was engrained in his mind. It was how he'd always remember him. With a deep breath and a shake of his head, he moved along.

After washing his hands, Cole joined his dad, who was watching the local sportscast in the living room. "Hi, Dad."

"Hey, Champ. Thanks for coming over. Your mom loves the company."

Cole nodded, knowing his dad didn't mind his visits either. They watched television in silence until his mom called them to the table.

"How's work going?" She cut a slice of meatloaf with her fork and knife.

"Oh, pretty good. No complaints."

"Any exciting cases?"

Cole considered telling his parents about Emily, but he didn't want to get ahead of himself. He decided to focus the story on Tyler instead, and his history of abuse and foster care.

A few minutes later, his mom interrupted. "That reminds me. The other day, I read about this study they did on adults who grew up in the foster system."

As his mom listed off various foster-related statistics, Cole's mind wandered back to Emily. For whatever reason, she'd captured his attention. Her generosity and quiet beauty. Her compelling blue eyes. Her... *Stop it, Cole.* He had to find a way to tamp down his attraction to someone he hardly knew. After all, he didn't even know if she was a Christian, so to start desiring something more at this point was premature. All he wanted was to understand what motivated her.

27

Just spending time with her twice had made him want to be a better person, and that had nothing to do with her looks. How many other wonderful people had he overlooked in his past because they didn't fit a certain physical mold?

He wanted to ask her out, but it wasn't the right time. For starters, he didn't want to put Emily on the spot in front of Tyler and his foster mom. But more importantly, it probably wasn't appropriate to ask out a patient's... well... whatever she was to Tyler. Besides, he wanted to leave room for God to determine if and when the time was right to take that leap. And he didn't know if God was saying *yes* to Emily or not. He wanted to feel a peace about asking her out, not rush ahead out of a selfish desire. If he'd learned anything from his past relationships, it was not to rush things.

Shaking off his insecurities and doubt, he focused his attention back on the conversation at hand, hoping he hadn't missed anything important during his daydream. As much as he loved his parents, this was the first time in a long time he found himself wishing he was spending his Friday night amidst some female company instead. And a very specific female, at that. With thoughts like those, he'd likely spend the rest of the weekend praying for wisdom before Tuesday rolled around.

# CHAPTER 5

EMILY ENTERED THE FAMILIAR PEDIATRIC ONCOLOGY unit and headed straight for six-year-old Bryant's room. Seeing his bald head wrapped in bandages, she fingered the locket on her chest and swallowed the lump in her throat. The fear of breaking down in front of these kids was ever-present, but she forced a smile.

"Hi buddy!" She reached over for a high five, and the boy did his best to reciprocate, his strength zapped from a recent surgery to remove a tumor from his brain. His pale, emaciated body revealed how pitiful he felt, but he still managed to break into a wide grin upon seeing Emily that Saturday afternoon. The glimmer of joy in his eye was all it took to ease the knot in her chest.

Bryant's mom sat next to him, and she greeted Emily with a warm smile despite appearing a little ragged. Hanging out in hospitals worrying about your son would do that to a person.

"I can stick around for a while if you'd like to go grab a coffee or something." Emily put a friendly hand on the woman's shoulder.

She bit her lip, looked at her son, then the door, and then at Emily. "Are you sure?"

"Absolutely. I just have to be back on duty in a half hour."

Bryant's mom stood and hugged Emily. "I'll only take a few minutes to get some coffee. Thank you. You are a godsend."

Emily watched as she exited the room. "So, Bryant. Summer is just around the corner. What are you most looking forward to?"

The little boy smiled. "I can't wait to play at the park. Every day! And Mom says when I get better, we'll go to the zoo."

Emily almost teared up at his innocence, relishing the way his words came out since he couldn't say his *R's* very well. "That's awesome! What's your favorite animal at the zoo?"

Bryant thought for a minute. "The polar bear." His response came out sounding like *polo bayow*, and Emily forced back a giggle.

She spent the next fifteen minutes drilling him about the highs and lows of his past year in kindergarten, spotty though his attendance had been, along with discussing summer plans before Bryant's mom returned. "Thanks again, Emily. I owe you."

"Oh goodness, no you don't. I love talking to my bud." She smiled at Bryant. "You hang in there, okay little man?"

He nodded, then yawned and glanced at his mom. "I'm sleepy, Mom."

"It's okay, baby. You go ahead and take a nap."

Emily left the room and glanced at her watch. There was still a few minutes to say hello to eleven-year-old Charlotte. The unpredictable girl had leukemia and had been in and out of the hospital for months. Some days she was grateful for Emily's presence, while other times she was downright angry at the world and wanted nothing to do with any visitors. Of course, the emotions likely depended on how her cancer and medications made her feel. Although she never knew what kind of mood to expect, Emily didn't give up on her visits. They had been building a rapport, and she didn't want to lose that momentum.

Emily heard the sound of the television as she knocked tentatively on the door.

"Come in," came a deep male voice.

Poking her head into the room, she found the tween sitting up in her bed with her father seated nearby.

"Emily!" Charlotte flashed her a smile as wide as the arms she extended for a hug. Her head was wrapped in a bandana, the chemo having stolen all of her hair. Her eyes were slightly sunken in and her skin had an unhealthy pallor, but she was a fighter and Emily saw a spark of life in the girl. Not unlike the spark she used to see in her mom before the cancer took over.

Emily returned her embrace. "Hi, hon. I only have a few minutes, but I *had* to come say hello to my favorite eleven-year-old girl in the world."

Charlotte smiled, and Emily gave her a quick wink

before turning to face her father. "Would it be okay if I brought a little treat for Charlotte during my next shift on Monday?"

He frowned. "I'm not sure if she'll be able to keep it down, but I'm all about piling on the treats for my little girl." Charlotte rolled her eyes at her father's doting, but Emily could tell deep down she enjoyed the attention—quite possibly one of the only positive takeaways from her present situation.

Emily turned back to Charlotte and lowered her voice. "Did he visit?" Hopefully the girl knew who she was referring to.

Her smile confirmed it. "Yesterday, yeah. He was with a few others from our class, but he was the first through the door and the last to leave."

"I knew it! That is so cool. That boy has good taste, sister." She winked at her young friend. In the midst of her disease, Charlotte still had something small to look forward to, even if it was the simple giddiness of a crush.

"What's the first thing you're going to do when you get out of this place?"

Charlotte tilted her head up towards the ceiling as she thought. "Probably go to the mall. I haven't been shopping in months."

"Tell ya what," Emily said. "If it's okay with your dad, maybe I can tag along on a shopping trip and buy you a new outfit. How does that sound?"

Charlotte squealed in delight, turning her attention toward her dad. "You don't have to do that," he said. "But it's fine as far as I'm concerned."

"Yes!" Charlotte beamed.

After a few more minutes of chatting, Emily glanced at her watch. "Well, I better get going. But I can't wait to see you on Monday." She reached out and gently stroked Charlotte's face.

"Me too." Charlotte held Emily's hand in place on her cheek for a few seconds. The girl's mom had passed away a couple years earlier. Emily knew all too well how it felt to lose your mom so young, so she was compelled to fill in the gap in whatever small ways she was able. "Thanks, Emily," Charlotte added.

With a final wave, Emily slipped out of the door, her heart more than a little torn at the thought of how lonely and scary Charlotte's days were lately.

She returned to the ER to finish out her shift, thoughts of Bryant and Charlotte weighing on her mind. There had been other kids she'd reached out to over the years, but they always came and went. Thankfully, many were cured and went on to live healthy lives. Some transferred to different hospitals. A few had passed away, which she had taken hard. But that was the minority, and it had been a while since that had been the fate of any of the patients she'd befriended.

As hard as those moments were, she loved playing a small part in their lives. It was the least she could do after all the pain she'd caused others in her past. Because of those mistakes, she'd made a deal with God years ago to serve Him in all that she did. And that life of service had kept her in God's good graces for the past seven years. She didn't dare do anything to mess that up.

# CHAPTER 6

COLE STOPPED LOOKING AT HIS MENU to glance at his watch. It had taken his sister-in-law exactly three minutes to ask about his dating life. Good thing she wasn't there last night to bring up the topic in front of Mom and Dad. "Hey, maybe you should let me choose my order tonight before making me pick a wife."

Maria stuck out her tongue at him.

"Y'know, there was a time when you supported what I was doing."

She smiled. "I know, I know. And it served its purpose, Cole. But I'm just looking out for you. You aren't getting any younger, if you know what I mean."

Cole's brother chuckled, but he knew better than to add fuel to the fire. Tim was usually content to let his wife stir the pot, but it was all in good fun. Those two were Cole's best friends despite Maria's spunkiness.

"Well, I haven't really been looking, but no

prospects at the moment." Without warning, Emily's face flashed through his mind. A smile escaped his lips before he could stop it.

"Wait, what was *that*?" Tim asked with a probing glare.

"What was what?" He raised an eyebrow and prayed that he wasn't about to be subjected to an interrogation by his cop brother and the equally-inquisitive Maria.

"That smile. Like you're hiding something." Maria had apparently noticed his slip-up as well. She used her straw to swirl the ice in her glass as she stared deviously at Cole.

Cole rolled his eyes. "You guys read into things too much."

"He's not exactly denying it," Tim said to Maria, as if Cole wasn't there.

"Guys!"

"Just tell us the truth and we'll move on." Maria clearly enjoyed the drama.

Cole sighed. He might as well just tell them. It was futile to think he could dodge the topic for the remainder of the evening—and besides, he could use some advice. "All right, there's this patient of mine. Well, she's not really my patient, but she's..." He paused. He wasn't sure how to explain it, so he took a step back and relayed the whole story of who Emily was and how he'd met her. "So, I'm intrigued by her, that's all. Nothing has happened—and maybe nothing will. I mean, technically I'm not supposed to date a patient anyway. But for the first time in a long time, I... I kind of *want* to." The side of his mouth quirked up at the thought.

Tim groaned, never the type to be anything but blunt with his feelings. "I'm disappointed. I was expecting something juicier."

Cole reached over and messed up Tim's hair. "Sorry, little brother. That's all I've got. After the whole Heather experience, I've been content to lay low for a while. No offense," he added, addressing Maria. Heather was Maria's coworker from a previous job, so she had been the one to set Cole up with her years ago.

Maria held up her hands in defense. "None taken. Heather was fun to work with, but she was obviously not marriage material for a nice guy like you. And I think this Emily girl sounds sweet. You should totally ask her out. She would be crazy not to say yes."

A wave of relief washed over Cole at Maria's supportive words. "Thanks. I don't know, I guess we'll see. I think I just have to figure out how to approach her—or if I even can. She's so different from anyone I've met, I'm not sure how to handle it."

"Have you never heard of a thing called the internet?" Tim took a bite of his breadstick.

Cole stared at him. "The internet?"

"Yeah. You know, put her name in a search engine. Find out more about her before you jump in. First of all, you may discover she's not someone you want to get to know after all. But if she *is*, you could learn some key information to improve your chances. You know, her favorite restaurant or where she grew up. Something you could casually weave into conversation to make her sense a connection."

Maria glared at her husband. "What ever happened to good old-fashioned conversation?"

"Oh please," Tim replied. "Everyone researches people online nowadays. Employers, cops, and yes, even potential dates. Like you wouldn't have done the same if we'd met each other randomly instead of going to school together?"

A smile tugged on the corners of Maria's mouth. "Oh, all right. As unromantic as it sounds, you do have a point." She turned her attention to Cole. "Look, do whatever you think is right. But be prepared to find something out about her online that you'll have to explain later how you know what you know."

Cole furrowed his brow. Would Emily freak out or get mad if she found out he'd been poking around online? Maybe he shouldn't risk it. "Hmm, good point. Thanks for the input, guys. I think I just have to wait for the right moment and not force anything. If it's meant to be, things will work out when the time is right."

"Well, look who's turning over a new leaf." Tim smirked and leaned over to Maria. "Where was his restraint back when Heather had him wrapped around her finger?"

"Oh, shush." Maria swatted her husband. "Being single for a year has cleared his head. Sounds to me like he knows what he wants and is willing to wait on God's timing."

"Uh, guys? I'm sitting right here." Cole waved his hands in the air. Why were they talking like he was in the other room? He did have a history of making bad decisions in his romantic life—rushing ahead in relationships without his girlfriend being on the same page when it came to heading towards marriage, or at least a monogamous relationship. But that was before he'd gotten closer to God. He had a whole new outlook now, and more than anything, he longed for a woman with a generous heart like what he'd witnessed so far in Emily. He had to hit the brakes, though. First of all, if he didn't want to make the same mistakes as before, he'd have to find out if she was a Christian. And secondly, he'd need to read the employee handbook a little closer to see if it was really against the rules.

"Well, let us know how things go." Maria put her elbow on the table and rested her chin on her fist. "This is exciting!"

Tim let out a short laugh through his nose. "Yeah, we can't wait to meet this little Mother Teresa."

Cole glared at his brother, then took a long sip of his drink. He wasted no time changing the subject to avoid more jabs from his brother, but for some reason, he couldn't get Emily's blue eyes out of his head for the rest of the evening.

HALFWAY THROUGH HER SHIFT on Monday, there was an unusual lull in activity, and Emily's supervisor gave her the green light to steal away for a break. She used the time to stop in the staff lounge for a quick snack and to get the treat she had bought for Charlotte. As she climbed the stairs to the fourth floor, she glanced at the cupcake and admired the decorative frosting, wishing she had that kind of culinary talent. A minute later, she arrived at Charlotte's room and knocked on the open door. But there was no one there to greet her—only an empty bed with messy covers. Her breath caught in her throat. She didn't want to think the worst, but she *was* in a cancer ward after all.

She found the closest nurse. "Do you know where Charlotte is?" She tried to keep her voice steady.

"Yeah, she's been going a little stir crazy, so we let her dad wheel her around the hospital for a bit."

Emily let out a sigh of relief. "Well, would you mind giving her this cupcake and let her know Nurse Emily will come visit at the end of my shift?"

The nurse took the cupcake and nodded, and Emily returned to the ER where the lull appeared to be over. They were flooded with cases that afternoon, which made the rest of her shift fly by. Days like this always caused mixed feelings. Patients allowed Emily to do what she loved, but at the same time, it meant people in pain.

When her shift finally ended, she remembered her promise to meet up with Charlotte and prayed on her way up that the girl would be in her room—and in good spirits. But this time, as Emily approached Charlotte's room, it was completely empty. It wasn't that the *bed* was empty like it had been at lunchtime; it's that the bed itself was not even *there*. Once again, she rushed to the nurse's station to find out where Charlotte had been taken.

The nurse on duty checked Charlotte's chart online and frowned. "It looks like there was hemorrhaging in her brain. She was taken to the OR for emergency surgery."

The room began to spin and a pit formed in her stomach as she sat in a nearby chair to steady herself. *God, what's going on? Please intervene and save Charlotte. She's been through so much as it is. Please help her to lead a long, healthy life. I'll even take her place if You'll let me. You and I both know I don't deserve to be here. But Charlotte does. Please. Save her.*

After praying, Emily clasped her locket and made her way toward the operating room. Nobody would be able to tell her anything yet, but she still wanted to be nearby. When she reached the closest waiting room, she found the poor girl's dad sitting in a chair, his head in his hands. "Hi, Mr. Jarvis." She gently put her hand on his shoulder.

He looked up with puffy eyes, his face showing indescribable misery. "Emily," he said as though he was about to say more. But no more words came. He bowed his head and covered his eyes with his hand. He needed space, but she hoped her presence might bring a small ounce of encouragement.

"I'm praying," she whispered, and then she walked away. Down the hall, she peeked into the room where Charlotte lay. Several doctors and nurses scurried about, trying to fix the hemorrhage that threatened Charlotte's life. Hopefully, they had discovered it in time.

She choked back tears as she walked to her car. Once in the driver's seat, she put her hand on her locket and sighed. Grabbing her phone, she pulled up the Bible app and searched for Psalm 23, which always seemed to calm her nerves at times like this. She knew the words by heart, but seeing them displayed on the screen somehow quenched her thirst for the Truth. "Even though I walk through the valley of the shadow of death, I will fear no evil, for you are with me." *I know this, God. I trust You Lord.* It was out of her hands now. She had to believe that all her good deeds—befriending cancer patients, serving the homeless at the Mission, paying for a little boy's physical therapy, helping her elderly neighbor—would be enough to convince Him to pull through for her... this time.

# CHAPTER 7

THOUGHTS OF CHARLOTTE INVADED EMILY'S MIND when she woke up on Tuesday morning. She logged into the hospital network and entered the girl's Patient ID, taking a deep breath before her shaky hand clicked enter. She whispered a prayer as the hour glass indicated her request was being processed. *God, prepare me for what I'm about to find.*

A wave of relief washed over her when she saw that Charlotte had made it through the night, but after reading through the subsequent details, she bit her lip. Her initial relief was overshadowed by the serious complications documented in the file. It didn't look good. Shutting her laptop, she bowed her head. *I know You can save her, God. Please, please work a miracle in her life.*

Emily distracted herself for the next several hours with errands, laundry, and housework until it was almost time to pick Tyler up for therapy. But she had a nagging desire to get an update on Charlotte. The girl's condition weighed on her mind, and she didn't want to go the rest of the day without knowing she was okay.

Pulling up Charlotte's file again, she scanned the words on the screen. *Time of death – 11:43.* She blinked a few times to make sure she'd read it right before her mouth went dry and her stomach turned.

No matter how many times she'd had to deal with death in her lifetime, it never got easier. Especially when it was a child falling victim to the evils of cancer. The tears began to flow, her whole body shaking from the sobs. She thought of the expression on Charlotte's face when she'd visited on Saturday, her arms wide open, her excited smile discussing the cute boy who'd visited her. Her whole countenance lit up. Somehow her young soul had still managed to find joy despite her circumstances. At least, on her *good* days. But then there were times the girl could barely muster a smile. Just like Emily's mom.

*As soon as the school bus stopped, Emily was out the yellow door in a flash, her twelve-year-old feet hitting the pavement with increasing frequency and not stopping until she was inside her house. She poured a glass of apple juice from the fridge and stacked a few saltine crackers on a plate — the only things her mom could stomach these days. The chemo had sucked all the life out of her, and to make a cruel situation that much worse, even a delectable treat could not overcome the nauseating side effects.*

*As she neared her mom's bedroom, Emily's chin quivered, but she coughed to loosen the emotion clogging her throat and* reminded herself to be strong. She'd made the mistake one too many times of breaking down in front of her. It had only made her mom sad, and the one time her dad had caught her blubbering on, well… it hadn't gone well for Emily either. She despised the man and couldn't imagine life without Mom by her side. God would never do that to her, would He? She shuddered at the thought, then put on a brave face as she stepped into the room.

"Hi, Mom." She forced a smile into her voice as she set the juice and crackers on the nightstand.

Her mom gazed up through halfway open eyes. "Is that you, Emily?"

"Yeah, I just got home. How are you feeling today?"

Her mom was silent for a moment. "You're old enough to know, Em." She took a shallow breath. "You know it won't be long, right? Just a matter of time."

A lump formed in her throat at the thought of her mom dying. At the thought of being left alone with her father. "You don't know that," she said, choking back tears.

Her mom reached over to hold her hand with a sad smile. Emily was startled by how cold her mom's skin was. "It's going to be okay. Dad will take good care of you."

"No, Mom. Mommy, don't leave me." She cried steadily now, no longer able to hide her tears. Hopefully her dad wouldn't come home anytime soon. He would chew her out big time for losing it in front of her mom again. Maybe even get out the belt and punish her again for being a burden to her dying mother.

"It's out of my hands," her mom said softly. A single tear slid down her mom's cheek. "I promise, you will be fine without me."

*Emily shook her head, unsure what else to say but knowing somewhere deep down that this would be one of the last memories she would have of her mom.*

*"Open the top drawer of my dresser." Without saying a word, Emily obeyed. "Do you see that locket on the silver chain? Bring it here, will you sweetie?"*

*Emily handed her mom a chain which held a silver, heart-shaped locket. Her mom's bony fingers clumsily opened the clasp to reveal a tiny photo of Emily as a baby in the arms of her much younger, smiling, carefree mom. "I want you to have this, Em. To remember me by."*

Emily clasped that very same necklace hanging around her neck as she thought about what Charlotte's dad must be going through. Losing her mom had been the first of many gut-wrenching losses in her life. But to lose one's child? It was hard enough having yet another person she cared about die. The thought made her tremble.

Wiping another tear from her eye, she sucked in a deep breath and shook her head in an attempt to regain her composure before picking up Tyler. Would she be able to hold it together for his physical therapy appointment? She wasn't sure, but she didn't exactly have a choice. There would be a time to mourn, but for now she had to put her game face on—for Tyler's sake.

When Emily and Tyler walked through the doors of PT Possibilities, she forced a smile as she greeted Cole at the clinic. He didn't need to know she'd been an emotional wreck only an hour ago. Over the years, she had gotten fairly good at keeping things hidden from the outside world; there was no reason today should be any different.

Emily observed the intensive physical therapy session through the glass window like before, but she barely registered what was happening in there. It was all a blur as her thoughts were preoccupied with the fragility of life. Charlotte. Her mom. So many others along the way. Images of their faces flooded her mind. She swallowed the lump in her throat as she tried to focus on Tyler so she could compliment him on his progress on their drive home.

After the session was over, the guys met up with Emily, who stood to walk back to the front office together. But Cole appeared to study her face and didn't move. What was he staring at? Did she have something in her teeth?

"Do you have a few minutes to chat while Tyler sits in the waiting area? Our front office staff will keep an eye on him."

Emily raised her eyebrows, then nodded and followed him to a private room halfway down the hall. What did he need to talk to her about?

"Is everything all right?" Emily took a seat on the nearby chair.

"Funny, I was going to ask *you* that." Cole tilted his head, a slight frown on his face as he stared into her eyes.

"What do you mean?" She shifted in her seat, uncomfortable with the intensity behind his eyes, almost as if he could see into her soul. Did he know more about her situation than he let on? Or was this perhaps about Tyler?

"Something's bothering you. I could tell during Tyler's session."

"Oh!" Had her face inadvertently revealed her heartache?

"I only bring it up because if there's something going on with Tyler at his foster home, or something in his life that might adversely affect his treatment and recovery, I feel I should know about it. And I would think you would want that as well, since you're financing all of this."

Emily took a deep breath. "I can assure you, nothing is wrong with Tyler's situation that I'm aware of. I mean, other than *everything* being wrong with his situation. But nothing more than last time." She paused and glanced up at him with a small laugh. Why did she have to become a blathering idiot now? "Does that make sense?"

Cole chuckled. "I think so. So, everything is okay with Tyler, then. But what about with you?"

She swallowed. Was it his question, or the look in his eye that made her feel like he truly cared how she was doing? No one had looked at her that way in years, and it was too much. Too soon. Her nose stung with suppressed emotion, but this wasn't the time or place to discuss it. Assuming Cole was even someone she'd want to confide in. Even if his intentions were as genuine as they seemed, she hardly knew the man.

She stood. "Yes, everything is fine. I mean, I just found out some sad news, but it's completely unrelated to any of this, so…" Out of nowhere, her eyes began to water. "Oh, wow. I'm so sorry." She quickly wiped away the tears before they fell down her cheeks. She had not been prepared to cry in front of this man. What was wrong with her?

Cole touched her shoulder. "Forgive me, Emily. I didn't mean to hit a nerve. Would you like me to give you a minute? Or do you want to talk about it?"

Emily peered up at Cole, meeting his gaze. For the first time, she recognized how masculine his face was and yet how gentle and caring his eyes appeared. For a moment, she couldn't find any words to say, and she was keenly aware of the warmth of his hand on her shoulder. "I... It's just..." Her chin began to quiver.

"Have a seat." Cole's voice was soft, his expression sympathetic. "Tell me what's wrong. I mean, if you want to."

Emily certainly didn't *want* to, but her knees buckled and it didn't take much convincing for her to sit and start talking.

"There's this little girl at the hospital—Charlotte. She's a cancer patient, and she had to have emergency surgery on her brain. And I... I just found out she didn't make it." She fingered her locket while staring at the opposite wall, shaking her head at how stupid she must sound. Cole handed her a tissue and rested his hand on her back.

"So, you lost a patient of yours?"

Emily shook her head. "Not *my* patient. But I got to know her during visits on breaks and after my shifts at the hospital. I'd gotten close to her since she was in and out of the hospital so much. She was fine when I saw her on Saturday, but yesterday, she..." Emily stared off into the distance as Cole's hand stroked her back. She sniffled, then faced Cole again. "I prayed so hard for that girl. I just don't understand why God would have let this happen."

Cole frowned. "I wish I had an answer for you. But I'll definitely keep you in my prayers, if that's okay. And this girl's family."

She tried to smile at his kindness, then took a deep, shaky breath. *Get a grip, Emily.*

Clearing her throat, she sat up straight in her chair. "I am *so* sorry. This has absolutely nothing to do with Tyler, or physical therapy, or anything like that. I literally found out an hour before we came, so it's fresh in my head. But not your problem. I really do apologize."

"Don't even worry about it. I care about my patients, that's why I asked. And not just my patients, but also their families and… well, ex-nurses?" He tilted his head with a mixture of confusion and amusement on his face.

She grinned, grateful for a lighthearted transition away from the previous topic, then stood to leave.

"Well, again. Please excuse the emotional mess you just saw. Thank you for listening, and for caring. It's nice to know Tyler is in such good hands."

Cole grinned, then led her through the doorway and back out into the waiting area where Tyler watched cartoons.

"Ready to go?" Emily did her best to mask any evidence of the emotional outburst she'd had moments ago.

Tyler stood and hobbled to the front door, giving a fist bump to Cole's outstretched hand on the way. Emily mouthed a silent "thank you" as she passed by.

As Cole put away the resistance bands he'd used with Tyler, his boss, Frank, tapped him on the shoulder. "Do you have a minute to talk?"

Cole suppressed a frown. It wasn't often his boss requested a one-on-one. He glanced around the room at two patients still working with their therapists. "Sure, what's up? Should we talk in your office?"

Frank nodded. "That might be best." Once they were seated in his office with the door closed, Frank folded his hands atop his cluttered desk. "I noticed you pulled a patient's mom aside to chat in private. Is everything all right with that kid?"

Cole furrowed his brow. He wasn't about to tell his boss about the personal struggles Emily had shared with him. "Yeah, everything's fine. Our talk wasn't even about Tyler's therapy, so there's nothing to worry about."

Frank's eyebrows raised. "That brings me to my next question." Cole cringed as he realized how his words may have sounded. "I trust you're familiar with our fraternization policy as it relates to patients and their family members? Is it possible you're getting a little too close with this woman?"

Cole's mind raced as he licked his lips. All he could do was speak the truth. "No, I assure you the conversation was entirely professional." But he hoped for something more to come out of their next conversation, and he had to know if he was in the clear. He took a deep breath for courage. "But Frank, the patient is a nine-year-old boy. Emily isn't even related to him. She *is* the one paying the bill, but she's literally known him for, like, a few weeks. She was his nurse and just wanted to help him out. I'm curious what the policy says about that kind of arrangement." He held his breath as he waited for the answer.

The way his boss stared at him made him feel like he was back in middle school in the principal's office. Finally, Frank's face broke into a crooked grin. "I'm fairly certain our policy doesn't address that particular situation."

For the first time in their conversation, Cole breathed easy. At least his boss wasn't ruling out the possibility altogether. "If I did find that things might progress romantically during the timeframe I'm working with Tyler, would… would that be a problem?"

Frank scratched his cheek and sucked in a breath. "Well, I suppose I'm the one who writes the rules, huh?"

Cole flashed him a hopeful smile.

"Do you think your potential relationship would interfere in any way with Tyler's care?"

Cole shook his head. "Absolutely not. I'm a professional, you know that."

Frank stared at him a moment longer before slamming his hand onto his desk. "Well, all right, then. But I prefer that you not conduct your personal business on company time. Understood?"

The relief was instant. "Of course. But honestly, at

this point, there's no personal business to be had. I'm intrigued by her, but it's not like we've gone out or anything, just so you know." Considering there was no personal business going on, he'd sure thought and prayed about Emily an awful lot. But Frank didn't need to know that.

His boss waggled his eyebrows. "And just so *you* know, I happen to think you guys look good together. So, keep that in mind, Cole. Have a good night."

After saying goodbye to his boss, Cole tidied up his work area. Their conversation had gone better than he'd hoped. And Frank even thought they looked good together—but looks weren't everything. If they were, he'd still be with Heather. No, Emily had a lot more to offer than outer beauty, and her display of raw emotion today was humbling.

As he headed home, memories of Emily's tear-stained face were fresh on his mind. Hopefully he'd been a comfort to her—that she was able to recognize his honest intentions and sincere desire to help. But only God could truly heal a broken heart. Did she believe that? She had *mentioned* God during their conversation, but that was only one step in the right direction.

*God, please help Emily get through this rough time. Help her to know that even though we don't understand Your reasons, we trust You to make things right in the end. And Lord, if she and I are meant to be together, will You help us both to be obedient to whatever You want us to do? I'm starting to really like her, but I don't want to be blinded by my own desires.*

Maybe he was reading too far into things. Maybe

they weren't meant for each other. But couldn't he at least get to know her better? Glean from her generosity? Point her closer to Christ? If only he knew where she stood in her faith.

# CHAPTER 8

WHEN SHE DROPPED TYLER OFF AFTER therapy, Emily decided to walk him in and give Barb an update on his session. Barb held the front door open and grinned at Tyler, who walked inside and disappeared.

"How'd he do?" the woman asked.

Emily stood on the front stoop, not planning to stay long. "Really good. Cole is challenging him to push through the pain, but he's not overdoing it." She lowered her voice to make sure the boy wouldn't hear. "Tyler even laughed out loud a couple times, so it's nice to see him have a good time."

Barb covered her mouth with her hand. "I'm so glad. I can see a difference in him already, and I know this therapy is only going to build on that momentum. Thanks again for making it work."

Despite her emotions about Charlotte, knowing that Tyler was improving in more ways than one made

Emily's heart soar.

"When are we making it?" called a young voice from inside. Tyler appeared, looking up at Barb with a hopeful expression.

"We'll make it right now, but you'll have to have some patience. We need to eat supper before we can have any."

Tyler lifted his shoulders up and down with an exaggerated sigh before he walked away. Barb turned to Emily with a slight shake of the head. "We're making homemade ice cream tonight. Children need good memories, don't you think?"

Emily gave a slight nod. "Aw, that's nice. Have a good night." That was all she managed to get out before the lump reappeared in her throat. She escaped to her car, but she couldn't escape her thoughts as she drove home. She didn't have happy memories of her childhood. Since her mom had been diagnosed with cancer when Emily was seven, their relationship had been strange. While her friends had birthday parties, shopping trips and tea parties with their moms, Emily was literally spoon-feeding hers, especially since her dad wasn't around much. The cancer finally overtook her when Emily was twelve and things with her dad had gone downhill even more after that.

One night, after she'd called him a drunk, he'd snarled and told her he wished she'd never been born. He constantly berated her for making her mom's life miserable, like she'd been a burden to her dying mother instead of a source of joy and love. She couldn't deny she was far from perfect, but his insults drove her further and further into rebellion. She would act like his words had no effect on her, but deep down they pierced her soul. In retrospect, she knew his attacks were borne out of grief, in his own lost way. But even if she'd been wise enough to realize it at the time, it wouldn't have made his anger and spite any easier to handle.

As she drove, she passed a liquor store. It was funny how the sight still gave her a sour taste in her mouth. Her dad's drinking had escalated after her mom died, and it only made things worse. No wonder she'd started sneaking out of the house, defying her father every chance she got.

*"Where are you going?" Dad sprawled in his recliner, a cheap can of beer in his hand.*

*She rolled her eyes. "Out." She sensed his glare on her back as she put on her shoes.*

*"We haven't eaten dinner together all week."*

*"So?"*

*"So... I was hoping we could talk." His words were slurred. This wasn't his first beer of the evening.*

*She sighed and paused before turning towards him. "About?"*

*"Your geometry teacher called. Said you've only been to class twice in the last two weeks." He stabbed his cigarette butt in an ash tray on the arm of his chair before reaching for another from the pack in his front shirt pocket.*

*"Geometry is pointless. I learned my shapes in kindergarten."*

*"Don't talk to me like that, young lady. If your mother was still alive—"*

*"I'll be at Shelly's. I'll be back by 9:00." She slammed the*

*door behind her. He didn't understand, and it wasn't worth getting into it with him. She would need to start changing which classes she skipped so it didn't raise a red flag with any one teacher. But the thought of sitting through geometry class multiple times a week? Ugh! It made her skin crawl and her eyelids droop.*

*Part of her felt bad for ignoring her dad, but another part knew he really would rather be alone anyway. He didn't actually care if they had dinner together—who was he trying to kid? She wished she had a normal father who actually wanted to spend time with his daughter. But if kicking your high schooler out of your house was legal, he probably would have done it by now.*

*They hadn't been on best terms even when her mom was alive, but at least the love they had for her had served as a common bond. Without her, the two of them were merely co-existing until Emily was old enough to be on her own. She couldn't wait until graduation when she'd finally escape his drunken binges forever.*

Emily watched the liquor store disappear in her rearview mirror as she tried to shut off the flood of memories. They were too painful. There was too much heartache. Too much regret. And that's why she spent her life focused on the Charlottes and Tylers of the world. Whenever the intensity of her past became too much to take, she found another life to impact in the here and now. Another soul to save. It was all she could do to push back the guilt which daily threatened to hold her captive to her past.

Turning left at a stop light, she passed an ice cream shop and smiled. Tyler was probably turning the crank of the ice cream maker right now. Creating happy memories, just like Barb said. She'd had *some* good times as a kid, hadn't she? She concentrated on conjuring up some fun outing or vacation when it finally came to her. For as long as she could remember, up until she turned ten, she spent a week at her grandparents' house every summer. They lived near a lake, so they went to the beach every day. She loved the sand, and she usually ended up with so much in her clothes and hair that her grandmother said she found sand around the house for weeks after her visits.

She smiled at the thought. Her grandmother had passed away the fall after her last visit, and her grandfather went into a nursing home not long after that. She hadn't been able to visit him there, due to her mom's cancer and her dad's unwillingness to travel. He'd died alone a few years later.

Emily sighed as she pulled into her driveway, home at last. It had been far too long since she'd thought about her family. Since she'd talked to them or even talked *about* them to anyone. She simply wasn't comfortable opening up to people, especially about things so personal. So painful. Which is why it confused her so much how and why she had let her guard down in front of Cole the other day. And now that she had, would she allow or desire that kind of exchange with him more often?

No. Her life was too messy for anyone to understand, and as long as she kept pulling off the facade of normalcy and having it all together, everyone was better off.

Once home, she threw her keys on top of a stack of papers, too drained to care about the disarray. She rubbed her tired eyes with her palms, remembering all the tears she'd shed earlier that day. How crying in front of Cole had seemed to actually help, how he'd made her feel like it was completely normal. His response was downright endearing, not to mention how his hand on her back had made her feel so warm inside.

The memory of Cole's warm hand still invaded her thoughts at work on Thursday. When she visited the pediatric oncology unit, she overheard two women at the nurse's station mention Charlotte's name. She wandered over. "Are you guys talking about the Charlotte that just passed away?"

One of them turned to face Emily. "Yeah, services are tomorrow at St. John's. Were you planning to go? Visitation starts at 4:00, funeral at 6:00."

"I'd like to, yeah. Thanks for the info. Maybe I'll see you there." She excused herself and squeezed her eyes together. She wanted to attend the funeral to support Charlotte's grieving father, but it conflicted with Tyler's appointment. What should she do?

Biting her lip, she tried to be rational. The way she constantly replayed Cole's kindness and sensitivity from last time, she could probably stand a little distance from the man. After all, she couldn't let those feelings begin to develop. She knew what happened whenever she got close to someone, and she wasn't going to make that mistake again. He didn't deserve that.

She got out her phone and pulled up Barb's contact info to send a text. MIGHT YOU BE ABLE TO TAKE TYLER TO

THERAPY TOMORROW? I HAVE A FUNERAL TO GO TO. I'LL MAKE IT WORK IF NOT!

She watched the screen in hopes of a quick reply. She wasn't asking too much, was she?

Barb's response displayed on her screen a few minutes later. YES, THAT'S FINE. IT'S THE LEAST I CAN DO AFTER ALL YOUR HELP.

Emily breathed a sigh of relief before replying. THANK YOU SO MUCH! AND DON'T WORRY, THIS SHOULD BE A ONE-TIME REQUEST.

Barb: NO WORRIES. HE'S BEEN DOING HIS EXERCISES. IT'S HELPING!

Emily grinned and replied with a thumbs-up emoji. It was nice to know Tyler was making the best use of her investment, though she wasn't doing this to get a pat on the back. She was also thankful for Barb's willingness to chip in. The distance from Cole might give her the perspective she needed to stop dwelling on his touch. His kindness. His eyes. But besides that, she wanted to pay her respect to Charlotte's family. Her dad deserved all the encouragement and sympathy he could get.

# CHAPTER 9

A S FAR AS COLE WAS CONCERNED, Tuesday couldn't come soon enough. He'd gone crazy last Friday when Tyler had arrived without Emily. Anticipating her visit had been what got him through the day, and although he loved his job and serving kids like Tyler, he couldn't deny his attraction to this woman. He tried not to get his hopes up today either, but when 4:00 rolled around, he scanned the waiting room searching for her face. When the familiar *ding* of the door opening sounded, he jerked his head and saw Emily ushering in Tyler. He wiped his sweaty palms on his pants—the wait was over.

Emily wore a grey and white striped ankle-length cotton skirt, a white tank top and flip flops. He stepped out to greet them, trying to find an excuse to put his hand on her shoulder or back again, but he opted for the standard handshake instead. He was clearly getting ahead of himself. *Perhaps I should start by asking her out on a first date. Or finding out about her faith.* He was not about to slip back into his old dating habits. His next girlfriend had to be a Christian.

Emily reciprocated his handshake, then adjusted her purse on her shoulder. "It's good to see you again."

Cole gave Tyler a friendly pat on the shoulder, stuffing his giddy middle school emotions and putting on his professional face instead. After all, Frank had made it clear he had to keep things professional at the clinic, which only made sense. They walked to the back like usual. Emily's smile was bright and sincere, making her seem like an entirely different person from the last time they had spoken, a whole week ago now. A week was too long. He definitely needed to do something about that.

Cole worked with Tyler in the large room while Emily watched through the observation window. Tyler's range of motion was noticeably improving, and the pain he reported during his sessions was already starting to subside. It was clear he'd been doing the requested exercises at home. As much as Cole didn't want to lessen the frequency of their sessions, soon Tyler could get away with only coming to the facility once a week for follow up and assessment.

After his session ended, Cole's heart started to beat faster as he wondered how he could justify asking Emily out without going against his boss's rules. Frank had said he preferred that Cole didn't conduct personal business on company time. Well, Tyler's session was over, and his next appointment hadn't shown up yet, so… Was he splitting hairs here? Besides, asking Emily to talk in private again was proving more difficult than he thought it would be.

To his surprise, Emily solved that dilemma for him. "Tyler, can you watch television while I talk to Cole?" The boy nodded, and she turned to Cole. "Do you have a minute?"

"Yeah, of course." He led her to the same room where they had talked the previous week, casting a glance toward Frank's office on the way. If asked, he'd just explain that this private conversation was per Emily's request.

Emily spoke right away. "I wanted to re-apologize for last week for crying all over you. I'm normally very reserved when it comes to those sorts of things. But I guess I was caught off guard with the news of Charlotte, and you were the first one to notice something was off."

Cole held up his hands. "Like I said, no worries."

"Thanks." Emily flashed him a sheepish grin. "Also, I want to thank you for the work you're doing with Tyler. It's obvious he needs good influences in his life. I know he's here for the therapy, but I like that you're someone he can trust and look up to, too. I mean, he used to not say two words to me in the car, but all I heard on our drive over today was Cole-this and Cole-that."

Cole's face grew warm from her affirming words. But if she thought so highly of him already, maybe she'd be willing to get to know him better. He had to take advantage of this opportunity. He'd deal with Frank later if it came to that. "That's awesome. And I'm flattered that you think I'm an okay guy. In fact…" He pointed his finger in the air and swallowed hard. "I'd like to get to know you better, and I wondered if you'd like to have dinner with me sometime. Um, maybe even tonight, if you're not busy."

Her eyes grew wide upon hearing his invitation. In fact, she seemed downright fearful at the prospect, making Cole's stomach plummet.

She blinked several times, opening and closing her mouth like a fish. "Oh."

Cole couldn't help but laugh at her flustered response, despite the blow to his ego. "Or if not dinner, how about coffee?"

Emily's face turned red, and she dropped her gaze to her feet without speaking.

Why was she unwilling to take the simple step of meeting up for coffee? Of course! How selfish of him not to even think that someone like her might already be taken. "Wait, do you have a boyfriend?" He blurted out the question before giving it any more thought.

When Emily shook her head, he relaxed a bit—but what to say now? "Tell you what. I'm going to go to the coffee shop next door after my next appointment, so I'll be there around 6:30. I'd love it if you happened to be there as well. But if not, it's all good. I don't want to make you feel uncomfortable." He paused and scratched the back of his head. "Truth be told, I'm a bit intrigued by your generosity and figured the least I could do is buy you a cup of coffee while you tell me what motivates you to do what you do."

Staring at the ground, Emily pressed her lips

together.

"Sound like a deal?" All he wanted was some kind of verbal response. This was not going as planned.

Emily nodded unconvincingly. "Okay," she finally spoke. "Um... thanks, Cole." A moment later, she turned and walked out to the waiting room where Tyler was ready and waiting.

*What just happened?* Cole dragged a hand through his hair and tugged on the roots. She had been happy and poised when she said her kind words to him, but as soon as he'd mentioned meeting up, her whole demeanor had changed. He had a sneaking suspicion he would be drinking coffee alone tonight. But he would still show up, on the off-chance that Emily changed her mind.

AS SHE WALKED OUT of the clinic with Tyler, Emily hoped no one noticed the way her hands trembled. While Tyler chattered all the way home about how cool Cole was, she wrestled over her decision. Being asked out was flattering, but also a bit unsettling. She had rejected guys before, but somehow this was different. She really liked Cole, and from anyone else's perspective, she had no reason to turn him down. But knowing what she did about her past, the fact that Cole was such a good guy was all the more reason she had to keep her distance.

What would it take to get to the point where she would even consider an offer like Cole's? He was gorgeous. Caring. Talented. Passionate about what he did. And apparently available and interested. And based on his offer to pray for her, he seemed to be a Believer. But she simply couldn't invite him into her life. If only he knew what that would mean.

After dropping Tyler off and heading home, Emily drummed her fingers on the steering wheel. Her stomach was in knots. She wasn't going to the coffee shop Cole had invited her to, but a small part of her wondered what that scenario might be like. She hardly remembered what it felt like to be attracted to a guy — the giddy butterflies that fluttered in her stomach; the heat that emanated from her body when their legs inadvertently touched; the feeling of acceptance when she heard the words *I love you*. Was she giving up all those wonderful sensations for no reason, or was she right to push aside those desires and focus solely on the good that God could do through her for those in need? Surely He expected her to hold up her end of the bargain.

Once home, she made herself a turkey sandwich and pushed a pile of papers to one side of her kitchen table, making room for her measly dinner-for-one. She sighed. At thirty years old, did she want to live the rest of her life as a single woman? Because if the answer was *no*, then one of these days she would need to actually accept a date. Was this the right time? Was Cole the right guy? Would God allow her the hope of a lasting relationship again? There was no way to know for sure.

Up until the last week or so, she had been completely content with her life. Lonely, maybe, but fulfilling nonetheless, the way she was able to get involved in the lives of those who needed her. For all the pain she had caused others and for all the mistakes in her past, she needed to give back, to make up for the hurt, and perhaps tip the scales once again in her favor.

Deep down, she knew *karma* wasn't theologically sound, but it sure seemed logical sometimes. She stuffed a bite of her sandwich into her mouth as she recalled all the good deeds she had done since the accident. They'd certainly made her feel better about herself.

No, she couldn't risk undoing all the good she had done. And if she hadn't yet fully made amends for her past, she couldn't risk bringing Cole into the mess she had made of her life—that would be a selfish decision on her part, knowing everyone she loved in the past ended up getting hurt. And *seriously* hurt, not just a mild heartbreak.

She shoved another bite of sandwich into her mouth as she continued justifying her choice to decline Cole's offer. If he only knew, he would surely thank her for keeping her distance. Not that he *would* ever know, of course. And she had no idea what she was going to say to him when she saw him next. But he had made it clear it was her choice whether or not to meet up with him and promised there would be no hard feelings if she declined. It was settled then. This was her final decision. She simply couldn't go down that road. Not now, anyway. Maybe never.

The bite of sandwich turned to sawdust in her mouth, and she had to choke it down.

# CHAPTER 10

COLE BOUGHT A CUP OF DECAF coffee with cream and sat at a table for two inside the quaint coffeeshop. The woman at the table next to him was sipping a frappe, and he cringed at the memory that drink evoked. Hmm, maybe coffee and women weren't the right combination for him. His cringe turned into a smile as he gazed into the distance and wondered what kind of drink Emily would order if she actually showed up. Not that he expected her to. He only wished he knew why she was so reluctant.

Was she not attracted to him? Had she just gotten out of a relationship and wasn't ready to date again? Maybe she *was* interested but already had plans that night and didn't know how to tell him.

There any number of reasons she would choose not to come. But as he carefully sipped his hot coffee, sending up a prayer for clarity and wisdom, he couldn't deny that it felt right to him, the two of them together. Maybe it was because he was finally ready to end the dating drought in his life and she was the first true prospect he had run into. Or maybe he was just so intrigued by this woman who seemed to pour her life into others that he was misinterpreting his fascination for attraction. Her extravagant selflessness wasn't something he was used to.

Two cups of coffee and forty-five minutes later, he resigned himself to the fact that Emily wasn't coming. After finishing the scone he'd bought halfway through his visit and reading the news on his smart phone, his brother's voice suddenly entered his head. *Use the internet.* Cole's brain started racing.

Maybe if he looked her up online, he could find something that would convince him she wasn't who he thought she was. Maybe she had secret drug charges or had been married and divorced four times by the age of thirty. That would certainly help get him past his little fascination, wouldn't it? And if he found nothing but positive feedback online, then maybe there would be some sort of clue to help him appeal to her in the right way, or to help him understand why she was so guarded. Or maybe she'd been lying about being in a relationship, and he'd find pictures on social media that revealed a boyfriend.

Throwing caution to the wind, he went back to the clinic to look up her full name for his search. A pang of guilt stabbed him when he realized he was using client files for personal reasons, but he pushed past it. This was a case of the end justifying the means. He turned on the desk lamp in his office and fired up his computer. A few minutes later, he found the "emergency contact" section in Tyler's file and sure enough, there was Emily's full name and address staring back at him—Emily Jenkins, living in Everly, Kansas on the outskirts of Kansas City.

He copied and pasted her name into the search engine on his computer and pressed "Enter." Several results turned up, but once he weeded through the ones that were obviously not hers, one article stood out to him. It was from seven years ago and described a terrible car accident in which the passenger of one car— Emily's husband, according to the article—had died. The drivers of both cars, one being Emily herself, were taken to the hospital and in critical condition at the time the article was written. Emily had obviously survived, but the article was silent about the fate of the other driver, a woman named Sylvia Gonzalez. Pictures of the mangled cars were included on the screen.

Cole leaned back in his chair and let out a long sigh, slowly rubbing his chin in disbelief. There was a pit in his stomach as the shock of the article sank in. A fatal car crash. That was enough to affect a person for life. His family knew that all too well.

According to the article, she was only twenty-three back then. Was this the reason she was so hesitant— even fearful—to go out with him? Because she'd lost her husband in such a traumatic way? Did she feel trapped by the loss, unable to move on? Surely, she had been on dates in the past seven years, hadn't she? Someone as young, beautiful, and kind as Emily. So why not with him?

He realized with sudden clarity that what Maria had predicted had come true—what was he supposed to do with this information he'd uncovered? It wasn't like he could confront her about it or tell her he understood the pain from her past. That would certainly make him seem like a stalker. He considered calling up his brother and reaming him out for his advice, but the truth was, he had chosen to follow it. He had no one to blame but himself.

*God, more than ever I ask that You be with Emily. She lost a husband, and she deals with tragedy all day at her job. Is that why she's so reserved? Please bring her emotional healing. Thank you for this amazing person's presence in my life. I don't think You want what we could have to end before it even begins, but I'm willing to wait on You for the ifs and whens.*

He wanted to listen to God and was willing to do whatever He asked of him. To pursue or pull back. To move on or wait patiently. He just hoped that Emily was willing to follow God's lead in the same way.

ON WEDNESDAY, AN AMBULANCE delivered the first of several victims from a car accident, and Emily found herself handing sutures to the attending physician as he closed the first of several gaping abdominal wounds. A pile of bloodied gauze fell from the operating table to the floor. When she reached for a fresh pile to replace them, her red-stained gloves caught her attention. Breathing through her mouth to avoid the metallic scent, she focused on her training.

From the corner of her eye, she noticed Nan, another ER nurse about twenty years older than Emily, giving her a funny look as if she was trying to figure something out. After the patient was all stitched up, he was rolled out to a recovery room while Emily and Nan headed to the scrub sink to wash up.

Nan was a Kansas transplant from Alabama, so her southern drawl stood out from the rest. "You get different when this kind of case comes in, Emily."

The intensity of her words caught Emily off guard, especially since she was normally so playful when it came to their interactions. "What kind of case do you mean?" She tried to forget the visions of blood before they triggered memories she didn't care to relive today. "Different how?"

"An accident—a bloody, traumatic one. You get focused. Serious. Invested. Am I right?"

Nan's perceptiveness was uncanny. The older woman didn't know much about Emily's past, but she knew there were some demons lurking there, and she wasn't afraid to try to draw them out of her. Of course, Emily never allowed her to make much progress. Except, as good as she felt after crying to Cole last week, maybe it would be nice to have someone listen to her for a change. Especially one with a strong faith, like Nan. They went to the same church ever since Nan had invited her a few years back, and their bond was stronger than she shared with the other nurses.

Emily shrugged and dried her hands on a paper towel. "I guess it just reminds me of my own car accident, and I feel more connected to the patients that have gone through the same sort of thing as me."

Nan nodded. She knew about her car accident, but Emily never shared the details—certainly not the outcome of the others involved. Though for someone as insightful as Nan, Emily's silence was probably almost as telling as knowing the full story. Thankfully, Nan knew when to stop pushing. "Take the time you need, hon. I'm praying for you."

Emily didn't respond, but headed to a quiet place so she could take a few moments to compose herself. Nan was right. Patients like this one always triggered unwanted memories. She glanced down and noticed a spot of blood on the front of her scrubs. Her stomach churned, and she leaned her head back.

*She opened her eyes, dazed and confused. It didn't take long for the numbness and shock to wear off and pain to take its place. She couldn't move her legs, and a quick glance down confirmed what she already suspected. Though her vision was blurry, she saw the blood, and lots of it. Pain coursed through her body.*

*What had happened? She was driving to dinner with Derek, and then… Derek! She glanced over at the passenger side of the car to find her husband, out cold. Was he even breathing? A sinking feeling swirled inside her before she heard the sirens and closed her eyes, seeing nothing but black as she mentally slipped away.*

*The next thing she knew, she was staring up at nothing but white. Was she on the other side? Would she soon see angels or Jesus or... something? Instead, a friendly female face appeared, checking a monitor next to her bed. Oh. She was in a hospital. "Where's my husband?"*

She swallowed hard against the memory. At the time, that accident had proven to her that God's vengeance hadn't been fulfilled yet. Of course, karma had always been fresh on her mind thanks to her husband, who never let her live down the ways things had ended with her father. But as quickly as that notion came to her mind, she scolded herself for even thinking it—after all, she was the one who was alive. Derek, on the other hand, hadn't made it.

Although she knew the emotional pain was deserved, she couldn't live in a state of permanently reliving the past—while it shaped a proper perspective, it also hindered her ability to make a difference in the present. She had patients to tend to, after all, and coworkers to assist. Starting with giving Nan a break. Surely she could put her own misfortunes aside and attempt to assuage their hurts and troubles, couldn't she?

# CHAPTER 11

Emily opened the supply room door and almost jumped when she saw Nan writing something on a clipboard. "There you are. I've been looking for you."

Nan didn't look up. "Well, I'm right here, hon. What do you need?"

Emily bit her lip. This had sounded like a better idea before she was face to face with her mentor. "I, uh... I wanted to apologize for shutting you out earlier, and then abandoning you in the ER. I shouldn't have left like that."

Nan stopped what she was doing and raised her head. As she searched Emily's eyes, it was as though she was reading her like a book. Nan obviously knew the truth. That Emily had lost someone in her accident. That she blamed herself for it. That she had never truly moved on. Did she really have to say the words? To Emily's relief, Nan just nodded and returned to her

75

clipboard.

"Can I help you with your inventory to make it up to you?"

Nan gave her a scolding look. "Emily, dear. You don't have anything to make up to me. But I sure wouldn't mind your help just the same." She handed her a printed page from under the piece she was using. Emily had helped with this task before, so she knew the drill. She grabbed a pen from her pocket and began counting syringes.

"Did I mentioned I'm taking off next week?"

Emily was relieved at the change of subject. "What? No, I didn't know that. Going somewhere exciting?"

"Mm-hmm." Nan waggled her eyebrows. "Terrence and I are going to Niagara Falls for our anniversary"

Emily gasped. "No way! Good for you guys. Congratulations."

"Yep, celebrating thirty years. I can't wait." She checked a box on her paper and focused her attention on the next shelf. "And what about you, missy? Any hot date prospects for the weekend?"

"Actually, I could have had a hot date last night." Emily bit her lip. Should she have guarded that information a little more closely?

"What?" Nan stopped writing and faced her. "Tell me more."

She shrugged. "There's really nothing to tell. Cole— the physical therapist I'm taking that boy to—asked me for coffee."

Nan's eyes bulged. "And you turned him down?"

"Yep. I don't really want to get involved with

anyone. And I'm not into flings, you know that."

"Honey, tell me again the part about how handsome he is." Nan was a free spirit and always razzed Emily for not getting into the dating scene. She admired the woman's energy and loved her stories. They had worked together ever since Emily started at Kansas City Med five years ago, and Nan always encouraged Emily to get out and meet someone. Her southern accent somehow made the nagging seem more endearing than overbearing, and Emily rather enjoyed their lighthearted banter most of the time.

"Oh, Nan. I know. On paper, he's perfect. And I'm sure I'm a fool for not seeing it. But any time I've ever been close to someone, it's not ended well. And I really don't want to put either one of us through that heartache." *After all, everyone I get close to ends up dead.*

Nan shook her head. "But you haven't even tried in all the time I've known you. I don't understand why you wouldn't at least take that first step. You are so cute and smart and fun. From where I stand, you deserve this. You *need* this. You'll end up an old lonely soul with no one to take care of you."

Emily rolled her eyes at the exaggeration. "I hear you, Nan. I do. And maybe my resolve to remain single is coming down, because I have to tell you, I did consider his offer. But... I don't know, it's hard to explain without knowing all I've been through."

"So? Tell me, darlin'. What exactly have you been through?"

Emily stared at her coworker. Did she really want to share her burdens with her friend? Might she feel better afterward, like when she'd cried to Cole? No, it was too much to get into right now. "Let's just say a lot of crazy stuff, okay? Lots of death and tragedy. And I'm not talking about on the job, either."

"And what does that have to do with going on a date?" Nan asked matter-of-factly.

Emily knew Nan meant well, but there was no way to get her to understand. "I don't want to fall in love with someone only to lose them. Besides, I really think I'm better off single. And I'm not crying myself a river about it either. I *like* my life the way it is. It's a lot less complicated." Even if she sometimes felt enslaved by mistakes from her past.

Nan smiled. "Well, I can understand that for sure. But complicated isn't always bad either. I just want to see you happy, that's all."

Emily pasted on an overly fake smile to prove a point, and Nan laughed. "Ah, very convincing."

Just then, the intake specialist knocked on the supply room door and held up a file. "Elderly man brought in with chest pains. Room C. Who's got it?"

"I'll take it." Emily grabbed the file. "I need to escape this lady's interrogation."

"I'm just watching out for you!"

"Yeah, yeah," Emily called back. She suddenly felt a weigh lifted, as if sharing just the little that she did, revealing just enough so Nan knew she had some complex layers under the surface, somehow eased a burden or two. And maybe Nan was right about giving Cole a chance. For the first time in years, the idea of a relationship—or at least a first date—was starting to sound appealing, as much as she'd been trying to repress the thought. But she really wasn't sure if she was ready. Or how she would even know what *ready* felt like.

After a chaotic afternoon in the ER, Emily was asked to stay late to help with the influx. By the time she got home, it was too late to make it to her weekly Bible study—which was unfortunate, because she could have used the distraction. Somehow, she had to dispel the guilt from the sudden onslaught of memories the earlier accident victim had triggered, but she wasn't quite sure how to make that happen.

It's not that she was trying to earn God's love or His favor, per se, but she couldn't shake the notion that she still had to make up for the horrible choices she'd made as a teenager and in her early twenties. Would she ever feel like she was right with God? She believed He died for the sins of the whole *world*—so why didn't she believe His death and resurrection were enough to conquer *hers*? What made her offenses so unforgivable?

Without the distraction of her Bible study to fill her evening, Emily scrounged her bare pantry shelves for something to eat. After deciding to stop at the grocery store after work tomorrow, she changed into her pajamas and settled on the couch to watch an old movie.

The romantic theme caused her thoughts to drift to Cole. How would she act around him at Tyler's next physical therapy appointment on Friday, given how she had blown off his invitation last night? Why was he into her, anyway? They had only talked on a few occasions, and certainly not long enough to develop a strong connection. There was no denying he was a good guy with a caring heart, but why was he so drawn to her of all people? And why did she feel more drawn to him than any other guy who had asked her out over the past seven years?

*God, please give me wisdom as I figure out what You want for me—and* from *me. Sometimes I feel like I have to keep making up for my past, but at the same time I know You don't hold my sins against me. Why can't I live in the freedom so many people talk about? Is it possible to truly move on from the things I've done?*

Emily knew God listened to her, but why was it so hard to hear Him speak in return?

# CHAPTER 12

AFTER HIS SHIFT ON THURSDAY, COLE went straight to the grocery store to grab a few items. In addition to the staples like bread and milk, it was his turn to bring in Friday office treats, so he had to pick up a box of pastries or donuts. He'd also run out of car window cleaner, so he figured he'd get it all at one place. After putting a loaf of bread in his otherwise empty basket, he glanced down the aisle containing cleaning supplies and pet products and did a double take. A woman knelt on the ground reaching for a huge bag of dog food on the bottom shelf.

He swore the woman was Emily, but then again, his eyes might be playing tricks on him. After all, he did have Emily on his mind lately. Even if it wasn't her, this woman clearly needed help lifting the large bag, so to lend a hand—and to get a closer look—he walked down the aisle with his green plastic shopping basket in hand.

Sure enough, his hunch was correct. She wore lavender hospital scrubs and her hair was tied back in a messy ponytail. Even in her work clothes, she was beyond adorable. A wide grin grew on his face, which he tried to dampen before getting her attention. "Emily?"

She glanced up upon hearing her name, then shock covered her face. "Oh, my goodness! Hi, Cole." She tried to stand up with the gigantic bag of dog food wedged between her hands and legs, but she was unsuccessful. The bag slid off her legs as she tried in vain to catch it.

Cole instinctively reached out to help, but he was too late. Emily laughed as the bag plopped to the ground.

"Let me get that for you." Cole put his basket down on the floor, grabbed the bag of dog food, and placed it on the bottom of Emily's cart.

"Thanks, I appreciate it."

"No problem. What kind of dog do you have, anyway?" He gestured to the large volume of dog food she was buying.

"Oh, I don't have any pets. I'm buying this for my neighbor. She wanted a giant bag so she wouldn't have to get more for a long time. She's like a grandmother to me and doesn't get around very well, so I help her out. You know, 'cause I'm so strong and can handle these things." She waved a hand at the bag of dog food she'd already dropped once.

"Clearly." Cole chuckled, thankful for this glimpse into Emily's life outside the clinic. It was also nice to know Frank wasn't looking over his shoulder. "You sure like to help people, don't you?"

Emily raised her eyebrows. "What do you mean?"

"Well, taking Tyler to PT. Your visits to cancer patients. And now... your elderly neighbor?"

Emily shrugged. "Well, anyone would help a neighbor like mine. She's so friendly. I really only do it for her homemade cookies. And as for the cancer patients? I mean, it helps that I work at the hospital. Why not get to know the regulars while I'm there, right?"

"I don't know. I'm sure most people would find slightly more selfish things to do with their time. But if you like helping people out so much..." He paused. Was this the right time or way to bring this up? "I could have used your help the other night." He winked, so she would know he was teasing her about standing him up.

"Oh, my word, I know. About that. I... I didn't mean to make you feel bad or anything."

Cole grinned. "No worries. I'll just take it up with my psychiatrist when we talk about my abandonment issues."

Emily giggled and lowered her gaze, blushing. Cole didn't mean to put her on the spot, but he found it a bit too coincidental that he had this timely opportunity to speak to her outside of the clinic. He couldn't let her off the hook altogether.

"Question for you," he said.

"Okay."

"Hypothetically speaking, if I asked you out again right now, would I get the same answer?"

Emily's head jerked up with a deer-in-the-headlights

look, her face growing even redder as she stared. She wasn't going to make this easy for him. He sensed her hesitation—it didn't take a rocket scientist to realize she struggled to find the right way to turn him down. But he really didn't want to believe that reality.

He finally let out a small laugh to ease the tension. "Oh man, rejected again. Good thing it was hypothetical and not a *real* question."

After a bit of an awkward silence which Cole decided wasn't up to him to fill, Emily exhaled and finally spoke, her expression serious, her tone gentle and kind. "Cole, listen. I'm really flattered. And really tempted, actually. But I... I don't know how to say this. I guess you could say I'm in a weird spot in my life. I have a lot of baggage. And I don't think it's fair to get you involved in my junk right now."

Cole tried to absorb her words. How true was what she was saying? The excuse sounded a bit generic, but he didn't take her for a liar. Still, it seemed odd to him someone could really think their own baggage was a reason not to give another person a chance. After all, who *didn't* have baggage? Then again, he didn't know what her baggage was, unless she was referring to her accident from seven years ago. He could see how that would make someone tentative about getting involved with someone new, but not dismiss the idea altogether.

Cole scrunched up his nose. "Don't you think that's something I should decide for myself? I mean, if that's really the reason."

Emily closed her eyes for a moment, then opened them and peered up at him. "I'm really sorry. I'm just not in a place to be in a healthy relationship right now. And I'm definitely not the type to get involved if a long-term relationship isn't the end goal."

Cole nodded but frowned, frustration creeping into his soul. Still, what else could he say? "Okay, I guess I have to accept that."

Emily gave him a sad smile and averted her gaze. He didn't know if it was wishful thinking, but something told him she struggled with her decision to turn him down. It gave him hope that she might change her mind someday.

"So, I'm guessing you're going to need help getting that dog food into your car, am I right?" Cole picked up his basket as they walked to the end of the aisle together.

Glancing down at the bag of food as if re-analyzing its weight, Emily glanced from the bag, to Cole, and back to the bag again. "There's a strong possibility," she finally said. A smile twitched at the corner of her mouth. "Care to help a girl out?"

Cole nodded. He'd pick up donuts on the way to work tomorrow instead—and who needed milk? He wasn't letting this woman out of his sight. "Do you have more shopping to do first?"

"A little. I need to pick up something to make for dinner. I'm starving and my pantry is bare."

"Well, I was planning to grab a bite on my way home, if you care to join me." At least, that's what he'd do if she agreed. Otherwise, he had leftover pizza in his fridge with his name on it. "*Just* as a friend, I promise."

Emily bit her lower lip, seeming to mull over his request and the motivation behind it. Cole could tell this was a losing battle. He wasn't sure why he'd even tried again—he had already been stood up and then rejected on his second *hypothetical* attempt at asking her out. Why had he set himself up for a third strike? Was he a glutton for punishment?

He wished he knew what was going on inside her head as she stared at him with narrowed eyes, almost like she sized him up. But without warning, her eyes softened and a smile came to her lips. "On one condition."

Cole tried to hide his shock at her acceptance. "Oh... kay. And what's that?"

"If I can be so bold, I'd like to pick where we eat."

He gasped as if her request was outrageous. Then he smiled. "Absolutely. Your pick. And my treat."

Emily tilted her head. Just in case his paying would make the night seem more like a date, he quickly defended himself. "I treat my friends all the time. Next time we hang out, I'll let you pay if you want. Really."

She continued to cautiously eye him up before finally giving in.

AFTER THEY FINISHED THEIR shopping, Cole followed Emily out to her car. She opened her trunk as he reached for the bag of dog food at the bottom of her cart.

After shutting the trunk and facing Emily, he resisted the urge to put his hand on her waist. This was going to be more difficult than he thought—not just when it came to rushing her, but also not getting too physical with his dates like he had before becoming a Christian. He had to keep things platonic. Although he failed to fully grasp why and how she felt the way she did, she had only agreed to dinner under the assumption it would be as friends, so he owed it to her to respect her wishes. He only hoped he could avoid being in the Friend Zone for too long.

"So, where are we headed?"

"There's this little hole-in-the-wall burger joint near my house. I know the owner, and he's struggling to keep it open. So, on the rare occasion that I eat out, I try to go there to support him."

Cole raised his eyebrows. "Sounds… suspicious."

Emily laughed. "I promise it's delicious. I mean, if you can get past the graffiti. Oh, and I don't recommend using the restrooms there." She smiled at Cole's expression. "Are you still in?"

He wouldn't have missed it for the world. "You bet. I'll follow you."

They got into their own cars, with Cole following Emily's sedan through town. Several minutes later, she pulled into the parking lot of a little run-down strip mall with only a few other cars in it. It wasn't the best part of town, but it had its charm. And it was only about twenty minutes west of where he lived. He parked his car next to hers.

"This is it, have you heard of it?" she asked as they emerged from their cars.

Cole peered up at the neon sign that read *Antonio's* and shook his head. "I haven't had a reason to come to this side of town much before." Until now. He hoped he'd be out this way a lot more often.

"Well, trust me. They serve the best burgers in town. And if you're not in the mood for a burger, they've got great tacos too."

"All right. Let's do this." He gestured for her to take the lead.

Once inside, Cole soaked in his surroundings. The place was small and dark, and soft music played in the background. He heard dishes clanking in the kitchen and the enticing aroma of fresh grilled burgers taunted him. It was exactly as Emily had described it.

There was no hostess desk, but Emily knew the drill as she weaved past a few occupied tables and toward the back corner where it was quiet and less cluttered. After Cole took a seat, Emily leaned over to speak. "I'm going to see if my friend is here. You can check out the menu in the meantime." She pointed at the plastic placemat in front of him with a small menu displayed across it.

As she headed toward the kitchen, Cole suppressed a smirk. If there was any question about whether or not he viewed this as a date, Emily had no doubt picked this place to remind him this was nothing but a meal of convenience. And he could only respect her for it, even though he secretly hoped this would eventually turn into something more.

After studying the placemat menu for a few seconds, he heard a deep voice call out, "Emily!" Not much in the kitchen was hidden from public view, and Cole saw Emily give the cook a hug from the side, avoiding the grease stains from his white apron.

"How's it going, Antonio?" She grinned.

Cole strained to hear their conversation. He could tell the man she was talking to had a slight accent, as if his primary language was Spanish. "Hangin' in there, girl. Haven't seen you in a while. Thought maybe you forgot about me."

She put her hands on her hips with a scolding expression. "Never. You know I love this place."

"You with someone?" He peered out at the handful of guests in the dining area. "You with *him*?" He gestured with his chin at Cole, who suddenly pretended to study his menu again.

"Yeah, he's just a friend. Thought I'd share with him the best burger in town. Maybe make a regular out of him."

"All right, I'll be sure to make you guys the best then. Call me sometime, Em."

"You take care. I'll let you get back to work."

As Emily returned to her seat, Cole tilted his head, his eyes narrowed. "I thought you said you knew the owner here. You know the cook too?"

Emily smiled. "They're one and the same."

Cole let that sink in. "Must be barely making ends meet, huh?"

"Yeah. Antonio's is great, but business is rocky. He's always saying all he needs are a few more regulars to keep him afloat."

Cole took a deep breath. "Well, I hope things work out for him. So, what are you going to order?"

"You said it's your treat, right?" Emily asked. "In

that case, I'll go with the lobster."

"Is that so?" He liked her sudden lighthearted vibe. This was a new side to her, and it felt like a bit of a victory to see her walls coming down. Despite their lackluster surroundings, even despite her very clear declaration that they remain friends, her teasing energized him. "Unfortunately, it appears the seafood portion of the menu did not fit on the placemat, so we might have to forgo the lobster."

Emily giggled. "Okay then, I'll go with the Tex Mex Burger. It's good if you like spicy food. If you're a fan of mushrooms, I recommend the mushroom and Swiss burger, too."

"Hmm, I'll go with the Tex Mex as well."

After the server took their order, Cole sipped his water and leaned back in his chair. "Thanks for keeping me company for dinner. And for introducing me to this place. To think I may have gone my whole life without ever knowing it was here."

"Ha, ha. I swear, the food is great. And I have a special bond with Antonio."

"Yeah, what's that about?" He leaned forward a little. "How do you guys know each other?"

Emily's gaze fell to the table. "It's kind of a long story. I met him several years ago. I felt responsible for some pain in his life and wanted to help out how I could."

Cole couldn't help but think about the inside scoop he had on Emily's accident. Was that perhaps what she was referring to? How did Antonio come into play? But he decided not to reveal what he knew. "Did you help him get this restaurant started?"

Emily unwrapped her silverware from the rolled paper napkin. "You could sort of say that. A few years ago, I casually asked him what his dreams were, and he spewed off this grand plan to open his own restaurant. I gave him the moral support and encouragement to pursue it, and then helped him through the financial aspect as well—like directly with donations, but also walking him through the loan process with the bank, since I could tell that wasn't something he was really comfortable with."

"That's cool," Cole said. "I'm impressed you took such initiative."

"Yeah, well I really owed it to him. And I believed in his dream." She shoved her hands under her thighs in the booth and shifted her body back and forth.

Cole was still curious about the details around the event that led to their friendship, but he wasn't going to pressure her into sharing more than she was comfortable with. Instead, he took the opportunity to take the conversation down a different path. "And what are *your* dreams, Emily? Do you have a bucket list?"

"Oh, not really. I'm a pretty simple gal. I mostly want to make sure I'm living the way God wants me to."

Cole fiddled with his straw wrapper and nodded, thankful for the confirmation of her faith. "Well, that certainly shows. But… I mean, isn't there anything you want for yourself? Just because?"

Emily's cheeks grew red as she stared at the table and shrugged her shoulders. "There is *one* thing. I mean, other than some travel destinations I'd like to see but probably never will."

"And? What is it?"

She seemed embarrassed by her response. "I've always wanted to learn how to decorate cakes. You know—like, fancy ones."

Cole almost laughed upon hearing her primary goal in life. Not because it was silly, but because it was so... within reach. "You realize how achievable that is, don't you? I mean, you've paid for a stranger's physical therapy out of pocket. Don't you think you can afford a few cake decorating classes?"

"I know, I know. But I can't justify spending that much money on myself. Besides, I wouldn't want to go alone, and I don't really have friends who are into that kind of stuff. Most of my friends either have jobs with crazy hours, or they have kids and zero time for pointless hobbies."

"I wouldn't call it pointless. I'm sure you could put those skills to good use, like, baking cakes for orphanages or something." He winked at her.

"Well, what about you?" She reached for her water and took a sip. "What's on your bucket list?"

He glanced her way and rolled his eyes with a smirk. "I'm not quite so selfless. I have a number of things on my list. For starters, I'd like to visit every continent. Plus, I've always wanted to go skydiving. And I want to see a baseball game at every stadium in the country. I'd also like to befriend a homeless person. That one might resonate with you a little." Cole paused and narrowed his eyes. "Do you get offended when I make light of how, like, selfless you are?" He suddenly realized how much he had been teasing her for her generosity.

"Oh, not at all. I know it's a bit out of the ordinary. But trust me, I'm no saint. You know that law of physics—for every action there's an equal and opposite reaction?"

Cole nodded.

"Well, that's kind of like my life. For every good deed you've seen me do, there's something equally awful in my past to counteract it."

Cole was about to ask her to elaborate when their food came. After their server left, he picked up his burger. "This looks so good."

"I told you." Emily spread her paper napkin in her lap. "I've been meaning to ask you, how is Tyler doing? Is he on track to a full recovery? Is my money being put to good use?"

Cole swallowed his first bite as he nodded, hoping he'd have a chance to revert the conversation back to Emily's veiled statement from a moment ago. "Definitely. It was really good he came in. He wasn't being pushed to reach his full potential, but now that I've set him on that path, I don't think he'll have any problems getting back to normal—and soon."

"That's great news. I was disappointed not being there last Friday, but I had another commitment, so I'm glad Barb could make it." Emily squirted hot sauce on her burger and took a bite.

"Oh yeah. That girl's funeral, right?"

She nodded somberly and swallowed her bite. "Charlotte."

"I didn't mean to bring up sad memories."

Emily stared straight at Cole, and he held her gaze for as long as she would let him. "It's weird." She finally turned her attention back to her food. "You are the only one I've been comfortable talking to about that. I haven't even told my Bible study about her. I don't understand it, but it's true."

Cole considered her words a compliment. "Well, maybe you sense I'm a caring person who won't judge you or betray you." That came off sounding more arrogant than he intended, so he tried to lighten the mood. "If I do say so myself."

Emily laughed as he'd hoped she would.

"But seriously, if you ever find you need someone to talk to or hang out with—maybe come to this fine establishment with again in the future—I'm happy to be that person for you." He let that sink in for a moment. "I promise I won't keep asking you though. I'm not trying to pressure you or anything. But I'm here if you need someone, so please don't hesitate to ask."

Cole wasn't sure what to make of the silence that followed, but hopefully she took his words to heart.

"Thanks," she finally said. "I appreciate that, more than you know."

Cole downed a few more bites of his burger. "So, you're telling me the next time I come here, I should try the tacos?"

Emily licked her lips. "Without a doubt. And that hot sauce there—" She used her chin to gesture to a red and green bottle she'd added to her burger. "It's the absolute best if you can stand the heat. Can't find it in stores, so enjoy it here while you can."

Cole put his burger down. "Well, why didn't you say so earlier? I like a little spice." How hot could it be, anyway? He reached for the jar and poured a dollop on his plate. With two fries in his hand, he dunked them into the sauce and shoved them into his mouth. Emily watched as he chewed, and it only took a second for the spice to permeate his tongue. *Play it cool, Cole. If Emily can handle it, you can, too.* His whole face grew warm until he couldn't take the burning sensation anymore. Reaching for his glass, he sucked down several sips of water.

Emily laughed, hiding her mouth with her napkin. "I told you it was hot."

Cole finished swallowing his bite, then panted. "That's an understatement."

"I feel bad, but that was totally worth it." She grinned and looked at him with her beautiful blue eyes. "Did I forget to mention a little goes a long way? And not to completely douse your fries in it?"

Cole shook his head with a jovial smirk, but he had to agree with her first statement. Seeing Emily having a good time was worth a hot sauce assault in his mouth. Before long, they were both stuffed and ready to go. As promised, Cole paid the bill, leaving a generous tip considering how special the owner was to Emily.

She caught Antonio's eye through the kitchen doorway and waved goodbye before heading out.

"Are you gonna need a hand with getting that dog food out of your car tonight?" Cole asked as they walked through the parking lot towards their cars.

While he wanted to be helpful, he certainly wouldn't mind extending their time together on top of his chivalry.

"That's nice of you. But I think I'll manage. At least it's up higher in the trunk so I don't have to carry dead weight from the ground."

His heart dropped realizing this was the end of their evening, but he tried not to let his disappointment show. "That's true. Well, thanks again for showing me this place."

Emily smiled. "I hope you liked it. I know it wasn't—"

"It was perfect." Cole's fingers ached to reach for her, to wrap her in a hug. But he knew that wasn't what she wanted right now—she'd barely agreed to dinner as friends—so he shoved his hands in his pockets instead.

They stopped next to the driver's door of Emily's car, and she dug in her purse for her keys. "Well, I guess I'll see you tomorrow for Tyler's appointment. You know how to get out of here?"

"Yeah, I'm good."

"Okay. Good night, then." She took a step closer to him to reach for her car door, and her shoulder brushed against his arm. The touch was fleeting, but the warmth that permeated his body was memorable.

He took a step back and watched to make sure she got out of the parking lot safely before he turned on his own ignition and drove away, thankful for the few minutes he'd get to see Emily the next day and hoping—praying—she would reach out for more.

# CHAPTER 13

A N UNEXPLAINABLE WARMTH RADIATED OUT FROM Emily's shoulder, where she'd accidentally touched Cole's arm, and reached all the way to her heart. Driving home from Antonio's, she pondered his offer to talk or hang out sometime. She was concerned at how tempted she was to take him up on it, but he was such a likable guy. Flirtatious and funny one second, serious and gracious the next.

She frowned. Had dinner been a mistake? She had known there was a chance agreeing to a meal together might have given him false hope, as he seemed interested in pursuing something she wasn't ready to give him. But when he'd asked at the grocery store, Nan's words from the other day had run through her head, urging her to take a leap of faith by having a simple meal with the guy. And if Cole was sincere in his willingness to treat her as a friend—something she didn't have a lot of—then it was a win-win.

Once home, she reversed her car into her neighbor's driveway and knocked on the door. The elderly woman answered, dressed in a long night gown. Emily glanced at her watch, hoping it wasn't too late. "Hi, Dorothy. Is this a bad time? I have your dog food."

"Oh, thank you, dear. Would you mind putting it in the garage? I'll open the door for you and close it when you leave."

"Sounds good. Let me know if you need anything else, all right? Have a good night."

The woman nodded. "You're an angel. Take care now."

A moment later, the electric garage door opened, and Emily heaved the bag of food from her trunk into the familiar corner of Dorothy's garage. She was glad the weight was manageable from the height of her trunk— though if not, it would have given her and Cole something to laugh about the next day.

As she made her way back to her car, she heard Dorothy's voice from the doorway "Emily? There is one more thing."

She turned to face her neighbor. "Sure, what is it?"

"I'm going to be out of town for Memorial Day weekend, starting tomorrow. I'm dropping Rex off at my daughter's and stopping my mail, but would you mind just keeping an eye on the place for me?"

"Oh, sure. I can do that." Her heart started to race. Right. Today was already May twenty-fourth. The end of the month had snuck up on her, and with it the anniversary of the fire. She said goodbye and got in the car to drive the block down to her house. Memories rushed in of another neighborhood on a night when she'd only been a block from home. A neighborhood she hadn't seen in years. No, she couldn't do this. Her stomach soured. *Think about something else, Em.*

Inside her house, she unloaded groceries, forcing her thoughts to stay in the present. She thought about the dog food. About Cole's muscles bulging beneath the sleeve of his polo. She smiled. Yeah, think about Cole. Her reaction made her realize that deep down, she must want things to work out between them. She'd enjoyed their time together. It had been so natural, but now she felt so invested. Was it possible God was changing her heart? Time would tell.

After getting ready for bed, she lay wide awake sprawled out on the mattress. Her restless legs repositioned multiple times, her mind going a mile a minute. She thought about her night, about Cole's smile while they ate and the look on his face when he'd eaten the hot sauce. There. That should bring on good dreams tonight. She finally felt herself fade.

*Even three houses away, the fire roared in her ears. The pit in her stomach grew larger and emptier with every step. Everything she owned was in flames. Her teary eyes scanned the gawking crowd. Where was he? Her heart hammered in her chest. This couldn't be happening.*

*Her stomach churned as she pushed past the soot-covered firefighters until a blistering wall of heat halted her advance. Why couldn't she find her father?*

*As if in slow motion, all sounds faded as she focused on the jacketed hero carrying a large body out of the inferno.*

*Nauseating cramps clawed at her middle and fought their way out until she threw up on the pavement at her feet.*

Opening her eyes with a startled jerk, Emily's pulse raced as she reoriented herself. She gazed around her dark room, realizing with a mix of relief and sadness that it was just a dream, even if the images were real memories.

And just like that, the nightmares were back. It happened every year, and she knew from experience she'd never get back to sleep now. Heart still pounding, she clicked the chain of the lamp next to her bed to illuminate the room and retrieve a book from the shelf. She might as well not waste the night with fits of restless sleep, so she selected a long, humorous story that would get her through the night and keep her thoughts focused on more pleasant things. That would distract her brain from the relentless and unwelcome memories of the fire. After all, there was no sense in reliving a past she couldn't change.

EMILY AND TYLER ARRIVED a few minutes early for their appointment on Friday, so they sat in the waiting area until Cole was ready. Emily propped her head on one hand with her elbow resting on the arm of the chair while Tyler watched the cartoons they always played on the television. She yawned, finding it harder and harder to keep her eyes open after every blink.

The sound of Cole's voice jolted her awake. "Hey

bud!" he said, clearly greeting Tyler.

There was no way Cole hadn't noticed her sleeping, so she flashed a guilty smirk his way, her cheeks growing warm. "You caught me."

Cole grinned. "No worries. It happens all the time."

The three of them headed back to the treatment area, then Cole glanced over his shoulder. "Did you get the dog food out of your trunk okay last night?"

Emily chuckled. "Yeah, I managed to drag it into my neighbor's garage. Thanks for checking."

"That's good."

Tyler's therapy began, and once again, Emily watched through the observation window. Before long—despite her good intentions to stay awake—her head rolled around like a dashboard bobble-head. Strange how sleep evaded her all night but as soon as she actually *wanted* to stay awake, her body finally gave in to the urge. Despite her drowsy state, she was alert enough to keep an eye on Cole. Hopefully he wouldn't catch her sleeping again.

After Tyler's appointment, they walked to the front of the clinic. "Did I keep you out too late last night?"

Emily rubbed her eyes. "No, I just didn't sleep well last night. I should probably be more embarrassed about dozing off in public, but I guess I'm too tired to care."

"Don't even worry about it." Cole put a comforting hand on her shoulder. "I hope you get a good night's sleep tonight."

Emily stifled a yawn. "Thanks, me too. And thanks again for last night. I had fun."

"Yeah, so did I." She was probably reading into

things, but Cole seemed to have a little twinkle in his eye as they spoke.

Her cheeks grew warm, and while she was tempted to continue the conversation, she also didn't want to lead the poor guy on. "Well, I guess we'll see you next week."

Cole nodded, the twinkle fading away.

"Bye," Tyler chimed in.

Emily was thrilled to hear Tyler's voice. She saw a smile on Cole's face too, probably having the same thoughts. Something about Cole brought out the best in that boy.

"Bye, guys. Have a great weekend," Cole called after them.

Emily waved goodbye and headed home, praying she wouldn't fall asleep on the way. Tyler's chatting kept her awake for a portion of the drive, and she managed to make it the rest of the way just fine. Once home, she made dinner and fell asleep to the drone of the television. But that sleep was quickly interrupted by another nightmare of the fire, and her resulting wakefulness once again lasted through the night.

In fact, she only slept in small spurts due to her overactive memories, and each day was a challenge to keep from yawning all through her shift at work or from dozing off even in the middle of a conversation. It didn't help that Nan was on vacation. While she wasn't sure she wanted her well-intentioned coworker prying as to the cause of her drowsy state, Nan's energy might have at least helped keep her on her toes. Pouring her fourth cup of coffee Monday morning, Emily yawned and slapped her cheek for an extra jolt. *Why can't I be this tired at night like a normal human being?*

By Tuesday, she had dark circles under her eyes, despite her attempts to cover them with foundation. She stopped for an iced coffee on the way to physical therapy and brought it in with her for Tyler's session.

Cole greeted them from the front counter. He glanced at her drink and a flicker of amusement washed over his face. But after he looked up at her eyes, his expression turned to concern. "Are you all right?"

"Me?" Yep, he'd noticed the eye circles. "I'm fine, just tired. Last night was rough—again. Sorry, I know I haven't been myself these last couple of appointments."

"No need to apologize since you're not the one doing the work." Cole led the way down the hall, then stopped in the doorway of the treatment room and waved Tyler inside with instructions to start stretching. He turned around to look at Emily, placing a hand on her shoulder. "Hey, are you okay?"

Emily swallowed hard, blinking a few times as she stared at him. True to form, Cole was concerned about her well-being. How should she answer a question like his? Something in his face told her he wasn't asking out of obligation or to be polite. But would sharing about her nightmares only open up the door to a whole lot more? Did she really want to reveal the source of her struggles?

She shrugged. "I'm fine. It's just… Well, honestly, I've been having these nightmares. It happens every now and then and keeps me awake for a while. It's really nothing, but a big bummer while it lasts. It'll pass, though. It always does."

Cole kept his eyes on her, his eyebrows narrowed in concern. "That's too bad. I wish there was something I could do to help. I mean, other than praying, which I've already been doing."

He'd been praying for her? That was really thoughtful. She waved her hand in the air to downplay the situation. "Thanks, but it's no big deal. I squeeze in naps here and there to make up for the lost sleep."

"Clearly." Cole gave her a teasing wink. "Well, I don't want to gyp you or Tyler of his time, so we better get started. But, let me know if you need to talk more about anything, okay?" His tone was as genuine as they came.

Emily gave him a nod. Who was she that Cole cared so much? It was hard enough letting Nan into her business sometimes, but she was out of town this week, and none of her other coworkers had noticed her sleepiness. So, to have Cole come out of nowhere and express such interest, such concern for her, was... pretty amazing. But the question of *why* kept circling her brain.

As she watched Tyler's weekly stretches and exercises through the glass window, she pondered her situation and Cole's kindness. Meanwhile, her eyes began to droop.

After the session, they stopped up front to chat. "I have good news for you." Cole leaned his forearms on top of the front counter, clasping his hands together. "Starting next week, I only need to see Tyler once a week. Shall we keep the Tuesday rotation? Does that work for you?"

Emily forced energy into her voice. "It sure does. Tuesdays at 4:00, and we get our Fridays back again. Cool, huh Tyler?" She elbowed the boy in the side.

"Yeah." Tyler flashed her a small smile.

"You're doing a great job, bud. Keep practicing at home and you'll be running marathons in no time." Cole peered down at the boy.

"Well, let's go tell Barb the good news." She turned to Cole and lowered her voice, resting a hand on his outstretched forearm for balance as she leaned in. "Thanks for being so kind. And not to sound like a broken record, but thanks for everything you're doing with Tyler, too. We'll still see you this Friday, right?"

Crinkles formed at the corners of Cole's eyes. "You bet. Take care, guys."

# CHAPTER 14

A S HE WATCHED HER LEAVE, COLE'S mind raced. Brushing him with her shoulder in the Antonio's parking lot had been an accident, but her touch on his forearm today—that was intentional. Had it meant anything? Or was he just that deprived of the female touch that an innocent, casual gesture caused a flurry of activity in his stomach?

Despite those positive signs, he was bummed that Emily hadn't shown an ounce of interest in having dinner together again—hadn't even alluded to the *possibility* of meeting up again. But even more than that, he was concerned about her physical and emotional state. She had proven to be guarded with her feelings, but it was clear she struggled with something—which likely caused her nightmares. What that was, he didn't know, but hopefully he would be able to get to the bottom of it. Not that she would make that task easy.

As he went through the motions of his job and personal life for the rest of the week, he realized he needed to see Emily for more than an hour or two a week if he had any hope of uncovering whatever bothered her. The only problem was, she wasn't exactly running with his offer to hang out. As promised, he wasn't going to pursue things with her or ask her out again, until or unless she showed interest first. He only prayed that would, in fact, happen. And soon.

Above all, he prayed for Emily to get the sleep she needed and that whatever caused her nightmares would subside. If she was still struggling when he saw her next, he'd have to take action. She may not respond to his efforts, but he had to try.

On Friday, Cole studied Emily from the moment she walked through the door of the clinic. Her shoulders were slumped, her face pale, her eyes glossy. The sight made his heart sink. Once they'd arrived at the treatment room door, he sent Tyler in to wait for him on a bench and turned to Emily. "I was going to ask how you slept last night, but it's obvious you're exhausted. I'd really hoped things had changed."

Emily shrugged. "It's okay. I've been through this before. It usually passes after a week or two, so I'm more than halfway there."

As she watched through the observation window, Cole stole occasional glances her way, wishing he could ease her pain. When he was done with Tyler's session, Cole asked the boy to sit in the waiting area while he talked to Emily at the front desk. Grabbing a business card out of a plastic shelving unit on the counter, he scribbled something on the back and then gave it to Emily, offering up a silent prayer in the process.

"What's this for?" She turned the card over in her hand.

"That's my business card. And *that*," he said, pointing to his scribbling on the back, "is my personal cell number."

He put his hands up, anticipating her protest. "I'm a bit of a night owl, so *just in case* you find yourself having trouble sleeping again in the near future, please feel free to call. Okay?" He concluded his plea with a hopeful smile.

Emily stared at the number on the card for a few long seconds. Cole hoped his offer would be well received, but he never knew what to expect with this woman or what was going on inside her head.

Gradually raising her gaze to meet Cole's, her expression softened. "Okay. I... I will." Her lips twitched up just a touch. "Thank you." Then she shoved the card in the outside pocket of her purse. She tapped Tyler on the shoulder, and the two of them left the clinic.

Cole had a spring in his step after that. Receiving a call from her was a long shot, but at least she'd taken his number and not stammered through some lame excuse about why she couldn't possibly talk to him on the phone. He chuckled at the thought, then prayed Emily would truly believe he was someone she could turn to. Because he knew deep down he was exactly what she needed to help her overcome her so-called baggage, just like she was helping Tyler get over his lingering pain. And maybe *she* was exactly what *he* needed, too.

"How's your leg feeling?" Emily kept her eyes on the road but tried to engage Tyler in conversation on their way home.

"Pretty good." The boy stared out the window. His words were positive, but his tone was subdued.

"Are you glad therapy will be over soon?"

Her question was met with silence. "Tyler?"

He sniffed and continued looking the other way.

Emily furrowed her brow. He wasn't the most talkative kid, but he was never one to ignore her questions altogether, especially over the past couple weeks. "Hey bud, what's wrong?"

Tyler lowered his head and turned to face the front. A single tear streamed down his cheek. "Oh, honey." She reached out and patted his shoulder. "Can you tell me what happened?"

"I just… I want to keep seeing Cole." He hiccupped.

His spoken desires broke her heart. "He's a good guy, isn't he? I know he really likes you, too." She wasn't sure what else to say. "Do you have an email account? Maybe you guys can stay in touch."

Tyler wiped his cheek and nodded. "Maybe."

Emily sent up a prayer for the boy and mentioned the conversation to Barb when she dropped him off before heading home. In a weird way, she could relate to Tyler. He'd been dealt a rough hand, just like she had. And every time she found someone to trust, they were taken from her. But was Cole different? She reflected on his offer to talk. She might have been trying to keep her distance, but the truth was she needed a friend. And if push came to shove, she'd probably find herself more than tempted to dial his number.

At home, she threw her purse and keys on the kitchen table and made herself dinner. After reading the Bible and watching television, she got ready for bed, wondering if tonight was the night that sleep would finally come. But with yesterday being the anniversary of the fire, it was too soon for that reprieve. Even if Cole's card and his caring words had given her a glimmer of hope.

It was early, but she stifled a jaw-splitting yawn and collapsed on her bed before drifting off to sleep.

*The mixture of smoke and ash stung her eyes. Tears streamed down her cheeks as she huddled in the corner of the wreckage of their house. Her dad glared at her, his face blistered from burns. Spittle flew from his mouth along with his curses. His evil frame drew closer and closer, his finger pointing right at her. "It's your fault your mother is dead. You. It's all your fault!"*

Emily awoke with a start, the pulse in her neck throbbing, her heart racing, her skin clammy. Just like she had every night for the past week. And yet, this time the dream was different. *It's all your fault.* Yes. *Her* fault her dad ran into a burning building. *Her* fault her husband died. Even her inability to sleep was her own fault.

But it was becoming hard to function this way, and for the first time in her life, she wondered if she needed professional help. *This too shall pass,* she kept reminding herself. Just like it had the last time, and the time before that. Besides, guilt was a natural response to the trauma she'd experienced—at her own hand.

Unsure of what else to do, she turned on the lamp next to her bed, an action that had become all too familiar lately. Getting out of bed, she walked to the kitchen for a glass of water, then sat at the table and rested her head on the cold surface. *Why, God? Even if I get past this round of nightmares, will I ever be able to fully move on with my life? Do I even deserve to?*

Tears stung her eyes. Twelve years since the fire, and it still haunted her. That's when she saw it, out of the corner of her eye. Cole's business card poking out of the side of her purse. She reached for the card and studied the number written on the back. She'd had no intentions of taking him up on his offer this soon, but it almost seemed as if she'd reached rock bottom—not that she planned to tell *him* that, of course.

Did it make sense to call? Would it be giving him the wrong impression? What would she even say to him—and how would he respond?

Glancing at the clock, Emily decided to get her phone. Something inside told her to give Cole a shot, and the fact that she even considered it made her wonder if maybe it was finally time to go down that road again. To let someone in and catch a glimpse of who she really was.

Even though it was past 11:00, he had seemed open to a late-night chat. Emily really didn't know what would happen if she opened herself up to this kind of conversation, but at this point, she didn't have much to lose.

Before she could change her mind, she tapped out a message.

# CHAPTER 15

COLE WAS DRIFTING OFF TO SLEEP when his cell phone buzzed on the nightstand. Why did he leave his phone on vibrate at night? It seemed to make more noise than his normal ring tone. He opened his eyes and sighed. Should he check it? Or wait until tomorrow?

He finally decided to take a quick peek, so he reached over and checked the screen. He immediately sat up, leaning his bare back against his headboard.

IT'S EMILY. ARE YOU AWAKE?

He couldn't prevent the grin on his face, or the increasing rate of his heart beating in his chest. *I am now.* Emily had finally reached out. His fingers typed out a quick reply. YES. WHAT'S UP?

Emily: CAN'T SLEEP.

Cole: NIGHTMARES?

Emily: YES. I KNOW IT SOUNDS STUPID.

Cole: NOT AT ALL. NO JUDGMENT. Cole hoped she

never got that impression from him.

Emily: THANKS. WHAT ARE YOU UP TO?

He chuckled, not wanting to tell her he had almost been asleep. NOT MUCH. TALKING TO YOU I GUESS. LOL.

Emily: HA HA.

Cole: WHAT DO YOU USUALLY DO WHEN YOU CAN'T SLEEP?

Emily: PRAY. READ. PACE. I'D GO FOR A WALK BUT NOT THE SAFEST HOUR TO BE WALKING ALONE OUTSIDE.

He pictured the rundown neighborhoods near Antonio's and wondered if hers was similar to what he'd seen. WHAT IF I WALK WITH YOU?

Emily: OH NO. I WASN'T DROPPING HINTS.

Cole sensed her embarrassment and humility through her text, but he hoped she would be open to his offer. I KNOW. BUT I'M HAPPY TO.

There was a lull, so Cole sent a second clarifying text. I CAN DRIVE TO YOUR PLACE OR MEET YOU SOMEWHERE. BEING SERIOUS HERE.

There was another pause and Cole held his breath. *Don't get too excited.* After all, Emily hadn't been very receptive to his offers in the past, so this invitation would likely yield the same result.

Then finally, her response appeared on his phone: I GUESS THAT WOULD BE NICE.

Cole's heartbeat raced. Was he actually about to see Emily outside of the clinic? Even though he knew it wasn't a date by any stretch of the imagination, the concept still sounded too good to be true. LET ME KNOW WHERE.

A moment later, Emily sent her address.

BE THERE IN TWENTY MINUTES. He threw on a pair of jeans, a plain white tee shirt, and tennis shoes in record time. After hopping in his car, he made a beeline for her house.

EMILY MUST HAVE BEEN watching for him, because as soon as he pulled into her driveway and got out of his car, she held the front door open.

"Hey there." A floor lamp in the corner of the living room gave off enough light to cause his heart to skip a beat at the vision of her beauty. He tried not to make it obvious how cute he thought she looked standing barefoot in her yoga pants and a T-shirt, her pink-painted toes shimmering against the tan carpet.

"I don't think we should do this." Her brow was furrowed as she spoke.

"Uh, oh… kay." Was she sending him packing already?

"I only mean, I don't think it's wise to walk around my neighborhood this late, even if you're with me."

"I see. Don't trust me, huh?" He grinned. Emily tilted her head as if she scolded him, but he ignored her lighthearted reprimand. "Well, is there any place open at this hour where we could go grab a bite or sit and chat?"

Emily shrugged. "We can sit on my back porch for a while if you want. I'd hate to waste your trip out here since I know you went out of your way to come over."

"I'm fine with whatever." *As long as you are part of*

*the equation.*

They walked into the kitchen, and Emily opened the fridge. "Can I get you something to drink? Tea? Lemonade?"

Cole cleared his throat. "A glass of water would be great, thanks."

"Oh, good." She closed the fridge and turned to him with a reddening face. "Turns out I don't have any tea or lemonade anyway."

Cole suppressed a laugh as she retrieved two glasses from the cupboard. The counter was covered in stacks of papers, which she shoved to the side in order to put the glasses down. A few receipts slid to the floor in the process, and Cole bent down to pick them up.

Emily sighed. A slight frown covered her face. "Thanks. Sorry for the mess. I'm a bit disorganized lately. Or maybe always." She shook her head and muttered something under her breath as she filled the glasses with water.

Cole wasn't sure whether to laugh at her absentmindedness and clutter, or to offer his sympathy for how sleep-deprived she obviously was, but hopefully she realized he wasn't here for hospitality anyway. She handed him a glass and then gestured to follow her outside.

They took a seat next to each other on the porch swing. A small porch light and the glow of the kitchen light through the back window illuminated where they sat just enough to make out each other's faces along with a single ash tree in the small, fenced-in back yard.

Emily took a sip of water. "I hope you don't mind

about the walk."

"Not at all. I understand." Cole gently swayed the swing back and forth with his legs, causing a rhythmic creaking sound to echo in the night air. Then he turned his attention to their surroundings. The yard was a cute, grassy space. There was a birdfeeder dangling from the ash tree, and he pictured Emily sitting out here on summer nights watching the birds and squirrels eat the seed. "It's nice out here. Cute little porch. Beautiful night." *Gorgeous girl.*

Emily nodded and gazed up at the star-sprinkled sky. "Yeah, I've been renting this house for a few years now, and I love it. Sometimes I'm able to sleep better out here than in my own bed."

Cole put his glass of water down on the porch railing opposite the swing. "Yeah, so about that. What exactly is my role here? I mean, do you want me to help you work through what's causing the nightmares? Distract you from thinking about it? Keep you awake? Lull you to sleep?"

Emily laughed, putting her glass next to Cole's on the railing. "I'm not too sure myself. This is new territory for me. I mean, the inviting someone I barely know over to my house late at night because I can't sleep, that is. The *nightmares* are old hat. Yesterday was the anniversary of something that happened years ago, so they get triggered around this time of year. But this isn't the time to get into the story behind them. That conversation would take far too long. Definitely not a wee-morning-hour discussion."

"Well." Cole nudged her with his elbow. "I guess

we're going to have to meet up during normal hours one of these days to talk about that."

Emily flashed him a sly smile but didn't give him the satisfaction of a verbal response. He couldn't help but wonder if the anniversary she was referring to was of that car accident he'd discovered.

"Okay, so I'll distract you then." Cole shrugged. He'd take what he could get. "Let's see. Why don't you tell me... what your favorite color is?"

"Oooh, starting out with the deep stuff I see." She leaned back in the swing. "I'd have to say yellow. You?"

For a second, Cole pictured a little boy in a baseball jersey riding his bike. "Blue. Royal blue." He cleared his throat and ditched the memory. "Okay, what's your favorite type of TV show?"

Emily bit her lip. "I like game shows. I know it's weird, but I even record some and binge watch them at night."

Cole chuckled, hoping this night would last forever. "Nice. No judgment from me. Okay, let's see... Tell me about your favorite meal."

"My favorite meal?" Emily asked, her tone incredulous.

"Yes. What's so odd about that?"

"I don't know. Random, that's all. And besides, usually people ask what your favorite *food* is, not an entire *meal*."

"Well, I didn't realize I had such a picky audience on my hands! I figure almost everyone's favorite food is pizza, so that question is pointless. But pizza isn't really a *meal*."

"Okay, okay. Good point. Hmm, my favorite meal. Oh! Well, when I was a little girl, my mom made the absolute best grilled cheese and homemade tomato soup. I don't know what she did, but to this day I have not been able to replicate it. She always made cheesy broccoli to go with it, too. And for dessert—peach cobbler." Emily's voice sounded dreamy, more joyful than anything he'd ever heard her say before. "Great question!"

"Ha! You went from doubting my entire word choice to complimenting my question? I don't know Emily, I'm finding it hard to trust your sincerity here."

Emily slapped his knee playfully. "No, I mean it. My mom died when I was twelve, and I'd forgotten all about that meal, so it conjured up some really good memories."

"Ah. I'm sorry to hear about your mom. But that explains your change of heart about my question." He loved seeing this side of her, especially when it involved her hand on his knee.

"Next question?" Emily's lips curved up.

She was clearly enjoying this, and although he didn't know her very well, he sensed it was out of the norm to let herself be the center of attention. He was honored to help her tear down that wall. *So* different from Heather. The two were like night and day.

Cole rubbed his chin with his thumb and forefinger. "Hmm. What is the craziest thing you've ever done?"

Emily tucked a strand of hair behind her ear. "I would have trouble picking only one."

"Really? I would have pegged you for someone who

couldn't think of *any*."

"I know. But I was actually a bit of a rebellious teen."

Cole angled his head. "*You*? Rebellious? I find that hard to believe."

"Well, I've changed a lot since then. I mean... a *lot*. This doesn't even scratch the surface of my deviance, but to give you an example, I dyed my hair black the summer before my junior year of high school."

Cole laughed. "Are you serious? I can't imagine your pale face with a head of black hair. No offense."

"Yeah, well. The color didn't take very well so it didn't last long. But I thought I was pretty cool for a few weeks." She reached for her glass of water and took a sip, then held it in her lap. "What about you? Any wild and crazy stories to share?"

Cole chuckled. "Nothing too far out there. I toilet papered a few houses in my day, got a couple speeding tickets. But nothing drastic. Typical teenage boy stuff."

"Sounds about right."

"Hey, I remembered something I wanted to ask you. How do you know Antonio?"

Emily squirmed in her seat, causing the porch swing to sway unevenly. "I'm going to have to pass on that one."

"What? Is that allowed?"

Emily studied her water glass for a moment, then reached over to put it back on the railing. "Trust me, that's a loaded question for another day."

Cole pursed his lips. "Okay, I'll allow it. But add that to the list of reasons we need to hang out again—

during the day." He paused to watch Emily's response to his insinuation.

She turned to look at him, her forehead wrinkled, then nodded before staring back down at her hands in her lap.

Cole let his words sink in before deciding to go back to distraction mode. "Let's see. What about your friends? How many close friends do you have and what are they like?"

Emily laughed and yawned at the same time. "Well, notice who I texted at 11:00 at night when I couldn't sleep. That might give you a small clue."

"What are you saying?" Cole hoped she could tell he was teasing. "Do you not value the friendship we have? I'm hurt!"

Emily gave his shoulder a playful shove. "You know what I mean. I honestly don't have a lot of *close* friends. I moved away from my hometown of Olivette, near St. Louis, after high school, so lost touch with most of my friends growing up. I didn't go to traditional college, just nursing school night classes once I figured out what I wanted to do with my life, so there are a few people from there I keep in touch with, but none that I hang out with regularly. We didn't get close the way people do when they room together on campus and stuff."

She paused to yawn again. He knew it was good if she could fall asleep, but he loved hearing her talk and didn't want their time together to end. "I'm friends with a few nurses from work, and one of them—Nan—goes to the same church as me. I'm also in a Bible study with some nice women, but… I don't know, I guess I haven't allowed myself to really click with anyone on a deep level. I try to keep myself available for people who really need me rather than filling my own desire for a social life."

Cole wasn't sure what to say. For someone who seemed to have an amazing, selfless heart, Emily's life sure sounded lonely. Rewarding and fulfilling perhaps, but lonely nonetheless. "Y'know, you kind of remind me of a book I read growing up—you might know it. The main character is a tree that gives away every last ounce of himself to make others happy."

With her mouth closed, Emily let out a thoughtful laugh through her nose, then lowered her gaze. "That might be true if, before giving everything away, the tree first causes unimaginable pain and destruction to those around it."

Emily's transparency took Cole by surprise. "Do you care to elaborate?" He expected her to say *No*, of course, but he wished she would be willing to share what weighed so heavily on her mind.

Emily fidgeted, then shook her head. "Sorry, I'm not even sure where that came from. Can we forget I said that? To make a long story short, I do have friends. But not very many I consider close. You know what I mean?"

Cole gave a small nod. He'd have to take some time tomorrow to reflect on everything Emily had revealed—and even more so the secrets she still kept. Like what was triggering those nightmares. "And do you like it that way?"

Head tilted up, Emily sighed. "I guess I feel like it's

the way it has to be. I know that's hard to understand, but I've made a lot of mistakes in my past relationships, and I feel like God is taking this season of my life to teach me some important lessons." She leaned her head back, yawned, and rubbed her hands over her arms, leaving Cole to wonder what mistakes and lessons she was referring to.

"Can I ask another potentially loaded question?"

A small laugh escaped Emily's lips. "Sure, why stop now?"

"When was your last relationship?"

"Oh, man. You really don't hold back, do you?"

Cole shook his head and waggled his eyebrows.

"Well, let's just say it's been quite a while since I've been in a relationship. And it's really not something I've sensed the need for."

"Y'know, I've been in the same boat," Cole said. "If it makes you feel any better, I haven't dated anyone in over a year."

Emily flashed him a devious smile. "Times seven."

"Times seven? What do you mean?"

"It's been over seven years since my last relationship."

Cole blinked and raised his eyebrows. No wonder she seemed so reluctant to accept his invitations if it had been that long since she'd had a man in her life. "Seven years?"

His mind raced back to the article he'd seen online. Emily's car accident—the one which had killed her then-husband—had been around seven years ago. He was sure that tragic end to her husband's life played a huge role in Emily's singleness. But come to think of it, he had seen snow in the photos of the wreck. That *couldn't* be what yesterday's anniversary was about. Besides, thousands of people dealt with the same type of loss and eventually moved on to find love again. What made her story so much different? "Emily, why?"

"Oh, Cole. I know it sounds crazy, but that's yet another—"

"Conversation for another day?" Cole finished for her.

She eyed him up with an amused expression. "How did you know?"

"Do you think we ever will?"

"Ever will what?"

He blinked. "Have those conversations?"

"Oh. Um... I don't know. Maybe. If you play your cards right." She winked at him, perhaps in an attempt to lighten the mood. A breeze blew through the porch just then, and Emily pulled her knees up to her chest, hugging her legs with her arms.

"Are you cold? I can go grab you a jacket or a blanket if you want." Cole didn't want to let her off the hook from what they were talking about, but his mother had raised her boys to be gentlemen.

"That would be great. There's a blanket on the couch in the living room if you don't mind."

He stood and returned moments later with the blanket. After covering her with its warmth, he sat and draped his arm along the back of the swing.

"Feel free to let me know whenever you want me to leave. I know it's late, and I don't want to wear out my welcome."

Emily pulled the blanket up to her chin. "Noted. So far, you're welcome."

"Good to know." There was a tingle in his stomach knowing she wanted him there. Perhaps it was only because of the late-night hour, but it seemed like he was making strides with this woman. Finally.

"What made you decide to become a physical therapist?" It was encouraging to hear Emily take on the role of the question asker. She laid her head on his shoulder, and sparks went off in Cole's stomach. She had to be sensing the same chemistry, didn't she?

He cleared his throat to delay his answer. The real reason he'd pursued this line of work was for the paycheck and prestige, but that sounded selfish seated next to such a generous woman. Now that he was more mature, he loved being able to use his job to help people like Tyler. But she deserved an honest answer. "Don't judge, but I basically just wanted a nice job, a big paycheck. I was willing to work for it too, and since I was good at science in school, I knew the medical field was the way to go. I'm in it for the right reasons now though, I promise you. I love my patients—more than my paycheck."

"That's obvious, Cole. And trust me, I'm in no place to judge." Another cool breeze blew in, and Emily lifted her head. Holding up half the blanket, she turned to face him. "Are you cold? We can share."

Cole only pondered her question for a moment—he was warm blooded by nature, but he certainly didn't want to pass up the opportunity to cuddle up next to

Emily under a blanket on a porch swing on this beautiful night. Nodding, he scooted closer to allow for the blanket to rest on his lap and cover his legs. Their thighs now touched, and heat radiated through his body.

"Is there anything else I can do for you?" Cole noticed with mixed feelings that Emily's eyes were starting to droop.

She yawned. "Oh, no thank you. You're a really nice guy, you know that?"

He let his fingertips brush the top of her shoulder as his arm rested on the back of the swing. "Nah, just your average Joe."

She shook her head, and her hair tickled his neck. "Well, I know I haven't had much recent experience, but I still feel qualified to tell you that you are definitely not average."

Cole closed his eyes, soaking up her words. "Well, Miss Emily. You are one to talk. I can honestly say I've never met anyone quite like you. And I mean that in the best possible way."

Emily didn't respond, but instead leaned her head against Cole's chest. He dropped his arm from the back of the swing to cradle her shoulder. This felt right. *More* than right. And he hoped she had the same thoughts. But before he knew it, he heard her rhythmic breathing, and a quick glance told him her eyes were closed. Well, he had succeeded in his mission. She was asleep. Now all he had to do was figure out what on earth to do next.

# CHAPTER 16

EMILY WOKE UP THE NEXT MORNING and rubbed her eyes. Peering around, it only took a second to realize she was on her living room couch. The blanket Cole had gotten the night before was draped over her, and her glass of water was on a coaster on the coffee table. A smile formed on her lips as she recalled their conversations out on the swing. When he'd brought her the blanket, she'd become instantly warmer—but she suspected it had more to do with his arm around her shoulders and their close proximity than the actual blanket itself. His protective arm made her feel safe. Treasured.

It didn't take long for her smile to fade as she contemplated their emerging relationship. She knew now that she really liked Cole, but was she ready to go down that path after all these years? She had truly believed relationships were a thing of the past for her, but this possibility seemed right. Her heart had gotten excited sitting next to Cole, catching a hint of his scent when the wind blew, hearing his voice, sensing his concern.

If she could bring herself to be in a relationship at all, she was confident Cole was the right one to be with. But that was a big *if*. For over seven years, she'd been fine on her own, caring for others and serving God through her support, donations, and hospitality towards those in need. Given the pain she'd caused so many in the past, it had seemed like her destiny. Or penance, maybe. Was it okay to focus on her own happiness for a change? She shoved those thoughts aside and moved on with her day. Relationships were far too weighty a subject for a Saturday morning. It *was* morning, wasn't it?

A glance at her cell phone on the coffee table told her she had gotten the sleep she'd needed for days. It was 10:15! Good thing she worked second shift today. It hadn't even occurred to her to set an alarm, but she was glad she hadn't. Her body needed the extra sleep. Sleep that had started outside on the swing with Cole.

As she got up and folded the blanket, her mind wandered to the last thing she remembered from their night together. Cole had been talking about what led him to his job, and she thought she had drifted off after that. But then... how had she ended up in here? Cole must have had something to do with that.

Reaching for her phone, she decided to text him. WAKE UP.

Cole: I'M AWAKE! WHAT'S UP?

Emily smiled. She couldn't deny she was smitten by this man. She dialed his number and smiled even wider when he answered. "What did you do?"

"Uh... Sorry?"

Emily laughed. "Oh, my word, Cole. I slept like a baby last night. In fact, I just woke up. What time did you leave?"

"Well, I wanted to make sure you were really asleep, so I let you lay on my shoulder for about a half hour while I enjoyed the peace and quiet of the night. That was probably close to one?"

Emily's eyes widened at the revelation. "I was asleep for a half hour with you out there? How embarrassing. And then what? Don't tell me you carried me into the living room." She cringed at the thought of her drooling on his shirt.

Now it was Cole's turn to laugh. "What, you don't think I'm strong enough?"

"No, it's not that. I'm just surprised I don't remember it, that's all."

"Ah. Well, I did carry you, and you were out cold. I locked the back door and turned off the lights. Locked the front door behind me, though I couldn't bolt it since I didn't have a key. I hope that wasn't a big deal." There was a soothing nonchalance in his voice.

"No, of course not. I'm still amazed at how well I slept. I really needed this." Especially when she normally had nightmares for another week after the anniversary instead of only one day. "You must be the miracle drug I've been looking for. You don't mind stopping over every night around midnight until I fall asleep, do you?" She meant the words to be teasing despite the buried truth and was relieved when Cole laughed.

Emily nestled back into the couch cushions, remembering how comfortable it had been snuggling with him on the swing. "So, did I scare you away with my crazy self last night? I hate to think of what all I told you in my semi-sleepy state."

"Ha! Nothing you said scared me away. I'm actually a little intrigued by some of the things you *didn't* say."

"Oh yeah?"

"Yes ma'am. Do you want to catch up later today and discuss the *loaded questions* you claimed I asked?"

Emily bit her lip. This was what she'd been afraid of when it came to getting close to Cole. Though she had to admit, his request didn't scare her nearly as much as she thought it might. "I have to work today." Should she suggest getting together tomorrow instead? No, she had to... Oh. That would be perfect! "But if you're free tomorrow afternoon, I'm doing something I think you might be interested in. It might even cross something off your bucket list."

"A trip to Australia?" Cole didn't miss a beat. "Heck yeah, count me in!"

Emily giggled. "No, not quite that exciting. But dress comfortably and meet me at my house at 2:30 tomorrow if you can make it."

"That's all I get?"

"That's all."

"Okay, count me in."

Emily breathed a silent sigh of relief. "Good, I'm

glad. Hey, I better go get ready for work. See you tomorrow?"

"You bet."

Fifteen minutes later, as the shower beat down on the back of Emily's hair, she closed her eyes and soaked in the warmth of the water—but even more so the warmth of the feeling coursing through her body. It had been so long since she'd experienced the giddiness of a budding relationship. Not that she was convinced that's what this was. In fact, she was still very cautious about taking things to the next level. After all, Cole hadn't even touched the surface of who Emily really was, what she had been through, the pain she had caused, the life she had lived. No, she couldn't confidently move forward with things until he had an inkling of what he was getting himself into. She'd made that mistake before. And she tried not to get her hopes up, because she knew once he did gain access to that information, there was a very real chance he would choose to walk away. And she could hardly blame him if he did.

But for now, she couldn't deny her heart was a little bit fuller at the mere thought of this man who had somehow wriggled his way into her life. The smile on her face was impossible to wash away.

EMILY PLOPPED A NEW box of non-latex gloves on the counter of the nurse's station while humming a worship song she'd heard on the radio that morning. Seated in front of the computer, Nan looked up from the screen. "Well, aren't you chipper today."

Emily grinned. She did have an unusual spring in her step, thanks to a good night sleep—and more likely due to an energizing night with Cole. And it was good to have Nan back at work, too. "Yeah, I finally slept well last night."

"Was that man involved in any way?" Nan raised her eyebrows.

Emily coughed and stared at her in disbelief. "Excuse me?"

"I'm just saying—that kind of energy, that joy I'm seeing in you. Usually a man is involved. Or God. But that particular twinkle has *handsome man* written all over it." Nan winked.

*Wow. Nan is good.* "You can really tell?"

"I knew it! I'm so happy for you. Tell me everything."

Emily giggled. How much should she share where coworkers might overhear? "There's not much to tell, really. It wasn't a real date or anything. He only came over to keep me company during a bout of insomnia. Nothing happened—all we did was talk. But I have to say, it was pretty awesome. It seemed like he really wanted to get to know me. Like there was no hidden agenda, no secret motives."

"Mm-hmm."

"Nan!"

The woman held up a hand in defense. "No, no, I hear ya. But I suspect there's more to it. Not in a bad way, hon. In a good way. I can't wait to see what becomes of this, that's all. I'm really happy for you."

"Nan!"

"What?"

"I—I don't know, but you have to stop, young lady."

Nan laughed. "Young lady? Oh, Emily. It's been years since I've been called that. Don't you worry. It's an old woman's hunch, nothing more. And I'm happy you got some sleep and that you found someone you can talk to. For now. That's all."

"Well, okay then." Emily was still uneasy about her coworker's insinuation, but her intentions were innocent enough.

"So, when are you seeing him again?"

Staring at the ground, Emily slurred her words with her hand over her mouth. "Tomorrow."

"Excuse me? Did you say tomorrow?" Nan's tone implied she'd caught Emily red-handed.

A smile slowly crept to Emily's face. Okay, maybe things weren't quite as platonic as she let on. She really did feel safe with Cole, and maybe it *was* finally her time to find someone. To move on. To start over with another relationship and be happy again. But tomorrow was most certainly not a date, as Cole would soon find out. She only hoped he wouldn't be too disappointed with what she had planned.

# CHAPTER 17

FOR MOST OF SATURDAY AFTERNOON, COLE couldn't wipe the grin off his face. As he washed his car in his driveway, he thanked God for the previous night. It had been a while since he'd felt this way about someone. Sure, Emily may have had a few skeletons in her closet, but who didn't? He only hoped she would let her guard down and give their relationship a chance. That obviously wasn't something she did easily, and he was honored she'd given him some transparent answers to a few of the questions he asked. Still, there was a lot she'd left unanswered, and he wasn't sure if he'd ever get to the bottom of it all.

Inviting him somewhere on Sunday was a good sign. What was it they'd be doing? It was in the afternoon, so it probably wasn't church-related, unless hers had an afternoon service. Besides, she'd said it was something from his bucket list. Could it be skydiving?

Probably not, unless she thought so far ahead as to book two spots at a skydiving center and trust he was available. A baseball game? That sounded more likely. He wasn't sure what her plans were, but he didn't care. The fact was, he got to see her again, and that was a win in his book any day.

Since Emily was working Saturday night, Cole decided to hang out with Tim and Maria. He couldn't wait to share with them the progress he'd made with Emily, small though it may be.

Maria plopped down on the couch next to Tim, who was scrolling on his phone. "Pizza's ordered and will be here in twenty minutes."

Cole wiped sweaty hands on his cargo shorts. No time like the present. "I've got some news."

"Let me guess." Maria waggled her eyebrows. "It's about that girl from the clinic."

He rolled his eyes. So predictable. "Is that all you think about, Maria? My love life?"

Maria flashed him a devious grin. "Yes, Cole. You are my *life*, man."

"That's what I thought. Well, you happen to be right."

"I knew it!" She punched her husband in the arm, as if to say *I told you so*.

Tim put his phone on the coffee table and rubbed his arm. "Ouch!"

"So? What's the news?" Maria leaned forward. "Did you finally ask her out?"

For as long as he'd fended off Maria's interrogations in the past, it was nice to have something exciting to share for once. He shrugged, a smirk on his face.

"Oh stop." She threw a couch pillow at him. "You did, didn't you? How many dates have you had?"

Cole enjoyed having a captive audience. Even Tim appeared interested in his response, though that interest would surely dissipate when he learned Cole hadn't actually progressed *that* far. "Well, I wouldn't say we've had an official date, per se, but we went out to dinner a week and a half ago. And then last night, we hung out at Emily's place until she fell asleep on my shoulder."

Maria tilted her head, her eyes glossed over. "Aww, Cole! That's so sweet. How did you manage that?"

"Well, she hasn't been sleeping well, so I gave her my number in case she needed a late-night chat."

"Smooth." Maria gave him a thumbs-up.

"Next thing I know, she's inviting me over." Cole paused and averted his gaze, a thought suddenly occurring to him. "Or maybe I invited myself over. Hmm. Not really sure now that I think of it. Never mind that—the point is, we talked until the wee hours of the morning when she fell asleep on my shoulder, thank you very much."

"Wow." Tim's tone sounded unenthused as he gave an exaggerated eye roll. Cole expected as much, but he wasn't going to let his brother kill his mood.

"Yeah. Wow." Maria sighed as she sunk back into the couch cushions.

"And get this. We're seeing each other again tomorrow."

"Wow!" This time, Tim's tone contained a little more excitement, making Cole laugh.

"Well I'm super excited for you, and I can't wait to meet her."

Cole was glad for Maria's support. "Thanks, I'm pretty stoked myself. She's so different than anyone I've known, in a really good way. She doesn't seem to care what other people think of her, and she's always trying to help people, putting others first. I know it sounds cheesy, but I want to be a better person because of her."

"Ugh! Cole. Dude. Your *Man Card* has hereby been revoked." Tim closed his eyes and shook his head.

Maria laughed as Cole squinted at Tim. "My what?"

"You heard me. Stop talking that way. You're ruining my appetite."

"I think it's sweet." Maria bunched her shoulders and giggled. "He likes her! Maybe even falling in love with her. And it sounds to me like he could do a heck of a lot worse."

Cole wasn't sure about the "L" word quite yet, but at least he had an ally in Maria. He couldn't tell if revealing his developments with Emily was a mistake or not—it suddenly seemed like they were both making fun of him, on different levels. But he wasn't ashamed about his feelings for this woman. He wouldn't apologize for wanting to find love.

Thankfully, the doorbell rang a moment later, turning their attention to paying the delivery driver and digging into a large, deep-dish pizza loaded with pepperoni and sausage. Cole was determined to avoid any more chatter about his potential relationship with Emily for the rest of the evening. Things would progress on God's timetable, and he didn't need his brother's approval to pursue who he hoped could be his future wife.

THAT NIGHT, EMILY GOT home from work after 11:00. She changed into her pajamas and turned the living room TV on low, hoping to fall asleep on the couch while watching whatever late-night talk show happened to be on. She looked forward to the next day, taking Cole to a place that was truly special to her. No sooner had her thoughts turned to him, then her phone chimed, alerting her to a text. She smiled when she saw it was from Cole.

HI EMILY. WANTED TO CHECK IN.

Emily: HEY THERE. JUST GOT HOME FROM WORK.

Cole: GOOD DAY?

She thought about her cases. NOTHING TOO CRAZY, CAN'T COMPLAIN. HOW ABOUT YOU?

Cole: PRETTY GOOD. HUNG OUT WITH MY BROTHER AND HIS WIFE.

Emily: NICE. DO YOU GET TO SEE THEM VERY OFTEN? Emily suddenly realized she didn't know that much about Cole's life.

Cole: YEAH, TIM'S PRETTY MUCH MY BEST FRIEND SO WE HANG OUT A LOT. WHAT ABOUT YOU, ANY SIBLINGS?

Emily: I'M AN ONLY CHILD.

Cole: COOL. CAN YOU GIVE ME A HINT ABOUT WHAT WE'RE DOING TOMORROW?

Emily took a deep breath. How much should she reveal? DRESS DOWN. AND LOWER YOUR EXPECTATIONS.

Cole: HA! YOU MAKE IT SOUND SO ENTICING.

She giggled, her eyes glued to her phone, thoroughly enjoying their exchange. I TRY. IT WILL BE FUN, I PROMISE.

After a short pause, another text came through. ARE YOU GOING TO BE ABLE TO SLEEP TONIGHT?

Emily: HOPE SO. THINK SO.

Cole: I'VE BEEN THINKING OF YOU.

Thankful he couldn't see her blushing, Emily hesitated for only a moment. ME TOO. OF YOU, THAT IS. LOL

Cole: AW SHUCKS. DO YOU NEED ANYTHING?

Emily: NO, I'M GOOD. PRETTY TIRED, SO HOPEFULLY WILL FALL ASLEEP FAST.

Cole: WELL, I WON'T KEEP YOU THEN!

Emily: NO WORRIES. I ENJOY TALKING TO YOU. Emily was surprised at how bold she was when hiding behind a screen. Texting was more dangerous than she'd realized.

Cole: SAME HERE.

There was a sudden warmth in her heart, and she knew if she asked him, he would be at her place in an instant. But nightly visits were a bad habit to start, and she decided she'd better cut this off for now. HAVE A GOOD NIGHT, COLE. CAN'T WAIT UNTIL TOMORROW!

Cole: ME TOO! SWEET DREAMS. LITERALLY.

Before she had a chance to offer up a flirty or witty response, or invite him over again for comfort, she turned her phone off for the night. Her heart longed for his company, but her head told her she had to take it slow. And he certainly needed to know the truth about her past before things progressed any further.

# CHAPTER 18

AFTER CHURCH ON SUNDAY, EMILY CHANGED into a
pair of jeans and a plain black V-neck tee shirt, then
threw her hair back into a pony tail. She was looking
forward to the day with Cole, but she hoped he didn't
have grand expectations about what the day would
hold. In retrospect, she probably should have told him
what they were doing. But he seemed like someone who
might enjoy this outing if he gave it a chance, and she
didn't want him to have too much time to think about it
and decide to back out.

At 2:30 on the dot, Cole's car pulled into Emily's
driveway. She met him at the door and couldn't help but
notice how cute he was in jeans and a T-shirt—
essentially the same thing he'd worn to her house Friday
night, but somehow in the light of day, it was downright
adorable.

"Glad you could make it," she said.

"Well thanks for inviting me. To..." he trailed off.

"You'll see." Emily wiggled her eyebrows. "Seriously, though, it's probably not what you're thinking. In fact, I've only invited one other person to do this with me—a friend from nursing school—and let's just say, she was less than excited about it."

"Uh-oh." Cole's eyebrows bunched together. "I'm starting to realize which item on my bucket list you were referring to."

Emily bit her lip. "You got me. We're going to serve dinner to the homeless at the Mission. Are you okay with that? You can back out now, no judgment."

Cole was wide-eyed. "Of *course* it's okay. Do you seriously think I'd bail?"

Emily shrugged. "I don't know. I suddenly realized maybe I tricked you into volunteering. That's not the way it should be."

"Emily, I love the idea. In fact, I used to serve there as a kid with my parents around the holidays. But as an adult, well... I guess I never really gave it a second thought. I suppose *life* got in the way. C'mon, let's do this." He reached over for a friendly side hug.

"Okay. Do you wanna drive?"

"Sure."

On the way, she glanced at Cole in the driver's seat. She was blessed to have this new friend in her life. Hopefully he didn't expect more from her and ruin such a perfect day.

After they entered the Mission, Emily introduced Cole to a few of the regular volunteers and gave him a quick tour. There wasn't a lot of time to spare, as dinner had to be prepared and ready to serve by five, which only gave them a little over two hours.

They ended up in the kitchen, where she threw him an apron and tried to hide the smirk on her face. After seeing him at the clinic so often, it was nice to see him outside his comfort zone for a change.

"Hey, Em. Nice to see you." An African American woman spoke from the doorway, her voice upbeat.

"Hi, Tracy. I hope you don't mind I brought someone to help out. This is Cole. Cole—Tracy. She's the kitchen manager here." Cole took a step toward the woman and extended his arm for a handshake.

"That's fabulous. The more, the merrier." Tracy had a contagious smile on her face as she shook his hand. "Today, we're serving beef and gravy, corn, mashed potatoes, rolls, and pies for dessert. I'd like you two to be in charge of the mashed potatoes and gravy." Her voice echoed above the chatter of the other volunteers in the middle of the large, industrial kitchen. "The Mission received a large donation of potatoes recently, so we're making them from scratch this week."

"Sounds good. We'll get to it." Emily went to the counter where the potatoes were piled up, then turned to Cole. "Do you want to peel, or chop?"

Cole shrugged. "I guess I'll chop."

Emily showed him where the knives were, then took a seat on a tall stool next to a large garbage bin and began peeling. She handed each one to Cole to chop up and put into a pot of water. They had two ten-pound bags to get through, and after filling two large pots with the chopped potatoes, they set the burners on high heat to boil. The manual labor combined with the heat of the stove made the kitchen extra hot, and sweat began to pool on her back. She hoped it didn't soak through her shirt.

"Those must be the cans of gravy." Emily pointed to the nearby counter. "Let's heat them up." They dumped a half dozen large cans of gravy into a massive pot and fired up another burner.

Cole glanced around the kitchen at the others who were hard at work. "What next?"

She wiped her forehead with the back of her hand. "Help me set the tables?"

With a nod, Cole followed Emily to the dining area. They lined the tables with paper table cloths and added a fake floral centerpiece on each one. After the tables were set, they checked on the potatoes and began washing the cutting board, knives, and other prep utensils they'd used, Cole at one sink washing the dishes, Emily right beside him drying them. The mundane tasks were so much better with Cole by her side. She usually hated washing dishes, but today was different.

Partway through, Cole casually reached over and put a dollop of soap suds on Emily's nose. She blinked in surprise, then jerked her head toward Cole and caught a twinkle in his eye. Before she could overthink it, she retaliated, flicking suds on his handsome face. The carefree action filled her heart with joy. She hadn't felt this free in years. Cole grinned, and she couldn't help but laugh, knowing she looked just as silly.

Just then, she caught a glance from a nearby

volunteer. Pressing her lips together to stifle the laughter, she reached for a towel and wiped her face dry, then handed it to Cole to do the same.

After the dishes were done, Cole excused himself to use the restroom while Emily wandered back to the stove. Tracy scurried over to where she stood. "Girl!" Despite keeping her voice low, others in the room turned their heads at the sudden echoey sound. "You need to dish."

"Pardon me?"

"Don't you 'pardon me,' missy," Tracy said in her signature sassy style. "You know what I'm talking about."

Emily looked down at the serving dishes for the potatoes. Had she grabbed the wrong ones? "I really don't, Trace. What's going on?"

Tracy cleared her throat and batted her eyes. "*Who* is that man and *why* have I never seen him before? You two dating?"

She inhaled a sharp breath. "Oh, you mean Cole?" This was what she'd secretly been dreading. How was she supposed to respond to this type of inquiry? *Friends* wasn't quite accurate, but they weren't really dating either. And whenever someone heard *it's complicated* or *somewhere in the middle*, their imaginations went wild.

Emily glanced over her shoulder to ensure that Cole wasn't back yet, then confirmed no one else was intently listening to them before responding. "No, we aren't dating. He's just a friend. I met him while taking a patient to physical therapy, and we started talking, but we're not… we're not a thing. Trust me, we're just friends."

"Mm-hmm." Tracy rolled her eyes. "Well, y'all are cute together, so if you ever re-think that *friends* thing, I say you go for that hunk of a man, ya hear me?"

Emily couldn't help but laugh. "Yes, ma'am, glad I have your stamp of approval."

"Aight, Em. Mash those potatoes and get 'em on out. We have guests in fifteen minutes!"

Emily turned her attention back to the pots of potatoes, poking them with a fork to see if they were ready to mash.

"Now what? Everything on track?" Cole's voice startled her. He was back fast. What if he'd heard her conversation with Tracy? She studied his face, but from what she could tell, she was in the clear.

"Yeah, it's great. Wanna help me mash the potatoes?"

"Sure thing, just show me what to do."

Emily handed him a hot pad, and together they drained the excess liquid from the large pots of potatoes, then dumped them into a huge mixing bowl where they mashed them up with butter, salt and pepper. She sensed Cole watching her out of the corner of her eye as she mashed the potatoes, pouring a splash of milk in with the other ingredients. Together, they transferred the final product into the large, metal serving bins, covered them to help keep the contents warm, then rolled the bins out on a cart into the serving hall where everyone else was assembling their final contributions.

They went back into the kitchen to dump the gravy. As Cole poured the pot into a serving container, it sloshed over the sides and splattered both of their legs. "Oh, man!" Cole cringed.

Emily reached for two towels, then handed him one as she leaned down to wipe off her pant leg. "It's all good. We can get most of it off now and worry about the rest later."

They finished with the gravy and wheeled out the bin just in time. Tracy let out a whistle above all the chatter and clanging of dishes. "Gather up in the kitchen, folks. It's almost time." A minute later, she led them in a prayer and reminded them of the serving protocol.

As they were dismissed to their stations, Emily fanned her glistening face and bit her lip as she gazed up at Cole. "You ready?"

He took a deep breath. "I think so. Thank you. For including me in this."

"Of course." She glanced at the other volunteers before lowering her voice. "I really wanted to spend this time with you." She was glad Tracy was on the other side of the room by then. No sense in getting her imagination all riled up again.

# CHAPTER 19

COLE WATCHED EMILY STIR THE BIN of mashed potatoes with latex-covered hands. He might have hoped the afternoon would entail a baseball game instead of volunteering in a soup kitchen. But after wishing and praying for a reason to spend time with Emily, he'd just be thankful for the chance, no matter the location. He remembered the carefree smile on her face as they'd washed dishes. It was refreshing to see the joy that came from serving. He was ashamed it had been so long since *he* had volunteered in a similar capacity and vowed to make it a higher priority.

Tracy walked by, giving one final inspection to the food line before heading to the door to open it for the hungry crowd. The sight of the kitchen manager made Cole narrow his eyes. Even *Tracy* had seen how well he and Emily fit together. So why was Emily, even in perceived privacy, unable to admit she might have feelings for him? Not that he was eavesdropping, but the metallic kitchen magnified sounds, and he couldn't help but overhear what they'd said as he was walking back from the restroom.

Then again, she had made it clear early on that she wasn't interested in a romantic relationship, so he only had himself to blame for getting his hopes up. But hadn't she felt the same spark he had when they were alone together on her porch swing the other night? Hadn't they made some headway with their intimate conversations and texting?

After Tracy opened the door, an influx of hungry men, women and children lined up. The first person was a man wearing a torn flannel shirt and a baseball cap that looked about twenty years old. Emily gave him a genuine smile with his scoop of potatoes. Then Cole held up a ladle. "Would you like gravy?" The man gave a grunt and a nod, so he added some to his tray.

Cole tried to keep a natural smile—after all, he greeted strangers at his clinic every day. But he was overwhelmed by the sheer number of people and seeing them up close. It was interesting to observe how they all responded so differently as well.

"Gravy?" A young man gave a simple nod, no eye contact.

"Gravy?" A middle-aged woman yanked her tray away, offended at the notion.

"Gravy?" An elderly woman smiled. "Yes, please. Thank you so much, young man."

As he finished ladling gravy on a little girl's potatoes, he heard a hoarse voice to his left. "And who is this new face?" Cole looked over and saw an older gentleman flashing Emily a toothless grin but pointing an arthritic finger in his direction.

"This is my friend Cole," Emily said. "Cole, this is Wayne."

"Nice to meet you, Wayne." Cole gave a short wave with his gloved hand.

Wayne's belly jiggled a little as he laughed, and there was a gaping hole in his mouth where he missed a front tooth. "Your friend, huh?" he said.

Emily licked her lips and gave him a nod. Wayne then turned his attention to Cole. "Is that true, young man? You folks friends?"

Cole's face grew warm. "Yes, sir."

Wayne laughed again, leaning toward them as if trying to keep his teasing between the three of them. "You ain't foolin' no one." Then he moved along in line, turning his neck to add, "Thanks for the food, darling."

Emily blushed, and Cole returned to his gravy duties. By the time everyone had gone through the line, those who'd eaten first had already dispersed from the dining area. Tracy motioned to Emily, who then turned toward Cole. "Would you like to eat?"

Cole blinked. "Here?" Emily tilted her head and narrowed her eyes, making Cole grimace. That probably sounded condescending. All he'd meant was that he was hoping to take her out somewhere they could talk, without an audience making her uncomfortable around him. But why hadn't he run that response through some sort of filter first?

"Yes, here. You saw the food made fresh. The tables

are clean. And I seem to recall you wanted to befriend someone who could possibly be in this very room."

Cole held up his hands. "I know, I'm sorry. That's not what I meant. You're absolutely right. Yes, let's eat. I'm starving."

He followed Emily as they loaded their foam plates with everything but dessert, since the pies were all gone. He trailed behind her as she headed for two empty seats next to a middle-aged couple.

"Hi, I'm Emily, and this is Cole. Mind if we sit with you?"

Cole shifted his weight from one foot to the other, praying that God would give him an open mind so he could be more like Emily.

The couple gestured to the open chairs, so Cole and Emily took a seat. Emily picked up her fork as she spoke. "What are your names?"

"I'm Joe, and this is my wife, Sandy."

"Nice to meet you. How long have you been married?"

Cole ate his roast beef, amazed at Emily's ease of interacting with them and chiding himself to treat these folks like anyone else at his clinic.

"We've been married twenty-six years." Joe glanced at the floor and then at his wife before continuing. "We haven't been coming here long. We just fell on hard times after our travel agency went out of business. Ended up losing our home too, thanks to all the debt, so we're staying with Sandy's sister-in-law until we can get back on our feet."

Sandy let out a chuckle. "It's a tight squeeze, but we

get by."

Cole swallowed. Joe and Sandy were just average citizens that ran into some bad luck. They were fortunate to have a relative take them in, and to have programs like meals at the Mission to help sustain them. He glanced around the room at the others still eating and visiting. Had he misjudged them too?

"I'm sorry to hear that." Emily took a sip of water. "So, your sister-in-law... does that mean she's your brother's wife, Sandy?"

The woman nodded. "Yeah, my brother died a few years back. He was a Kansas City police officer."

Cole's ears perked up. "Really? My brother's a cop. How long was he on the force?"

As their conversation progressed, Cole grew more at ease asking questions and opening up a bit himself.

The longer they talked, the more he realized how blessed he was, which led to a deeper conviction to lend a helping hand when opportunities arose. Before long, the couple stood to leave, and Cole made a point to shake their hands. Getting to know their story had changed his mind about the homeless. And all thanks to Emily, who had brought him here and showed him how to serve. Wait... Emily. Where had she gone? At some point during his conversation, she'd disappeared from his side.

Cole looked around the room and noticed almost all the tables and chairs were cleaned off and stacked neatly around the perimeter. He checked the clock and was shocked to see it was already almost 7:00. He found Emily sweeping on the other end of the serving hall.

"Hey, are you guys all done cleaning up?"

She glanced around the room and shrugged. "Pretty much."

"I feel so bad. I was totally planning to help. But I guess I got wrapped up in my conversation with Joe and Sandy. Their story was heartbreaking. Still, I did not mean to slack off on my duties."

"Don't worry about it." Emily emptied her dustpan in a nearby trash bin. "Interacting with the guests *is* part of our duties, in a way. I for one am glad to see you took an interest in them. I've never seen them here before, so I'm sure it made them feel welcome."

"Well, thanks. But I promise next time I'll be available to do the heavy lifting."

Emily took a deep breath and surveyed the room. "Well, we should be able to head out now. Let me just go say goodbye to Tracy."

"I'll come with." They walked into the kitchen to find Tracy and two others washing the last of the serving dishes and wrapping up leftovers.

Tracy raised her eyebrows. "You two heading out?"

Emily joined her at the sink and gave her a sideways hug, since her arms were plunged in sudsy water. "We are. Thanks for letting us serve. Good turnout tonight."

"I appreciate your help, Em. And thanks to you, too." Tracy gestured to Cole with her chin and gave him a smile.

"My pleasure." Cole waved.

Once they got in Cole's car, Emily buckled her seatbelt and turned to face him. "So. Bucket list?"

He started the engine and took a moment to fully

appreciate her question. "Pretty much, yeah. That was awesome. So, what now? Can I buy you dessert? Coffee?"

"Oh, I don't know. I could really use a shower. It was so hot in there, plus I have gravy on my jeans." She gave his arm a lighthearted punch.

"Yeah, okay." He was bummed, but her excuse was valid. And given the time, his invitation had been a long shot.

"Would meeting up at 9:00 be too late? To give us a chance to wash up? I mean, I know we both have to get up for work tomorrow."

Cole's shoulders relaxed as he drove, and a smile grew on his face. "Not at all. 9:00 works for me. Name the place."

# CHAPTER 20

AFTER COLE DROPPED HER OFF AT her house, Emily wasted no time getting into the shower to rinse off the sweat and grease from the day. As she rinsed the soap off her skin, her reluctance to give Cole a chance started to rinse away with it. He had definitely captured her attention, and she didn't want to be a mess when they hung out later. Her stomach did little flips as she thought about their time together.

But there was still that shred of doubt. Was she leading him on? Giving him false hope? Why was this so hard for her? Most women would be elated to have a date with a man like Cole—and he certainly seemed interested in her. She lathered up her shampoo, feeling like her thoughts were all up in a tizzy as well.

Deep down, she knew it was because of what inevitably happened to those who were close to her— and because he didn't know her past. If there was any hope of a future relationship together, he had to know the truth. So, he could walk away now instead of feeling trapped by her baggage later. And she suspected Cole wasn't going to beat around the bush when it came to the topics he'd brought up the other night. Normally, the thought of talking about that stuff terrified her. But the fact that opening up to Cole tonight *wasn't* that scary was probably the most frightening thing of all.

Hearing the truth might change his attitude towards her—and perhaps *that* was the real reason she wasn't jumping at the opportunity to move this relationship forward. For fear of what he would say or what he would do when he learned the truth. She rolled her eyes. She was *tired* of fear holding her back. But she couldn't escape the mistakes she'd made. The pain she'd caused.

After stepping out of the shower, Emily toweled off and glanced at the clock. Time had gotten away from her. She wouldn't have a chance to dry her hair if she wanted to be on time. She threw on a pair of capris, a tank top, and flip flops along with a touch of lip gloss— the only shine on her now makeup-less face. Grabbing her purse, her keys and her cell phone, she locked up behind her and drove to the ice cream shop she'd selected for their rendezvous.

Once there, she scanned the dark parking lot. Cole pulled in a second later and waved as he got out of his car. He appeared freshly showered, and as he approached, his intoxicating scent overtook her. "You smell nice." If only she had a stronger filter between her brain and her mouth.

"Thanks." His gaze drifted to her hair. "You *look*

nice."

Emily flipped her still-damp hair over her shoulders. "Sorry, I didn't have time to dry my hair."

Cole laughed. "I complimented you, y'know. You don't need to apologize."

"Right! Sorry." She squeezed her eyes shut, willing away her awkward apologies. "C'mon, let's go order. Then maybe we can walk to the park down the street and eat there."

"Sounds good."

They stood in line until it was their turn. Then, with ice cream in hand, they walked the couple blocks to the park. When they sat on a bench, Emily was careful to leave a little space between them. No sense in clouding her judgment. She took a bite of her sundae and looked around. They were surrounded by old-fashioned lamp stands which illuminated the entire area, making it the perfect setting for a nighttime chat.

"Thanks again for today." Cole sipped his chocolate shake. "I'm honored you invited me to something like that. It was a lot more satisfying of a way to spend my Sunday afternoon than watching sports, I'll tell you that."

"Oh good, I'm glad. I wasn't sure how you'd feel about it. But I volunteer there at least once a month, so you're welcome to join me anytime." It was nice having someone to serve alongside. Derek would have never gone with her. Not that she'd been one to serve back then either, but still.

"Awesome. I'll remember that." Cole took a deep breath as he stared at his shake. She braced herself for what was coming. "So, has it really been seven years? Not even a single date?"

A short laugh escaped her lips. "Nothing like crazy personal questions to kick off the evening, huh?" She was teasing, but the time had come to start telling him her story. She shifted on the bench and tucked one leg under the other to face him.

Cole scrunched up his nose. "I don't mean to offend or pry, but I'm so intrigued by you. Figured I had nothing to lose by asking."

"Well." Emily paused to think through how detailed her response should be. "If you must know, I have literally had one—*one*—solitary date in the past seven years. It didn't go well and only confirmed why I don't have time to waste on finding my perfect match."

Cole's eyes narrowed. "Was it with Antonio?"

Unexpected laughter burst from her lips. "No! No, Antonio and I never even attempted to go down that road, nor *will* we. I think he has a girlfriend right now anyway. I'm not sure, I don't keep in touch with him as much as I should. No, my date was with some random guy about two years after my... after my last relationship ended."

"I see." He raised his eyebrows. "Can I ask who Antonio is then?"

She took a deep breath. It was a perfectly normal and acceptable question, but he had no idea how much weight was behind it. The answer was not quick, nor was it easy. She wasn't even sure where to begin. "Do you have a few minutes? There's quite a story around him."

"Yeah, absolutely. I'm all ears." Cole's voice was nothing but kind.

"Okay. Well, there's something you don't know about me, and it's kind of huge." She paused before continuing, giving him a chance to prepare himself for the news. "I got married when I was nineteen. I thought I was in love, though I know now that's debatable. We were immature, but I was eager to put my past behind me and move on with my adult life, and I guess I thought marriage was a step in the right direction." She paused again, trying to gauge his reaction, but Cole just nodded, not the least bit shaken by her admission so far. His acceptance helped her relax as she continued.

"Anyway, we were married four years when something awful happened. Something that haunts me to this day. We were going out to eat—I was the one driving. I was stopped at a red light and as soon as it turned green, I pressed the gas and entered the intersection. The next thing I knew, I was pinned under the steering wheel of my car, glass everywhere, with my husband lying unconscious in the passenger seat next to me."

"Oh, wow." Cole put a hand over his mouth. "I can't imagine what that must have been like."

She blinked a few times to clear the crash images from her mind. "I was the only survivor. My husband was for all intents and purposes dead on the scene, and the other driver was in critical condition for a couple days before she finally passed. I later learned they think she had fallen asleep at the wheel. But the accident was my fault. I should have been paying closer attention."

Emily stared at the sundae melting in her hands. Cole set his shake on the ground and scooted closer, placing a comforting arm around her shoulder. She leaned into him and forced back a tear, trying to contain her emotions as best she could.

"That's not true. You can't blame yourself for something like that." Cole's voice was calm, soothing. "And Antonio? How does he fit into all of this?"

"Oh, right. The driver of the other car was Antonio's mom. He and I met at the hospital, and I felt compelled to comfort him and follow up after all the dust settled. He was only a year younger than me, and absolutely devastated by the loss."

"That was really nice of you. I can't imagine going through what you did."

She pursed her lips together. "Anyway, I guess that's *part* of why I've been so content with my single status. I mean, I had love, but it's my fault my husband died. Just like everyone I've ever gotten close to. And I don't want to go through that pain ever again, or put anyone *else* through it, for that matter."

Cole's arm tightened around her shoulder. "But Emily, the accident *wasn't* your fault. You know that, right?"

She pursed her lips. Did she? "I guess, in a way. But being the driver and the only survivor, it's hard not to feel somehow responsible. You can understand that, right?"

"Maybe. But that guilt hasn't faded after seven years?"

Emily swallowed. "Somewhat, sure. I mean, life

goes on, you have to keep moving forward. But it finds ways of creeping in. It seems like every time I pursue something for my own pleasure, something else comes along to remind me my life came at a cost, and that joy is… tainted, or something. And it's next to impossible to reconcile how or why God let *me* live."

Cole gave her shoulder a small shake. "Well, I can tell you why you lived. You lived for Tyler. For Joe and Sandy. For Antonio. For that young cancer patient who died a few weeks ago. And for a second chance at a future of your own—one filled with love and happiness. God doesn't want to deny you those things just because of an unfortunate accident."

Emily angled her head to face Cole, struggling to keep her tears at bay. "Maybe. But I feel like God is teaching me some lessons from all of this, and wants me to… I don't know, suffer, in a way, for what I've done."

Cole shook his head. "Well, that's not the God I know. Wanting you to suffer? And *for what you've done*—what's that supposed to mean? You didn't *do* anything. It was an accident, Emily. Not to trivialize it, but accidents happen every day. Besides, Jesus took all that blame and punishment on the cross. You don't have to be held captive to your past—you're free and forgiven. He wants you to move on, and that's a good thing!"

Emily frowned, not convinced. If only he understood the whole truth. But she didn't dare reveal it all to him yet. Nobody knew *everything*. No one. "It's not just the accident though, Cole. There's too much to get into right now, but I do understand what you're saying."

"There's more? Is it related to your nightmares?"

"Yes." Her voice dropped to almost a whisper.

Cole squeezed her shoulder tighter, and she nestled her head by his neck, breathing in the fresh scent of his skin, enjoying the warmth of his body, and suddenly realizing that her defenses were fully down. She was in dangerous territory now.

"It's going to be okay." Cole caressed the top of her arm. "I want to know you—even the stuff you think I won't understand. I won't judge you. I won't be angry. And I promise to take things slow. But I don't want you to shut me out. Even the Bible says it's not good to be alone. You can't live like an island."

Emily tried to let his words sink in. How had she stumbled upon someone so caring? So sincere? In the past seven years, she hadn't felt as safe and loved as she did when she was with Cole.

Tearing apart from his comforting arm was difficult, but she knew she needed to look him in the eyes. She turned her body on the bench to face him, and he met her gaze. "I want you to know me, too. But there are lots of layers. You saw some of them today. But until you know them all, I can't just jump in."

Cole nodded. "I'm okay with that."

Emily caught a glimpse of his lips, then dropped her gaze. Did he want to kiss her? It was only a matter of time. But she was too out of practice for this whole thing. "It's been so long. I'm afraid I may not be any good at the dating game."

"I don't play games." Cole gently tilted her chin up with his forefinger so he could see her eyes. "All you have to do is be who you are. If you haven't noticed, I happen to like that person."

It was reassuring to know that she hadn't scared him off. That he was telling the truth. "Thanks." The word sounded trite, but she wasn't sure what else to say. She held his gaze for a few moments before remembering her melting sundae, and she grabbed it from the seat next to her.

Cole reached for his shake at the same time and took a sip. "It's getting late, but when do I get to hear the rest? Are you available Thursday? I have off in the afternoon since I'm working another open house Saturday. How about I make you dinner at my place?"

"Make me dinner?" Surely she hadn't heard him right. "I think I can count on one hand the number of times someone has made me dinner in the past... I don't know, five years?"

Cole's eyes widened. "Seriously? Oh man, that puts the pressure on me to deliver."

"Actually, it means you don't have much competition. If anything, I think it takes the pressure *off* of you."

He took another sip of his shake. "Is that a yes?"

Emily bit her lip at the realization that Cole was taking the reins and moving things along for them. She was torn between being comforted by his efforts and terrified by them. But something in his eyes and in his smile convinced her this was all happening for the good, so she took the plunge. "I could probably swing by after work. Around 6:30?"

"6:30 it is. I'll text you my address."

"Sounds good."

Cole pierced her with another caring gaze. "So, are we good? Taking things slow, but moving forward, right?"

"Yeah, I guess that's where we're at." She could hardly believe what she was saying. It was scary but exhilarating to finally move forward with a man like this.

Cole let out a small chuckle. "Whoa, don't sound so enthusiastic about it!"

Emily laughed. "It's just... I'm a little amazed you got me to this point, is all. But I'm glad. You make me feel safe, Cole. And valued. And less abnormal than the rest of the world makes me feel. So, all in all, it's a pretty good spot to be in."

"That might be the strangest compliment I've ever received." Cole raised one eyebrow and the hint of a smile tugged at his lips.

She slapped him on the knee. "Take what you can get. I told you—baby steps."

Cole reached over to put his arm around her again, and she leaned into his chest. As he kissed the top of her head, a weight lifted from her heart.

# CHAPTER 21

E MILY STARED AT THE TEXT FROM Cole on Monday after work. THINKING ABOUT YOU. JUST WANTED YOU TO KNOW. The warm, giddy feelings that accompanied the newness of a romantic relationship had lain dormant inside her for so many years, but Cole had awakened them in full force.

Giddiness aside, it didn't go unnoticed that with Cole in her life, her nightmares had all but disappeared. It was as if the added love and laughter in her life had chased away the demons haunting her for so long. But she knew she still had more to share with Cole if she wanted their relationship to start off on sound footing. The dread of that conversation still weighed heavily on her heart, despite the joy he'd otherwise brought to her life.

On Tuesday, she and Tyler arrived at PT Possibilities for his 4:00 appointment. She looked forward to what little time she'd get to talk to Cole in person—even though they would need to keep it professional since he was at work and would have an audience. After all, she didn't want to do anything that would get him in trouble. When she saw him from a distance in his monogrammed polo shirt, she was overcome by how handsome he was. He gave her a quick wink, and she couldn't hide her smile. Or stop her stomach from doing a little dance.

After Tyler's session, the guys met her in the observation area. "Tyler, why don't you go pick out a sticker at the front desk. We'll be right up to join you."

Cole put his hand on Emily's shoulder. "Do you mind? I wanted to talk. It'll only take a minute."

His touch sent warmth coursing through her body. "Of course."

Would this talk be one of a professional or personal nature? The look in Cole's eyes as he leaned toward her gave her a clue. "Do you want to grab a cup of coffee tonight?"

Emily let out a sigh of relief and flashed him a devious grin as they began walking toward the front.

"I know I probably shouldn't be asking you here, but seeing you for ten seconds and then not again until Thursday, well... that's not cool."

"You're sweet." Emily kept her voice low as she watched Tyler skip down the hall and turn the corner out of view. "And a little crazy."

"Hey!"

"But yes, I'd love to get coffee with you. At the shop next door?"

"If that works for you."

"Sure thing. What time?" She stepped to the side to avoid running into another therapist and patient coming from the other direction.

"Well, if you aren't offended by the blue polo, I could head over there right after work, around 6:30. The sooner the better. Oh, and I promise not to barrage you with questions tonight. I really just want to spend time with you."

Her smile grew wider as they neared the front of the office. "Okay then. See you in a bit." She gave him a slight wink and turned to leave. On her way out, her heart pounded a little faster at the thought of hanging out with Cole tonight. She hadn't planned on spending much time with him before Thursday, but his invitation was a pleasant surprise.

After dropping Tyler off and arriving at her house, she had about thirty minutes before she had to leave again for Oak Pines. It was a bit uncharacteristic of her, but with the positive mood she was in, due to her unexpected evening plans, she suddenly felt like dancing. Dancing! When was the last time she'd done that?

As she searched for her mp3 player amidst the piles of paper on her kitchen counter, she wondered how and why Cole's existence had suddenly made her feel so carefree. She hadn't felt this relaxed and lighthearted since... she couldn't remember when. Could it be that all this time, the antidote to her guilt and hardship was simply letting a caring soul into her life? Was Cole the key to escaping the confined rut her life had become?

She finally found her mp3 player, while vowing to tidy up the mess of papers soon, and searched for a lively tune. Cranking the volume, she found herself bouncing around the living room and giggling at the notion that she could feel this way again. She had thought for sure her dancing days were behind her. *God, thank You for letting me find this place again. Help it to last and help me not to ruin it. I pray Cole will accept me even after he knows the truth.*

EMILY POINTED AT THE little wooden pieces on the board between them. "That is so not a word!"

"Sure it is." Cole drew five more tiles from the box and placed them on his tray. "*Fixins*. As in, I like to eat Thanksgiving turkey with all the *fixins*."

Emily stared at him in mock annoyance. He was adorable, but he was wrong. "I know what it means, but that doesn't make it a true word. Do they have an official game dictionary here?" She glanced around the coffee shop, zeroing in on the bin of games customers could borrow while they enjoyed their caffeine.

"Tell you what, I'll poll the other customers and see what they think."

"No!" Emily suppressed her laughter. Who wanted to annoy their fellow patrons with a meaningless debate? "I'll let you have this one. But the next questionable one goes my way."

Cole laughed. "Ah, so that's your way of admitting

defeat. Well, all right, I'll take it."

Emily resisted the urge to lean over and slap his arm in protest, and instead focused her attention back to her tray of letters. "Wait, was that your revealing fact? That you like turkey with fixins?" They had made up a rule at the start of the game that with each word played, the one who laid it had to share something about themselves that was related to the word.

Cole rubbed his chin with his thumb and forefinger. "Well, that's true, but kind of lame. So, let me add this— Thanksgiving was my favorite holiday growing up. My parents always hosted our extended family at their house. Talk about *food*. My mom cooked every vegetable under the sun. They still host a feast, but there are fewer people that come so it's not quite the big deal it used to be."

As Cole shared his idyllic holiday memories, Emily recalled her less-festive ones. In fact, she remembered one Thanksgiving with her parents, when her mom had become quite sick. Their feast had consisted of three frozen dinners—turkey and gravy, of course, but not quite the spread they'd had in years past and that she knew her friends were having. After her mom died, microwaved Thanksgivings had become a ritual for her and her dad. As sad as it sounded, it had become her *normal*, and she had oddly come to cherish the stark reminder of her mom's last Thanksgiving with them.

"Your turn." Cole's voice jolted her back to the present.

"Oh. Right." Despite her mini walk down memory lane, she was truly enjoying herself, so she forced the sad memories out of her head and focused on the game and the amazing man before her instead.

Studying her tiles, she laid the word she'd already prepared. "Bowl." She paused for effect before providing her explanation. "I once worked at a bowling alley for some extra cash. Even with practically unlimited practice time, I only broke into triple digits twice, with an all-time high of one hundred seven. I usually scored in the eighties."

Cole chuckled. "One hundred seven, huh? Was that with bumpers?"

Emily gave Cole's leg a playful kick under the table. Hanging out with him was proving to be a blast. They had naturally talked about their day, their jobs, their likes and dislikes. And the game they were playing was not only lighthearted, but informative as well.

But they both knew that soon, she'd have to tell him more of the tough stuff. And she'd have to be tough herself, in case he decided to end what was starting to grow between them. She knew there was a real possibility of that once he knew what she'd done, who she really was. But for now, she'd focus on how he'd already taught her to push past the grief, tragedy, and guilt as she stepped back into the land of the living.

# CHAPTER 22

EMILY SAT AT HER WORK COMPUTER Wednesday morning and updated the electronic file of an elderly man they had just discharged. Nan approached a minute later, and Emily looked up to see the woman stretching her arms in the air while letting out a long yawn. Had Emily's insomnia been passed on to her coworker? "Did you sleep okay last night?" She returned her attention back to the screen.

Nan slumped in the chair next to her. "Not really. We got a new mattress the other day, and it's not agreeing with my back."

Emily winced. "Uh-oh. That's not good."

"Eh, I'll get used to it. But I'm going to grab a cup of coffee as soon as I can steal away. Would you like me to get you one?"

Emily stopped her typing and glanced up from the screen. She thought back to all the coffee she'd drank last night and did her best to suppress a smile at the memory.

"I saw that." Nan leaned closer. "Did you finally get coffee with that man?"

How on earth? She should know better than to think she could get anything past that woman. She gave a reluctant nod, and Nan clapped her hands.

"Did he hold the doors open for you? Kiss you good night?" Nan grabbed her arm, her eyes wide.

"Nan! No more questions. I really don't want to go into any more details than those you've already coerced out of me. But I will tell you, to ease your curiosity, that he's a super nice guy and we did *not* kiss good night. Or at all."

"But you wanted to, didn't you?" Nan studied Emily's face until it heated. "Oh! I knew it! You'll have to bring this man around. Inquiring minds want to meet him."

"Ha! I think it will be a while before I'm introducing him to friends and family. We've only had one date." If you could call an impromptu board game at a coffee shop a date.

"Oh, bother." Nan swiped her hand in the air. "I knew Terrence was right for me from day one. He met my friends on our second date, met my parents on our third, and proposed on our fourth. Love at first sight, I tell you."

"Aw, that's so cool."

Nan got called into a patient's room, leaving Emily to think about how fast things were moving with Cole—emotionally, anyway. It seemed her feelings had gone from zero to sixty in a matter of days. Was that too much, too fast? Or was it right where she wanted to be? Her mind wondered if it was the former, but her heart told her another story.

On her lunch, she bought a cupcake from the cafeteria. It was the perfect treat to bring Bryant, who was still a resident up on the pediatric floor. After Charlotte died, it was hard to step foot in that unit again, but she couldn't let her friends feel abandoned. They'd been affected by the news of the girl's death too, and they needed her presence now more than ever.

Thankfully, a busy workload kept her mind preoccupied for the rest of the day and the beginning of her shift on Thursday as well. But as the day progressed, her thoughts kept flashing to her evening plans. She bit her lip as she stared at her computer. It was all she could do to focus on the screen.

"What's on your mind, hon?" Nan reached for the sanitizer bottle at the nurse's station and squirted some into her hands. "Nervous for tonight?"

Emily jerked her head up, startled by Nan's voice. "Yeah, a little."

Nan patted her arm. "Be your own, sweet self. That's all you gotta do. Trust that God's got this."

She was right, but that didn't stop butterflies from taking residence in her stomach.

At the end of her shift, she raced home and took a quick shower. Wrapped in a bath towel, she stood in front of her closet to select her outfit for the night. So far, their encounters had been rather casual if not downright ragged—from hospital scrubs when they happened upon each other at the grocery store, to yoga pants the night he talked her to sleep, to old clothes when they volunteered at the mission. Sure, she'd changed for their ice cream outing, but she'd not even had time to fix her hair or put on makeup.

Tonight, she'd step it up a notch. She chose a knee-length, sleeveless floral sundress with comfortable but stylish sandals, mascara and light eyeliner to give her eyes a little pop, some lip gloss, stud earrings, and to top it all off, she sprayed a light spritz of her favorite, though seldom-used, perfume. It was the same kind her mom used to wear. Paired with her locket, they brought a sense of closeness and nostalgia that fueled her through anxious times. She gave her reflection a once-over, hoping she wasn't overdressed or overpreparing for the night.

On her way to Cole's, she saw dark clouds forming in the sky and wondered when the rain would inevitably let loose. The adrenaline coursing through her body reminded her of the way she used to feel as a little girl just moments before a looming storm—the anticipation, the wonder, the excitement. But her present state of mind had little to do with the impending storm and much more to do with the company she would be keeping.

Her heart beat double-time as she pulled into his driveway. She was such a different person than the Emily of her former dating years, and the dating scene had changed quite a bit since then. Still, Cole had said to be herself. Hopefully they were on the same page where it mattered most.

COLE CAME DOWN THE hall after his shower wearing a pair of faded jeans and a short-sleeved button-down plaid shirt with a white T-shirt underneath. He checked on the platter warming in the oven, then said a quick prayer as he glanced around the clean living room. As he adjusted the flowers he'd bought for the coffee table, he caught a glimpse of the storm clouds outside.

He heard a door slam and glanced at his watch, then walked to the front door to greet his guest. When he opened it, the sight of Emily took his breath away. She'd worked all day and still looked and smelled lovely. He couldn't stop the grin on his face, especially when a pink hue crept across her smiling cheeks in return, and he immediately gave her a hug. He had to force himself to let her go from his embrace.

Emily tucked a strand of hair behind her ear. "Sorry I'm a few minutes late."

"You're fine. And you look amazing, by the way."

Emily blushed. "Thank you."

"C'mon in, make yourself at home. I'll be right back."

He walked into the kitchen and stirred the pot of soup on the stove, then drizzled a saucepan of melted cheese over a bowl of broccoli.

"Can I help you with anything?" Emily called from the living room.

"No, dinner's almost ready." Cole straightened the place settings at the table and got two glasses from the cupboard. Then he walked to the doorway between the kitchen and living room. "I hope you don't think it's corny, but I made... well, you'll see in a bit. Are you hungry?"

Emily stood and walked toward the kitchen. "Very. All I had for lunch was a small salad from the hospital cafeteria."

"Good. What would you like to drink with dinner?"

"Water's fine, thanks."

"Okay, I think the food's ready. Let's head in."

Cole filled the two glasses with ice water, and when he turned around, Emily was touching a napkin next to one of the settings. "Cloth, huh? Ooh la la."

He chuckled. "Yeah, I got those a long time ago as a gift, and I rarely use them. Tonight's meal is not exactly an occasion to use them either, as you'll see. But hey, you only live once, right?"

Emily's lips curved upward, her hands resting on the back of the chair as she stood behind it.

"You can have a seat. I'll get the food—but don't laugh." Cole retrieved the platter of grilled cheese sandwiches from the oven and watched Emily's eyes widen as he set it in the middle of the table. He turned to carry the pot of tomato soup and placed it on a hot pad on the table, followed by a bowl of broccoli drizzled with cheese.

Emily's eyes jumped from the food to him to the food again as she covered her mouth with her hand. Had he messed up the menu choice? Or the execution? Was it callous of him to try to recreate this special memory for her?

She finally removed her hand from her mouth and beamed. "Oh, my word. This is the absolute sweetest thing anyone has ever done for me." He barely had a chance to realize her silence was *pleasant* surprise, when she stood and walked toward him, reaching out for another hug. He instinctively wrapped his arms around her, basking in the closeness of her presence, the smell of her skin, the feel of her body against his.

After she let go, she stared into his eyes for a few long moments, their faces inches from each other. As her gaze dipped to his lips, a flicker of fear washed over her face. She shook her head quickly and turned to walk back to her seat. Cole's heart dropped, but he knew it would take time for Emily to get used to the idea of being vulnerable with someone again—how could it not after seven years of solitude? He would have to be patient with her no matter how long it took. At least she was here, making steady progress in her own way. He would take whatever small steps she was capable of making and trust God with the rest.

"Thanks, Cole." Emily wiped a tear from the corner of her eye, her face red. "This is really special."

Cole nodded, unsure how to respond. He sat down across from her at the table and tried to figure out how to bring the conversation back to a normal tone again. No sense lingering on the sentimental aspect of the evening, or the fact that they had just missed an epic chance for a first kiss. Then again, maybe he was the only one thinking about *that*.

"Okay, I have no idea what your mom's secret was for these sandwiches, so I don't expect this will really be the same. But I figured it was worth a shot—and it's the thought that counts, right?" He flashed her a grin.

Emily laughed. "That's right. And lucky for you I'm really not a picky eater—plus, I'm starving. So, I'm sure these will taste wonderful."

"Great. Do you... do you mind if I pray?" He had never prayed with a date before, but he was a new man, and with Emily it felt natural to do so.

"Sure, that would be great."

After he said grace, Emily ladled soup into her bowl, served herself some broccoli, and took a sandwich from the tray. She spread the napkin in her lap, then took her first bite and closed her eyes for a brief moment. "Mm. Well, we were both right. Not a perfect match, but super delicious. And really so, so thoughtful." She caught his eye again over the table.

"Well, you are very welcome. I have dessert in the oven as well, so save room."

"I thought I smelled something sweet. Is that... is that peaches?"

Cole wiggled his eyebrows.

"You didn't!"

"Did you really expect anything else?" How could he not wrap up her favorite meal with the dessert she'd mentioned went with it?

Once again, Emily put her hand over her mouth in awe. "This is, like, the best date ever. You know that, right?"

Cole's heart almost burst with the surge of joy. Yes, he had to agree. Best date of his life.

# CHAPTER 23

ONCE THE INITIAL RUSH OF EMOTION over her favorite meal had passed, Emily was able to enjoy the lighthearted conversation they shared over dinner. After she'd eaten her fill, she helped clear the table while Cole pulled the cobbler from the oven. She passed by with the pot of leftover soup and paused to eye the bubbling dessert. "That looks amazing! You made that?"

"As a matter of fact, I did. But don't be too impressed. *I used canned peaches*," he whispered, as if his words were a secret confession.

"Is that so? Cheater." She winked.

"Shall we sit in the living room while we wait for it to cool off?"

"Sure." Emily grabbed her glass of water before heading to the living room and taking a seat in the middle of the couch. Glancing outside, she noticed the long-awaited rain had started to fall.

Cole put his water glass on the coffee table and sat down on one of the cushions next to Emily. Her mouth grew dry as she anticipated their conversation, so she took a sip of water before placing her glass next to his. Was she ready to share her story with someone? Was Cole the right person to unleash on? He was trustworthy and caring, but she wasn't used to opening up to anyone—it had been years since she'd done so, and it seemed everyone she let in only ended up getting hurt in the end.

Cole glanced at her from his side of the couch and wiped his palms on the front of his jeans. "I don't want to pressure you or anything, but I'd love to pick up where we left off on Sunday night. I was thinking about it, your nightmares and all. And I wondered if maybe *not* talking about it to anyone has only added to the problem, y'know?"

Emily bit her lip. She had already resigned herself to the fact that tonight was the night she would lay it all out there, but that didn't take away her nervousness about the whole ordeal. Still, she wondered if there wasn't some truth to what Cole said. When was the last time she had talked about what caused her nightmares? If just being with Cole had made them subside, might getting the details out in the open make them cease altogether?

As the silence began to grow too long for comfort, she cleared her throat. "I know this might be overwhelming, or make you feel like I've been hiding things from you or misleading you in some way. But this is hard for me to talk about."

Cole reached over to hold her hand. "It's all right. I'm not going to judge you or be scared away. Please don't be anxious about this, okay?"

His words were intended to comfort and encourage, but knowing what she knew—and what he *didn't*—they were not enough to assuage her nerves and guilt. "Thanks, but… please don't make any promises until you've heard everything."

With a serious expression on his face, Cole nodded, keeping his hand firmly holding hers.

Another deep breath and Emily began her story, her gaze aimed down at her lap. "As you know, my mom died when I was twelve, leaving me and my dad to fend for ourselves. He was an alcoholic, but he had it under control until my mom got cancer. That's when things turned bad, fast. He had a really short fuse and blamed me for everything that went wrong. And I just let him for a while, because I wanted to keep the peace for my mom's sake. It wasn't until after she died that I started acting out. Like I told you, I was a bit of a rebellious teen. I snuck out of the house, got in trouble at school. I was pretty rude to my dad, too, though his drinking didn't exactly make him Father of the Year. I was really going down a bad path after my mom died."

"I'm so sorry to hear that."

Emily took a deep breath. "Anyway, one night at the end of my senior year of high school, we got into another argument about me skipping class. At the time, I thought he was being unfair, and I really didn't care to follow any of his rules. So, I stormed out and promised to be back by 9:00, which was my mid-week curfew. Of course, I knew he'd be out cold long before then, so I planned to spend the night at my best friend's down the street. Her name was Shelly Olivette, and we lived in the city of Olivette. Can you believe that?" She paused as she remembered the fun times she'd had with her best friend, then shook off the memories as she got back to her story. "Anyway, I planned to sneak back in early the next morning. We weren't even doing anything special, just something to defy my dad."

She glanced over at Cole, who was listening intently, then swallowed over the sudden dryness in her throat. "This next part is kind of hard."

A loud clap of thunder shook the house making Emily jump. Cole squeezed her hand, scooted closer, and put his arm around her shoulders instead. The act was loving, but Emily was sick to her stomach at how much Cole seemed to like her without knowing the whole truth.

"Take your time." There was a gentle quality to his voice as he gave her shoulder an encouraging squeeze. "I'm listening."

"I'm nervous." She frowned, her voice barely audible above the pounding rain outside.

Cole stroked the top of her arm with his hand. He was trying to ease her nerves, but the gesture nearly brought her to tears instead. This man was doing everything in his power to get her to open up, and the time was now, no matter how painful.

She stared at the darkened television across from the couch and lifted her chin, determined to get it over with. "Around 10:00, Shelly's mom told us there was a fire down the street. We only half paid attention, but then a few minutes later her mom brought it up again and asked if I wanted to go see if it was *my* house on fire. For some reason, the thought hadn't occurred to me, and I was instantly nauseous as soon as she said it. I figured I'd better go check it out. And… well…"

"It was your house?" Cole asked.

She nodded, unable to look him in the eye.

"Oh, man. That's terrible!"

Did he suspect the weight of what she was about to reveal next? She forced herself to continue. "At first, I was completely frozen in place watching the blaze from down the block. But then, something snapped inside of me, and I ran as fast as I could toward my house. The firemen stopped me before I got too close, and that's when I asked where my dad was. They told me a man had come out of the house, all weak and dazed. But after asking where his daughter was, he ran back in with no explanation. He was too quick, and they couldn't stop him. That had been a couple minutes before, and they hadn't gotten him back out yet." Emily paused to take a shaky breath and Cole's supportive grip tightened around her shoulders.

"My heart almost stopped right then and there. I mean, my dad had gone back in to rescue *me*. And I wasn't even there because I had disobeyed him by staying out late. I didn't even know how to process what was happening. A minute later, a firefighter came out of the house with a man draped over his shoulders. I knew it was my dad. I ran in their direction, but the medics made it first. They laid him on a stretcher and put an oxygen mask over his face. His body was so burned, and his face was black from the smoke. But for a second, my eyes met his, glazed over as they were. And I knew that he knew—I was safe. I was okay. But I hadn't been home. He had sacrificed his life for a disobedient, ungrateful child."

Emily wiped a tear from her cheek and sniffed.

Cole squeezed her shoulder and waited a moment before he said anything. "That's an incredible story. I don't even know what to say. I can't imagine what you went through. I have to ask what happened to your dad, though. Did he... did he make it?"

Emily nodded, then she hid her face from him as tears fell from her eyes. She was grateful for his presence, his kindness, but he didn't need to see her so distraught.

"So, he's alive? That had to be a relief, huh?"

Emily lifted her head and took a shaky breath. "It was, at first. But..." She paused to find the right words. "He may have survived the fire, but it was made very clear to me that I was dead to him after that night."

Cole furrowed his brow. "Wait. Do you mean...?"

She stared straight into his eyes, her words sounding flat despite her emotional state. "I haven't seen my father since that night twelve years ago."

# CHAPTER 24

"EMILY, ARE YOU SERIOUS?" COLE TRIED to keep his jaw from gaping open. "Why on earth have you not seen him in all these years?"

Emily lowered her head. "I did try to see him, at first. He was in pretty bad shape, in and out of consciousness from his injuries. His sister—my Aunt Nora—was super protective of his visitors, and she'd heard about how things went down from the firefighters. How he'd gone in to save the disobedient daughter who wasn't home. That didn't exactly sit well with her. She didn't like me much to begin with, but it got worse after that night. She banned me from the hospital. She even intercepted my phone calls and didn't mince words in telling me to stay away. Forever."

Cole shook his head. "But that was just because of the shock of it all, don't you think? I mean, she can't still be harboring that kind of hatred, can she?"

"Well, I moved to Everly after graduating from high school a couple weeks later. Since I was already eighteen and so close to graduation, I was able to make arrangements to stay with my friend—the Olivettes—who offered to take me in for that short time. And I was a co-beneficiary of my mom's life insurance. It wasn't much, but it gave me enough to get started. Then I met Derek a few months after moving here. We got married in the courthouse after six months of dating, promising ourselves we'd have a big wedding once we could afford it. Not long after that, I figured I ought to tell my dad about my marriage and see how he was doing now that the dust had settled. I was super nervous, but I knew I had to try to patch things up."

Cole leaned toward her, intrigued by all that she was revealing. "What happened when you contacted him?"

"Well, I pulled in front of my old house, but the lot was empty. They hadn't re-built a house there. I looked up my dad's name, but the old house address and land line were all that was on file for him, so I literally didn't know how to get a hold of him. My only connection to him was my Aunt Nora."

"And did you contact her?"

Emily nodded. "*Stay away*. That was her message to me even over a full year later. She told me to stay away and let my dad live his life in peace. That he wanted nothing to do with me anymore."

Hearing the details of Emily's past felt like a dagger in Cole's heart. She didn't deserve that kind of pain, nor should she be torturing herself with this guilt. Her father sounded like a drunk, a toxic relationship a teenage girl had every right to try to avoid. It wasn't her fault he'd gotten hurt, even if she technically should have been home.

"That's awful, Emily. The whole thing sounds so traumatic. Especially the way your family just wrote you off like that." Compared to his upbringing, he couldn't imagine something so messed up. His family had had its share of tragedy, but he couldn't begin to comprehend how hard the years had been for her. He'd thought he could relate to whatever she was going to share with him tonight, but his situation would only sound trite in comparison. "Do they know what caused the fire?"

Emily blinked and turned to face him. "It's funny. I didn't even think to ask that back then. I guess I was too caught up in whether my dad would live or die, and how I would move on with my tattered life. When I finally did get curious about the cause, I called the fire department, and they told me the records were sealed."

Cole sat up straight and tilted his head.

"I know. Weird, right?"

He furrowed his brow. "Sure seems weird to me."

"After that, I gave up trying to find out the cause *and* trying to reunite with my dad. I figured what's done is done, no matter the reason. And it's not like my dad and I had a good relationship to begin with." She sniffed. "Maybe my Aunt Nora was right—maybe his life really *is* more peaceful without me in it."

"That's not true." Why was this woman believing such crazy lies? Anyone would be better off with someone like Emily in their life. "So, your nightmares.

Are they reliving the fire?" She'd said the fire had happened just before she graduated. So that must have been the anniversary she was referring to.

Emily sighed. "For the most part. Sometimes I'm in the fire. Sometimes I'm who *caused* the fire. Sometimes my dad is there, all burned and charred, blaming me for what happened or even for my mom's death." She glanced up at him. "I used to take care of her after school, but if I made her sad or we ran out of crackers and I forgot to put it on the grocery list, my dad let me have it. Which is why my dreams are usually coupled with an awful, indescribable sense of guilt."

Thoughts flooded Cole's mind. Did her car accident compound that sense of guilt? He wondered if she had nightmares around the anniversary of that tragedy as well. So much pain for such a kind soul. Cole caressed her shoulder and spoke with a tone that matched his touch. "Why were you so nervous to tell me this? Was it because of the sheer emotion of it all?"

His question made Emily stare at him, her blue eyes glistening with unshed tears. "Don't you think dating someone who single-handedly killed her husband and alienated her father, almost burning him to death, is sort of… I don't know, bad news?"

Cole's eyes widened. What was she talking about? She hadn't killed her husband, and from the sound of it, her father had alienated himself long ago with his actions. "Oh, my goodness, that is simply not accurate. You know you're not to blame for either of those things, right?"

Emily closed her eyes and lowered her head. "You

have no idea how responsible I feel. If I'd been paying more attention, I could have avoided the accident. And if I'd been home, my dad wouldn't have gotten burned. It *is* my fault. I'm responsible, so I've been trying to make up for it. But everyone I love keeps getting hurt, and I don't understand why. I don't understand what's wrong with me."

Cole lowered his voice "Nothing is wrong with you. None of this was your fault."

Emily shook her head. "Don't. I don't need anyone trying to make me feel better about something so obvious. If I hadn't snuck out that night…"

"Then you *both* might have been caught in the fire."

"But if he'd *known* I had snuck out, or if I had left my friend's house the moment her mom told us about the fire…"

"You can't do this to yourself. Every situation in life has a million *what ifs,* but you can't focus on those because it won't change anything. Besides, you didn't set the house on fire. And he *chose* to go back inside despite the firefighters being right there. Look, I know I can't understand how hard that all was for you, and I'm not trying to make light of it. But I do know it's in the past, and that's where it needs to stay."

Emily took a shaky breath. "Are you starting to realize what you've gotten yourself into? I know it's a lot to take in. I promise I won't think any differently of you if—"

"Emily." Cole's tone was stern. He put his thumb and forefinger on her chin and forced her to look him in the eyes. "I'm not going anywhere. What you told me doesn't make me like you any less or suddenly not want to be with you. Is that... Is that why you haven't dated in so long? You really believe people blame you, or think you have a curse or something?" He paused, his mind scrambling until he drew the only logical conclusion he could find. "Wait, is that why you volunteer your time and help out the way you do? When you said you were trying to make up for it, are you working to make things right with people who were hurt, like Antonio? Or with God?"

Emily bit her lower lip. He felt her trying to pull away and realized he should ease his grip, so he reluctantly removed his hand.

"Both," she whispered. "But mostly God." Then she dropped her gaze to her lap. "I tried to warn you about my baggage."

Cole let out an almost frustrated laugh. "I don't care about any of that. I care about *you*. About *this*. Our relationship right *now*." He was laying his heart on the line, desperately trying to get through to this woman he was falling in love with. "I don't believe in a God who punishes you for moving on or who makes people around you suffer because you made mistakes in your past."

Thunder crashed in the background, as if God Himself was agreeing with him. The sound of branches banging against the windows filled the living room. Cole watched as the storm raged on outside, echoing the turmoil Emily was obviously feeling right now.

With slow movements, she rested her head on his shoulder before speaking. "You're the first person to talk to me like this in years."

"I am?"

She let out a humorless laugh. "I saw a therapist for a short time after the fire, but he wasn't able to crack me, really. He was very soft spoken, and I think I needed more of a boot camp instructor than a passionate listener."

She lifted her head and turned to face Cole. "When my husband died, I found myself at a church instead of a psychiatrist. There was no boot camp instructor there either, but I guess God got a hold of my heart and somehow I found my way to Him."

Cole swallowed. She may have found God, but was she living in the freedom He'd intended for her? "Well, I'm glad you did. But you should know He welcomed you with no strings attached. He didn't agree to forgive you *if* you donated all your free time and money to good causes, or *if* you befriended cancer patients and foster kids." Cole held up his hand in defense. "Please don't misunderstand. I absolutely love that you do those things. But I want you to know it's not a pre-requisite. Y'know?"

Emily blinked and a sad smile formed on her lips. "Yeah. I do."

Cole narrowed his eyes. "Do you?"

She rested her forearm on Cole's shoulder, wrapping her hand around the back of his neck. As they looked into each other's eyes, Cole was thankful she'd shared all that she had. They still had a long way to go, but transparency was key in the progression of any relationship. And tonight, she'd been mighty transparent.

"Yes, I do." Moving her gaze from his eyes to his hair, her small smile gradually grew to an all-out grin.

He wasn't sure what to expect next, but as long as she didn't retreat or bail on him, he'd be happy. Emily removed her arm from his shoulder and took a deep breath. "I don't want to ruin this evening, so I'll tell you what *else* I know."

He watched her, wondering what she was referring to. "Okay, and what's that?"

"I know that peach cobbler is not going to eat itself."

Cole chuckled. On the outside, she'd gone rather quickly from emotional and lost to flirty and fine. But she'd been brave and open tonight, and the conversation hadn't been easy. He didn't want to belabor her pain, so he was willing to let her off the hook for now.

"I guess I should go get us some cobbler then." He rose from his seat.

"That would be fabulous." Emily batted her eyes in a teasing way.

"Ice cream?"

"Yes, please."

"And are you... are you sure you're okay?"

Emily pursed her lips. "Yeah, I'm fine. Thank you. You've been great. I really don't deserve you."

COLE RETURNED A FEW minutes later with two bowls of cobbler topped with heaping scoops of vanilla ice cream.

Emily hadn't had this dessert in years, and her stomach growled at the sight despite having eaten dinner not that long ago. "Thanks. You're a peach." Cole groaned.

She took her first bite and let the rich flavor wash over her tongue. "Oh. My. Word. This is absolutely divine."

"You like it? Good. I'm glad."

She focused on her dessert before taking a second bite. "Wanna know something, Cole? You're kind of a catch. So much attention on *my* situation. What's *your* story? Why have you been single for so long?"

Cole took a deep breath and exhaled loudly. "I wondered if we might get to that."

"Oooh, sounds like a juicy story. Do tell."

Cole laughed. "No, no. I mean, nothing like what you've been through. I just got tired of starting relationships that inevitably ended badly. My latest, which lasted almost two years, slowly sucked all the life out of me. Everything was all about her, no matter what else was going on around us. It was exhausting. And my ex before *that* cheated on me, which I totally didn't see coming. I'd thought we were pretty happy, and then found out what she'd been up to when she was supposedly *at the gym*." He used air quotes for effect. "And so on and so on. A real round of winners, I guess you could say."

Emily clicked her tongue. "That's terrible. I don't know why someone would risk such a good thing for something so fleeting. I'm glad to say I don't know firsthand how being cheated on feels, but I can imagine how horrible it must have been."

"Yeah. I took her back initially, but it wasn't the same. The trust wasn't there, and she didn't seem to go out of her way to repair it either." He looked up at Emily with a half-smile. "I'm a forgiving guy in most areas of my life, but that experience taught me to be very leery of giving someone who betrays me in that way another chance."

"I bet. So, what made you decide to try again? I mean, with me?"

"Fair question." He paused before continuing. "After my last relationship, I had come to the point where I knew I wasn't living how I should be, that my relationships hadn't exactly been pleasing to God. In fact, not much about my whole *life* was pleasing to God. I was a pretty self-absorbed guy up until last year."

Emily took a bite of her cobbler as she listened to Cole's confession—it didn't sound like him at all, but then again, she knew all about a changed life.

"So, I took a step back a little over a year ago. Decided to deliberately focus on anything and everything *not* related to dating. I went back to church for the first time since high school and have been going ever since. I started reading the Bible, writing in a journal." He glanced at Emily with a smirk. "I sound like a real manly man, don't I?"

She laughed. "That's not what I was thinking. I think it's amazing the way you decided to turn your life around. But that still doesn't answer my question. I don't want to get in the way of your spiritual progress— if *not* being in a relationship is what got you back on track, why risk losing that by asking me out?"

Cole thought for a minute. "The truth is, meeting you was like the culminating moment in my journey. Like, seeing how selfless you were with Tyler. It took me by surprise, in such a good way. I wanted to be like that. I needed to know you more. But I didn't know how to make that happen. And you sure didn't make it easy for me, missy."

Emily blushed. "I know! It wasn't on purpose, I swear." She held up her hand in defense. "But I'm glad you were persistent. This—what we have—is refreshing." She put her empty dessert bowl down on the coffee table, reached for her water glass, and leaned back into the couch to relax and take in the moment.

"Cheers to that." Cole took his glass and reached over to clink it against Emily's. He reclined back to join her on the couch, and she leaned her head on his shoulder. Reaching over with his free hand, he gently interlinked their fingers, resting their hands on her lap before kissing the top of Emily's head. She closed her eyes. *Thanks, Lord. For Cole's kindness and patience. For Your love and grace. I don't want this feeling to end. Help me to truly believe that You love me in spite of my faults.*

After another hour of conversation and cuddling, the storm had finally died down and Emily checked her watch. "It's getting late. I should probably get going. I know you have to work tomorrow." She reluctantly rose from the couch, and Cole followed her lead.

"When can I see you again?" He walked her to the front door.

"I have plans tomorrow night, but do you get a

lunch hour at work? Maybe I could bring a little picnic and meet you at the clinic to eat? Is that allowed?"

Cole bit his lip. "We'll make it work. I love that idea. My break is at noon."

Emily grabbed her purse and turned to face Cole in the front entryway. He rubbed the top of her arms with his warm hands. "Thanks for coming over."

"Thanks for having me. And for all the special plans. Again, it was really thoughtful." Her heart hammered at their close proximity. Before she got caught in a kiss she wasn't sure she was ready for, she wrapped her arms around him in a tight hug. With her ear pressed against his chest, she was pleased to hear his heart was racing every bit as fast as hers.

Her seven-year hiatus from dating had caused her nerves to act up even more than normal for a first date, but it helped to know Cole was also affected by the moment. She nuzzled her nose in his neck, inhaling the subtle scent of his cologne. This was by far the closest she had felt to someone in years. Or possibly ever. She enjoyed his strong embrace and savored the feel of his hands as they cradled her back. With her heart beating even faster now, it was time to put an end to their embrace.

Pulling away from him, she took a step back. "I'm sorry." That word had become all too common for her lately, it seemed. She wasn't even sure what she was sorry about—pulling away?

"Don't be." Cole eyed her lips, then puffed out a breath as if fighting for control. "I'm the one who should be apologizing. I promised to take things slow. You deserve the best, and I want to be that for you."

Her face hot, Emily swallowed hard, butterflies once again swarming her stomach. "You're quite the gentleman, Cole. Not sure what I did to deserve you."

Cole glanced at the ground, then back up again, staring earnestly into Emily's eyes. "Have you ever... have you ever fallen in love with someone you've never even kissed?"

Her eyes widened. Was he insinuating what she thought he was? How should she respond? "I... I don't think so. But I do know as a teenager, I wasted far too many kisses on guys who meant nothing to me. So, I feel like it's probably wise to be in love first. I mean, for me anyway. After waiting seven years, I'd like to think my next kiss really means something." She put her hand on the back of her neck as her cheeks heated up. What had he expected her to say?

Cole cleared his throat. "I admire your honesty." Then he grasped her hands in his, squeezing them gently as he leaned in to kiss her forehead. A moment later, he shoved his hands into the pockets of his jeans, an expression she could only describe as charming covering his boyish face. "Good night. I can't wait for lunch tomorrow."

Emily took another step backward. "Me neither." Then she opened the screen door and walked to her car, her feet dragging from not wanting to leave. From the car, she looked back at the front door and waved. She felt his watchful gaze as she pulled out of the driveway.

On the drive home, electricity coursed through her whole body. It had been so long since she'd felt this way about someone. And despite what she'd said, she had really wanted Cole to kiss her when they were saying goodbye. Most people in their situation would have been well past a first kiss by now, but she had spoken the truth where intimacy was concerned. It was far too easy to get physically involved with someone before emotions had a chance to catch up—although she was rather emotionally invested already. Still, given that this was her first relationship in years, it deserved the greatest respect.

Once inside her house, she changed into her pajamas and plugged in her cell phone to charge. That's when she noticed a light flashing at her. Apparently, she had missed an incoming text on her drive home. It was from Cole, and it warmed her heart. HOPE YOU GOT HOME OKAY. I HAD A REALLY NICE TIME TONIGHT. CAN'T WAIT UNTIL LUNCH TOMORROW!

Emily tapped out a quick reply. AW, THANKS, ME TOO. I'M SAFE AND SOUND. SEE YOU TOMORROW.

Her smile hadn't even faded by the time her head hit the pillow.

# CHAPTER 25

THE BEST NIGHT OF HIS LIFE. That was all Cole could think as he washed the dishes from the evening. They hadn't even kissed—it was certainly not the kind of date one bragged about to their buddies. But somehow, with Emily, it was the absolute best he could have hoped for.

He knew from a simple hug they had extreme chemistry. But her restraint, her composure, her confidence, was all so compelling to him. He'd seen the longing in her eyes as she'd backed away, but she stuck to her convictions. He had never been in a relationship where the physical aspect was put aside to explore all other connections first, and he was thankful for her ability to be strong for the both of them.

As he scrubbed a dried ring of tomato soup from a pot, he realized that his connection with Emily was what he'd been missing for so long, and what he'd put his love life on hold to find. She was clearly closer to falling in love than she ever thought she would be, but he knew it wouldn't happen overnight. He was in love with this woman, but he'd have to be okay with waiting until she was in a place to be able to reciprocate.

After placing the last dish on the counter to air dry, he drained the dish water and sunk into the couch, flipping on the television and thinking ahead to tomorrow as he channel surfed. Meeting at the clinic for lunch was pushing Frank's fraternization boundaries, but as long as they kept things professional until they went outside to eat, he could justify it. After all, his lunch hour wasn't officially *company time.*

The news he'd settled on was merely background noise, as his thoughts were consumed with Emily and all she'd been through. He hoped she was truly past her hesitations when it came to moving on from her past experiences. The fact that she had held off on dating for seven years because she thought it would ruin her rapport with God, and that guys would want to steer clear of her like she was a black widow, was absurd.

*It's all my fault. I'm responsible, so I've been trying to make up for it.* Cole shook his head at her logic. Given how abruptly she had changed subjects, he figured the conversation would come up again, and he wanted to be armed with the proper response if it did.

Not that she wasn't straight up a kind-hearted person, but her motives to appease God's supposed anger didn't sit well with him. Then again, what was his motive in helping her break free from the lies she'd believed? Was he only trying to get her to the point of loving him? He furrowed his brow and dropped to his knees.

*God, help me get rid of the selfishness that remains in my heart. I thought I'd moved past it, that Emily had helped me move past it. But I know now it will always be a struggle if I don't surrender to You. And please help Emily to see that You don't need her good deeds. That You love her for who she is, not what she does.*

As he turned the pages in his Bible, he couldn't imagine living life in a constant state of guilt or unforgiveness. For someone so amazing, Emily sure had a skewed perspective of God's grace. It also hurt his heart to know she hadn't seen her father in twelve years. How could he ever help her come to terms with something like that?

WHAT AM I DOING? Emily shook her head as she gazed into the bathroom mirror on Friday morning. How had she gone from seven years of solitude and contentment to suddenly longing to see a man whom she had only met a month ago? Was this really what God wanted for her? She wasn't sure, but the fact remained, she was enamored with Cole.

While a batch of cookies baked in the oven, she assembled sandwiches and put fruit, chips and bottled water in a small cooler for their lunch date. She arrived at PT Possibilities as Cole was giving a goodbye fist bump to a young girl in the entryway. The girl left, and

Cole smiled at Emily. "Perfect timing. Do you mind if we eat outside?"

"That would be great. It's a beautiful day."

"Okay good. There's a picnic table out back. One sec." He turned to the receptionist at the front desk. "Shannon, can you add these notes into Megan's file and make a copy of this form for me?"

The woman nodded as she took the papers from Cole. "Thanks. By the way, I'm clocking out for lunch now." Then he turned toward Emily. "All right, let's head out."

They walked to the back of the facility and out a rear door Emily didn't realize existed. She spotted the picnic table, and though it wasn't exactly picturesque next to a dumpster, it would do the trick. After placing her cooler on the table, she unloaded the food she'd packed. Out of nowhere, two hands gently slid around her waist from behind.

"I didn't get a proper hello." Cole's voice was lighthearted as he leaned his chest against her back, squeezing her tight.

"Ah, I was not aware of the rules. My apologies." Emily's breath caught in her throat at the unexpected backwards hug. Her hands stilled as she leaned back to enjoy the moment. "I hope you like turkey sandwiches."

Cole removed his arms and walked around to the opposite side of the picnic table. "Oh yeah, I'm not picky. Thanks for doing this, by the way. My coworkers noticed I was unusually excited for lunch today."

Emily suppressed a giggle, then handed him a paper plate and gestured toward the food. They loaded their plates and sat to eat. "How's your day going?"

"Pretty good. Though I gotta tell you, one of my favorite clients is no longer coming on Fridays. So, it will be kind of a let-down when I get to the end of my shift."

Emily raised an eyebrow. "*One* of your favorite clients? Should I be worried?"

Cole laughed. "Okay, okay, you're my favorite. Hands down. There, I said it."

"That's better. Yeah, I kind of liked our standing appointments as well. But at least we get to see each other outside of therapy, right?"

"Heck yeah. Even better." He winked. "Except tonight. You're leaving me stranded, Em."

"Hey, I don't normally have much of a social life, but it was something I couldn't get out of. I hope you understand."

"I know, I'm just razzing you. I'm really glad you decided to give this a chance." He reached over to hold her hand across the picnic table.

The warmth from his touch radiated up her whole arm. She stared at him, realizing with joy how sincere his face appeared. "Me, too."

Cole let go of her hand a moment later so they could keep eating. She couldn't remember ever dating someone as kind and humble as this man. Either God was finally letting her have a lasting relationship, or she was in for a rude awakening. She prayed it wasn't the latter. For her sake as well as Cole's.

All too soon, it was time for Cole to get back to work, so they walked hand in hand around the building to the lot where Emily had parked her car.

"Thanks again for meeting me here." Cole wrapped her in a goodbye hug, kissing her temple before releasing her to get into her car. "Have a good afternoon, young lady."

"You too, kind sir." She got in her car and drove home, unable to wipe the smile off her lips and enjoying the warmth that came from spending time in Cole's presence.

# CHAPTER 26

WHEN HIS 4:00 APPOINTMENT ARRIVED THAT afternoon, Cole's shoulders slumped at the realization that he would not be seeing Emily and Tyler. Their absence was disappointing, though he enjoyed his lunch with Emily even more than catching glimpses of her through the observation window. But Tyler was a neat kid, too. Cole was going to miss him once he no longer required physical therapy.

Somewhere in the middle of his last appointment, Cole got an idea. After his patient left, he looked up Tyler's files and made a phone call to his foster mom. To Cole's relief, Barb was open to his suggestion.

Several minutes later, he pulled into Barb's driveway. As Cole exited his car, the front door opened, and Tyler walked out with a smile on his face.

"Hi, Cole!"

"Hey buddy, how are you?"

"I'm good. Barb told me you were coming."

"Yeah, I hope that's all right. I thought maybe we could go for a walk and then play a game or something. How does that sound?"

Tyler ducked his head, but Cole saw the flicker of happiness on his face. The boy wasn't used to positive attention, and Cole was determined to be a steadfast influence for the long haul.

"Okay, let's go. We can go as slow as you need. How's your leg?"

"Better. I hardly limp at all now. I even got to chase the basketball from the sidelines in gym class a few times this week."

Cole glanced over at Tyler as they walked. "That's good to hear. Is gym your favorite part of school?"

Tyler shook his head. "I like it, but I like art better. And recess."

"Well of course." Cole flashed him a wide grin.

It was surprising how chatty Tyler was as they walked around the small neighborhood block. He had come out of his shell over the past several sessions together, and Cole was honored to be part of the boy's transformation. This feeling was probably why Emily enjoyed helping others so much.

After returning from the walk, they went inside to play cards before Barb announced it was time for dinner and invited Cole to join them.

"That's so nice of you. But I'd better get going." He held his hand out for Tyler to shake. Tyler limply reciprocated, clearly not used to a formal handshake, and Cole chuckled to himself. "Thanks for hanging out, man. Maybe we can do it again next week?"

Tyler nodded and waved as Cole left the house and got into his car. *Now what?* He didn't have plans and being with Emily wasn't an option since she was busy. His thoughts flashed to the Bible verses he had looked up the night before for Emily's sake, and a new plan formed in his head. He wanted to help Emily find closure, and he suddenly knew just what to do.

But first, he decided to stop for a burger on the way home, intentionally going to Antonio's restaurant to support and honor Emily. Antonio was working in the kitchen, and when he caught Cole's eye, it only took a moment for the recognition to sink in.

"Hey!" Antonio walked out from the kitchen to greet Cole in the barren dining area. "Emily's friend, right?"

Cole smiled and extended his arm for a handshake. "Yeah, the name's Cole. Nice to officially meet you."

Antonio gave his hand a firm shake. "Man, I was so glad to see Emily with you that night. She's been hesitant to move on since the accident. She acts like it was her fault, but it wasn't."

Cole sighed. "That's what I'm gathering. She sure thinks highly of you, though."

The other man smiled. "Thanks. She's a great person, man. You treat her right, you hear me?"

"Absolutely." Cole watched as Antonio walked back into the kitchen. It came as no surprise that Emily was right—this restaurant owner was a stand-up guy just trying to make ends meet. Cole was happy to contribute to that cause, once again leaving a hefty tip on the table after he paid his bill. Then he waved goodbye to Antonio from across the restaurant.

He drove the rest of the way home with newfound purpose, envisioning how surprised and grateful Emily would be when she learned of his efforts to help her get past the unfounded guilt she still endured from her past. While he appreciated how difficult it must have been to experience all that she had, he trusted that his research along with God's words would put everything into perspective. If anyone could make her realize she wasn't to blame for what happened in the past, and that she was loved exactly as she was, it was God.

Once home, he booted up his laptop and soon his adrenaline surged as he searched a certain name online. Once he got a hit, he took a deep breath in anticipation of the phone calls he planned to make.

EMILY KNOCKED ON TRACY'S door Friday evening, mentally preparing herself for a night of forced, awkward small talk. The supervisor from the soup kitchen was hosting a home goods party, which Emily normally would decline without reservation. However, this was also a fundraiser, with the proceeds going to the Mission, and everyone who volunteered there on an even semi-regular basis was invited. Since Emily wanted to show her support for Tracy and the Mission, she had decided this was one party she could make a point to attend.

After Tracy greeted her, Emily chatted with the others milling around. She recognized many of them as Mission volunteers, including a few she'd seen less than a week ago when she and Cole had served there. Had it really been less than a week? So much had transpired since then.

A few minutes later, Tracy was by her side and whispering. "There's someone here I want you to meet. He's a school teacher and his wife passed away a few years ago. I think the two of you would really hit it off."

"Oh!" Emily's jaw dropped at Tracy's boldness. "Wait, T-Tracy." She had to stop the introduction before it even began. It was early on in their relationship, but her heart was undoubtedly with Cole.

"Now, now." Tracy tugged her sleeve to get her to move. "You have been single for far too long and I will *not* take no for an answer."

Emily began to panic. "No, wait, Tracy. I have to tell you something first."

Tracy rolled her eyes. "All right, I'll give you fifteen seconds before I pull the plug."

Emily led her to a quieter corner of the room and lowered her voice. "I'm sort of seeing someone."

Eyes widening, Tracy gasped. "You *are*? Is it that man who volunteered with you last week? What was his name—Kyle? Cole?"

Emily blushed. "Actually, yes. And it's Cole."

"I knew it! You insisted you were just friends, but I knew it. Oh Emily, I'm so happy for you. So, where is he? Why didn't you bring him along?"

"Ha! We've hardly had two dates and you want me

to bring him to a home goods fundraiser? That would be sure to send him running the opposite direction."

Tracy stared at her with an offended expression, immediately followed by a softer one. "Okay, fair enough. Good call. Well, you keep me posted, little lady. I want to hear how things go with this man, all right?"

"You got it," Emily said. And like that, Tracy was gone, mingling with the dozen or so guests in her small living room. Emily looked through the catalogs. The only thing she could envision using was a cupcake container—she'd bought so many cupcakes for the kids in the cancer ward at work, it would be nice to make her own instead. And maybe someday, she'd learn how to decorate them the way the professionals did. As she surveyed the happy conversations and socializing going on around her, she couldn't help but wish she was spending the evening with Cole instead.

They ended up talking on the phone after her party and made a date for Saturday evening. All through work on Saturday, her thoughts were on their date. She felt like a schoolgirl, the way she couldn't stop thinking about the man. After leaving work, she raced home to freshen up. When the doorbell rang, her stomach did a happy flip.

Cole smiled when he saw her, immediately leaning over for a hug. It was reassuring how accepting he was about taking things slow—physically and emotionally.

They decided on dinner out. After their server took their order, Cole peered at her across the table, his lips set in a slight frown. "I wasn't sure when to bring this up, but my boss asked me yesterday if I'd fill in for him at a conference next week."

Emily took a sip of her soda. "That sounds interesting."

Cole stared down at his hands, then sighed. "It's in Sacramento."

Eyebrows raised, her heart dropped. "How long will you be gone?"

"I leave tomorrow afternoon and come back Thursday. One of my coworkers will take my cases this week. They'll be up to speed on all the notes in my files, so don't worry about Tyler."

"Oh." Emily was surprised at how disappointed she was that he was going to be out of town the next few days, but she tried to look on the bright side. "We can always call each other, right? And text. And email."

Cole chuckled, reaching over to put his hand on her forearm. "The eternal optimist."

Emily smiled up at him. "I wish I could see you off tomorrow, but I promised Tracy I'd help her sort donations at the Mission. I'll keep my weekend free for your return, though." And she'd look forward to another hug then, too, without worrying about him rushing the physical side of things in the meantime. Instead, they could bond over the phone without that temptation. Was that so wrong? Or was she just afraid to move forward?

They decided to check out a movie at a local theater after dinner. She leaned her head on his shoulder as they watched, her heart at peace—content. She wanted to savor the way simply being in his presence made her feel. As he rested his head atop hers, a flutter rippled through her body. She was falling, there was no doubt about it.

After they pulled into her driveway, he walked her to her front door. *Such a gentleman.* On the porch, he turned to face her and Emily's heartrate picked up.

Cole cleared his throat. "I'll be sure to let you know when I land tomorrow."

Emily swallowed the unexpected lump in her throat. "I'll miss you." It sounded juvenile, but it was true. When and how had she grown so attached to this man?

A gradual smile formed on Cole's face as he reached over and put a hand on her waist. "I'll miss you, too."

Emily's face suddenly warmed, and she didn't want the giddiness to subside. She took a step toward him, wrapped her arms around his back, and leaned her head on his chest, squeezing him tight. He had to wonder when he was going to get a kiss out of her—she halfway wondered the same. Why was she so reluctant to take things to that level?

As they separated, Cole kept his hands on her waist and stared straight in her eyes. There was passion in his gaze, a certain longing that made her want him more than anyone she ever wanted before. He brought his hands to her neck, just behind her ears, his thumbs gently stroking her jawline. His gaze landed on her lips for a few seconds, then raised back to her eyes. He squeezed his lips together. "Mmm. You have no idea what you do to me, Emily."

Warmth radiated through her whole body. *I think I have an inkling.* He shook his head quickly and hugged her again. Lifting her hand to his lips, he kissed her fingertips, then smiled and turned to leave. His restraint was commendable. But she knew without a doubt that she loved this man, and she wanted him to know it, too. "Wait."

He stopped halfway between her front door and his car and turned to face her. Holding his gaze, she advanced a few steps, closing the space between them until they were only inches apart. She opened her mouth, but no words came out. Still, she knew what would speak even louder than words. Wrapping her arms around his neck, she looked up at him with such intensity that he *had* to know what she was thinking. His hands found their way to her hips, and he lowered his head slowly. She had time to change her mind, but she met him halfway, leaving no doubt.

His lips were soft and warm, and his kiss was tender, just the way a first kiss should be. She had almost forgotten what it felt like to kiss a man, but Cole wasn't just any man, and this kiss was better than any she'd had before. Her lips lingered on his for a few seconds before she pulled away and opened her eyes. Could he tell her heart was beating out of control?

Cole stared at her intently, as if studying her thoughts and the motivation behind their kiss. His arms wrapped around her back holding her tight as he gazed down at her. "I love you, Emily. I have for a while, but I didn't want to scare you away by saying it too soon."

Emily couldn't hide her smile. "I love you, too, Cole. And here I was the one worried *you'd* be scared away by my past."

"Never." He squeezed her tight, kissed her temple,

her cheek, then the tip of her nose. "This is going to make being away from you this next week that much harder, y'know."

Emily laughed, though he was probably right. "It just gives us that much more to look forward to."

His answering smile held a mixture of love and sadness. Then she watched him get into his car and drive away, the realization that she wouldn't see him again until Friday kicking her gut. She walked inside and touched her lips, as if to hold the memory of their kiss in place. Maybe it would be good to have some distance after their first kiss. She didn't want the passion to pick up too quickly, as she longed for their relationship to honor God first and foremost. And the way they'd been staring at each other just now, she knew that could be a slippery slope. But oh, what a slope.

# CHAPTER 27

COLE'S FLIGHT WAS ON SUNDAY AT 3:00—just enough time to grab lunch with his brother after church.

Tim waved a hand in front of Cole's face across the table. "Where's your head, bro? Girl trouble?"

Cole blinked. He may have been physically present with Tim, but he couldn't deny his mind was focused on the night before. "Sorry, man. I'm..." He smirked. "Preoccupied, I guess."

"So, what's her story?" Tim took a long sip of his soda.

"That's a vague question."

"I mean, is she fresh out of a relationship? Has she ever been married? Does she have kids?"

Cole fidgeted with the salt and pepper shakers on the table. How much should he share with his brother? Tim was trustworthy, but he didn't want to infringe on Emily's privacy either. "No. Yes. And no."

Tim rolled his eyes. "Man, why so tight-lipped? I'm not gonna judge her—or you. And I'm not gonna embarrass her. Maria and I would like to meet her, and we want to know a little about her beforehand."

"Oh, all right. She got married when she was nineteen, but her husband died seven years ago in a car accident." He decided not to get any more detailed than that.

"Man, that's rough. Poor girl."

Cole always thought Tim sounded funny when he was being sympathetic, but he knew his brother was sincere.

"What else?" Tim closed his menu and leaned back in his chair. "I mean, that was seven years ago. Why has she not found love in seven years?"

"Well, I haven't found love in *thirty-three* years, so I don't think it's so odd she's gone seven years without dating anyone." *Oops.* He squirmed in his seat. That exact detail was not supposed to come out.

"Wait, are you saying you're her only boyfriend in seven years?" Tim's eyes widened.

"That's none of your business. Let's drop it, please."

"Wow. No pressure!" Tim waggled his eyebrows.

"That's enough, Tim. I mean it." Cole frowned. He wished he was having this conversation with Maria instead. She'd at least show some sympathy.

"All right, all right. I'm just yanking your chain. I can't imagine how tough it would be to get over the death of a spouse. Besides, she's too busy bandaging up maimed deer and feeding the poor to find love, right?" He popped a tortilla chip in his mouth.

Cole wasn't sure whether to laugh or to punch his brother in the face. "If this keeps up, I swear I will never let you meet this woman. And I don't even know if she'll agree to it. She's kind of reserved, so no guarantees."

Tim pretended to zip his lips with his thumb and forefinger. Despite his mouth being zipped shut, he still managed to speak. "Like I said, I promise I won't embarrass or judge. I want this to work for you, big brother. You seem like a changed man these days, so I know she must be a catch."

The uncharacteristically serious words from his brother made Cole relax. "Thanks, man. Just don't expect to meet her right away. I'm going to have to ease into that conversation."

Tim nodded and spread his napkin on his lap just as their server arrived with their appetizer. Cole sighed. Now how could he broach the subject of meeting his family with Emily? He had a sneaking suspicion she wouldn't be nearly as excited about taking that significant step as he was.

By Sunday evening, Emily finally decided it was past time to clean up the cluttered piles of paper on her counter. Normally, she'd have already tackled the monthly task, except lately her free time—and thoughts—had been centered around a certain physical therapist. But doing it now would give her something productive to do to keep her mind off the fact that Cole was halfway across the country.

She had just thrown away three sheets of expired coupons to local restaurants and filed away her bank statement when her phone rang. Seeing Cole's name on the screen, she turned her back on the teetering stack to answer her phone. "How was your flight?"

"Hey there! Not too bad. It was right on time, and I even convinced the flight attendant to give me an extra bag of peanuts, so I'd consider it a success."

Emily abandoned her attempt at organizing in favor of sitting on her living room couch. "Are you at your hotel?"

"Yeah, I just checked in. I'll probably order a pizza in a bit."

Emily looked at her watch. Time had gotten away from her while she'd conquered half the pile in her kitchen. "Sounds good. Maybe I'll do the same."

"I wish we could eat together."

She considered bringing up the idea of a video chat so it would seem like they were in the same room eating together, but her messy pony tail and tattered sweatshirt made her second guess that idea. "I know, I like being with you."

"I like being with *you*. I love you, Emily."

Her heart swelled at his words. It had been so long since she'd heard them, not counting last night. "I love you, too."

"Say it again." Cole's voice held a smile.

"I love you."

They talked for an hour, but the time flew by. "I better get going." Cole yawned. "I have to get something in my stomach before bed, and the conference starts bright and early in the morning."

"Of course, I won't keep you." Emily didn't want their conversation to end, but she had to work tomorrow, too. Besides, as much as she disliked organizing paperwork, she had to capitalize on what little motivation she had and get back to her mess. Now that it was getting late, she'd just throw a frozen pizza in for dinner.

"I'll text you tomorrow, sweetie. I hope you sleep well tonight. I love you."

Emily's grin spread wide across her face as she echoed his words and said goodbye. *Sweetie.* She liked the sound of that. It was what her mom used to call her. The familiar term made her heart beat harder in her chest. If only her mom could see her now.

The following days brought with them a number of flirtatious texts, each one sending electric shocks through Emily's belly. She took a few random selfies and sent them to Cole in hopes of breaking up his academic escapades with a dose of comedy or romance. Judging by his responses, she succeeded in her goal.

When Cole was back in town Thursday night, he texted Emily again. NO PRESSURE, BUT ANOTHER PICNIC LUNCH TOMORROW WOULD BE FINE BY ME. JUST SAYING.

After nearly a week apart, she could hardly wait to see him face-to-face again. WISH GRANTED. SEE YOU AT NOON.

On Friday, he broke into a big smile when she entered the clinic, but Emily was wise enough not to hug him in front of his coworkers and patients. Once they walked out back, he nearly knocked her over with his firm embrace. The intensity of his greeting made her dizzy.

"Whoa! Nice to see you too."

Cole loosened his grip and let out a small laugh, then sat at the picnic table and rested his chin on his hand as he gazed at Emily. "I know we talked like every few hours while I was gone, but I really did miss you."

Her heart skipped a beat. Such kind words. "Thanks. I missed you, too."

"Good." Cole winked at her, then took a sip from his water bottle. "Hey, there's something I wanted to ask you."

"Sure, what's up?" She took a bite of her sandwich.

"Well, I hesitate bringing this up, but… my brother and sister-in-law have been asking to meet you. If you're game, I was hoping we could do dinner with them tomorrow night."

Emily paused mid-chew. The bread and meat turned to sawdust in her mouth, and she took a sip of water to force it down. Wasn't it a bit soon to meet his family?

Cole must have sensed her hesitancy. "I promise to make it as minimally awkward as possible. They're really cool people, and my parents wouldn't be part of the outing, so no real pressure."

Emily still wasn't sure what to say. "Cole, I… uh. I mean, we've only been dating for like two weeks."

"I know, I know. I totally get it. But I've been attracted to you for longer than that, so they've been hearing about you for a while." He grinned. "And truth be told, Tim and Maria are really more like my best friends than family. If that helps."

Emily let his words sink in, and Nan's advice sprang to her mind. *Be your own sweet self. Trust that God's got this.* She inhaled through her nose. How bad could meeting his brother really be? "Okay. I suppose I could handle that."

Cole picked up a chip and pointed it at her before popping it in his mouth. "If you'd like, we could come up with a code word in case you're super uncomfortable and want to bail. Like, if you start talking about... I don't know, dish soap? That will be my cue to rescue you from the evening. Sound like a plan?"

"Dish soap?" Emily chuckled and shook her head. "No way. I wouldn't feel comfortable ditching your family like that. Don't worry, I'll be fine."

Cole shrugged. "Suit yourself. Can I pick you up at 5:30 tomorrow? We can drive over to Tim and Maria's together. They live about a half hour from you."

Emily took another sip of her water. "Sounds good. Oh, what should I wear?"

"Anything. It will be very casual, I promise."

"Are you sure? I want to impress them."

Cole reached over and held her hands in his. "Trust me. They're an easy sell. And you make a darn good first impression."

Her cheeks heated at his reassuring words. She hadn't felt this carefree in years. Five years ago, if she'd have let her heart get this close to someone, she'd just be waiting for the other shoe to drop. But now, she was hopeful that this time was different. *God, please let me be right. I know I don't deserve it, but I'm genuinely happy.*

*Please keep things going in a positive direction with me and Cole. Help our relationship to honor You in all things. Amen.*

# CHAPTER 28

EMILY TOOK A SIP OF HER sparkling water and leaned against Cole on the couch, his arm around her shoulders giving her confidence to hang with his family for the first time.

Across the living room, his sister-in-law tucked a stray curl behind her ear. "While we're waiting for the roast to finish, why don't you tell us a little more about yourself?"

"Nothing like putting her on the spot." Cole gave Emily a comforting squeeze, which helped ease her nerves.

"What? She doesn't have to bear all." Maria shrugged.

"It's okay." Emily patted his knee with her free hand. "I'm originally from St. Louis, but I moved here after high school. I work as an ER nurse at Kansas City Med. I assume Cole filled you in on how we met?"

"Yes, we were quite impressed, weren't we Tim?" Maria turned toward her husband who was in the chair across the room.

Tim looked up from his smart phone and quickly put it down on the coffee table with a guilty glance at his wife. "Uh, yes. What made you decide to go into nursing?"

Emily took a sip of her drink. How could she phrase her response in such a way that wouldn't invite more questions? The truth was, after her own emergency room experience from the car accident, she had decided it was the perfect way to give back, not to mention a necessary means of income since her husband had passed away. She had continued working in retail while she went to nursing school, but it quickly became clear that her heart was in the medical field. No sense in getting into all those details now.

"I've always admired the hard work and care nurses and other medical staff give their patients, and I'd witnessed it firsthand on a few occasions. It's so necessary, and so rewarding, I just knew it was for me." Her response, while vague and perhaps a bit cheesy, was certainly not a lie. She resisted the urge to wipe a sweaty hand on her leg.

"That's awesome." To Emily's relief, the oven beeped and Maria excused herself.

"Can I help you?" Emily stood even before Maria responded.

"Sure, that would be great."

In the kitchen, Maria pointed to a drawer next to the sink. "Silverware's in there, and here's a stack of plates if you don't mind setting the table." Emily placed the plates around the table, then made her way to the silverware drawer as Maria opened the oven to check the temperature of the roast with a meat thermometer. Satisfied, she heaved the pan out of the oven, kicking the oven door up with her foot and then closing it with her hip. Emily counted four of each utensil from the drawer.

"Cole really seems into you." Maria kept her voice low. "Have you guys been spending a lot of time together?"

Emily walked around the kitchen table positioning the silverware on a napkin at each place setting. "Well, he was out of town this past week, but we stayed in touch. And we've gone out a few times before that."

Maria carved the meat as they talked. "Cool. And what do you like to do for fun? When you're not at work or with Cole?"

Emily thought for a minute. "I read quite a bit. And I like to take walks. But I also volunteer a lot." That reminded her she wanted to show Bryant a magazine article on polar bears that she'd seen in the waiting room the other day. She'd have to make a trip up there on Monday. "And I go to a weekly Bible study. Nothing too exciting, I'm afraid."

Maria shooed off her comment with the wave of a hand. "Oh, stop. Sounds like a pretty peaceful and rewarding life, if you ask me."

Talking with Maria as they brought the food to the kitchen table somehow made her appreciate Cole even more—the fact that he had family she could relate to and that seemed to accept her right away. Just like Cole said they would. Her stomach twisted as she realized they were the family she wished she'd had growing up.

"Guys, c'mon in. Dinner's ready," Maria called. A moment later, Cole and Tim wandered in, and Emily caught Cole's eye. The way he stared back at her, a boyish grin on his face, made Emily feel like she was the luckiest woman alive. It was still a little hard to believe they were dating.

"How was work this week, Tim? Any exciting stories to share?" Cole asked after they'd sat at the table and began eating.

Tim took a bite of meat and put his fork down, an amused expression forming on his face. "Let me think." He propped his elbows up on the table and rested his chin on his folded hands as he chewed, a far-off stare on his face as if deep in thought.

"Uh-oh. I recognize that look." Maria wiped her mouth with her napkin. "I think we're in for some juicy details."

Tim wiggled his eyebrows, then shook his head. "Nah, actually there was nothing too crazy this week. Just a teen who thought it would be cool to break into an electronics store and instead of stealing anything, he took a hammer to a dozen TVs. Why anyone would think that's cool is beyond me."

"That's terrible! Did you catch him?" Emily's eyes widened as she put a bite of meat in her mouth.

"Yeah, the store had a security camera. We brought him in, along with his dad. Not sure if there's a mom in the picture, but the dad seemed to be pretty upset. I hope they have a good lawyer. I mean, the kid deserves to be punished, but I don't want it to ruin his whole life."

Emily furrowed her brow. "Well sure. So young, I hope he can still be set on the right path. If so, then someday he'll look back on this and be able to tell people how he worked his way up from rock bottom."

Cole put a hand on her knee under the table and her heart did a little flip. His subtle support spoke volumes. Emily knew not every story could have a happy ending, nor did she consider herself a prime example of turning one's life around, but she was certainly a better person now than she had been growing up. If she'd been caught doing half the things she'd done back then, her life could have turned out much different.

"Anyway, other than that incident, my week wasn't too shabby. Mostly a bunch of people driving under the influence." Tim exchanged knowing glances with Cole, who swallowed hard and dropped his gaze, giving an unusual amount of concentration to his roast beef. What thoughts had Tim's statement triggered? Had Cole lied to her about his own teenage shenanigans? Had he done more than toilet paper a few houses like he'd said?

Maria put her water glass down. "For once, my job proves to be more exciting than yours."

"Oh yeah?" Tim stabbed his fork into a pile of green beans. "How so?"

Maria glanced at Emily. "I'm an Art teacher. Summer school started this week, and one of my classes is preschool through second graders. There's this little boy who I was warned puts everything in sight into his mouth. Well, we were making a collage of fireworks using glue and sprinkling glitter on top, then shaking out the excess glitter."

"Uh-oh." Emily imagined the end result.

Maria cringed. "Oh, my word. You have never seen such a sparkly mouth. And have you ever tried to get glitter off a tongue? I wonder what his parents will think when they see glitter in the toilet tonight."

Emily and Cole laughed, exchanging amused glances. Tim groaned. "Thanks for that image."

After a few more stories, they finished eating, and Maria turned to Emily at the table. "Would you like to help me with the dishes? I got this new dish soap I can't wait to try."

Emily almost spit out her drink but managed to swallow it quickly instead. Seeing that this was Cole's proposed code word, she wasn't sure how to engage in this conversation without giving him the wrong idea. "Um. Of course, I... I can help with the dishes." She stole a quick glance at Cole, who raised his eyebrows and shrugged.

After another moment of silence, Maria broke out laughing.

Emily stifled her own laughter as she pointed her finger at Cole. "You rascal! You set me up!"

Cole's eyes widened, revealing an air of innocence. "Who, me?"

Emily then addressed Tim and Maria. "I'll have you know, the whole *code word* idea was Cole's idea. I told him it wasn't necessary, but he seemed so worried about my feelings."

Maria leaned over to touch Emily's hand. "Oh

honey, we know. We were just having fun. And you handled it so well." Maria winked at Emily, and any remote feelings of betrayal or confusion melted away, knowing she was fully accepted by Cole and his family.

Later in the evening, Emily helped brew coffee and prepare dessert—Maria plating apple pie while Emily added ice cream. "I love your necklace." Maria gestured toward Emily's neck before putting another slice of pie on a small dessert plate.

Emily fingered the locket, an image of her mom running through her head. She would have loved Cole's family.

"In fact, you seem to have really good taste all around." Maria nodded at Emily's outfit. "I'm going shopping after church tomorrow. I need a dress to wear to a friend's wedding in a couple of weeks. Would you like to come with me? I could use a second female opinion."

Emily stopped scooping ice cream. Didn't Maria have closer friends than someone she'd just met to accompany her on her shopping trip? "Me? Really?"

"Absolutely. I'll even buy you lunch for fortification beforehand."

"Oh, that's not necessary." Emily turned back to her scooping duties. "Um, I suppose I could come with you. Should I meet you somewhere?"

"Cole said you live in Everly, right?" After Emily's nod, Maria continued. "I'm heading to Everly Pines Mall, so we can either meet there or I can pick you up if you prefer. I'll just need your address."

Emily jotted down her address on a piece of paper,

still a little dazed at the fact that she was going to be hanging out with Cole's sister-in-law.

The group ate their pie over more lighthearted conversation, and once they were finished, Cole announced he and Emily had to head out.

"Well, it was super nice meeting you, Emily." Maria reached over for a hug. "Pick you up tomorrow around noon?"

Cole shot Emily a look of confusion, but she ignored him. "Sounds good. It was nice meeting you both, too."

Once inside Cole's car, he stared at her. "What was that about? You're meeting up with Maria tomorrow?"

"Oh, yeah." Emily was excited to explore a new friendship, though she hoped Maria wouldn't interrogate her further while she was trapped at the mall. "She asked me to go shopping with her. You don't mind, do you? We didn't have plans, right?"

Cole chuckled to himself. "No, you're fine. But you don't have to hang out with my family, y'know. I hope you didn't feel obligated."

"Oh, no. Oddly enough, I didn't. I really like her, and Lord knows I could stand to get out more."

"Well, I could take care of *that* dilemma."

Emily suppressed a laugh. "And I'm happy to let you do so. But you know what I mean. *Girl*friends. Girl talk."

"Ah, okay. Well then, you won't find a truer friend than Maria. Hope you guys have fun. Would you be interested in catching a movie or something after your shopping excursion?"

"Sure, that would be great. I'll call you when we're

done?"

"Sounds good."

When they got to Emily's house, she stifled a yawn.

"I better let you go, missy. I know you've had a long day and you need to rest up for tomorrow's epic shopping journey."

Emily raised her eyebrows. "Oh, I didn't realize I was in for such a massive event."

Cole reached over to touch her knee. "I hope you had fun tonight. I know *I* did. Tim and Maria loved you."

"I enjoyed myself. I really did. Your family is great. I wish I had a family to introduce *you* to." She bit her lip as that reality set in.

Cole squeezed her knee. "I'm sorry if any part of tonight was insensitive to that."

"No, no. That's not what I'm saying. Truly, it was great. Every last bit of it."

"Good. Well, let me walk you to your door." He unbuckled his seatbelt and opened his door, leaving the car running in her driveway.

When they got to her front stoop, he reached over to grasp her hands. His lips curved up at the edges as his gaze penetrated her eyes, making Emily weak in the knees. She enjoyed the tenderness of his touch. Then without warning, he shifted his hands to her waist, gently nudging her toward him as their lips met in a gentle kiss. It was light and tender, but then he pulled her closer and deepened the kiss. He pulled away too soon, leaving her practically panting for more. She'd forgotten how quickly things could get out of hand.

They'd have to be on guard.

Cole wrapped his arms around her back and pulled her into a warm embrace before whispering in her ear. "I love you so much. But I don't want to rush this, and I want to honor God with our relationship more than anything. I hope you know that."

Still recovering from their kiss, Emily pulled away from his arms, then gazed into his eyes. "I love you, too, Cole. And I couldn't agree with you more."

Cole took a deep breath, then leaned over and gave her a simple kiss on the cheek before turning to leave. "Have a good night."

Emily scrambled inside and watched from the living room window as Cole climbed into his car and pulled out of her driveway. She closed her eyes, remembering how his kiss made her feel inside, and how his godly words that followed raised her respect for him even more than before. She sighed. The near perfection of their relationship and the bliss of this moment were precisely the reason she was just waiting for something to go wrong.

# CHAPTER 29

EMILY SLID INTO THE PASSENGER SEAT. Her seatbelt was barely buckled before Maria backed out. "Have you eaten yet?" With a glance over her shoulder, Maria pulled out onto the street and they were on their way.

"I had a late breakfast, so I'm fine for now."

Maria waved her hand in the air. "Well I'm starving, so I'm gonna buy you a world class, top of the line, shopping mall food court lunch."

"You really don't have to do that."

"Trust me, you're going to need the energy to shop with me."

Emily wasn't sure whether to be amused or intimidated, but she decided to take Maria up on her offer.

After they sat down with their sub sandwiches and sodas, Maria immediately started grilling her. "Okay, so tell me. What is it you like most about Cole?"

Emily shifted in her seat. "I don't know. I guess... I mean, I guess it's how caring he is."

Maria beamed. "He's a great guy, isn't he? I went to middle school and high school with him, same grade. Didn't know much about his brother Tim until our senior year. He was a freshman then. We got to know each other through the high school play, and we kept in touch my freshman and sophomore years of college since I attended nearby, at the University of Missouri in Kansas City. We finally officially started dating when Tim was a senior and I was in my third year of college. We dated on and off for two years, then exclusively for another two before he proposed."

"Oh, so you were the older woman, huh?"

Maria cackled and crunched on a potato chip. "Yeah, it was kind of weird at first. But we were such good friends, it just felt natural to take it to the next level. We really clicked—kind of like you and Cole. I can tell you guys make sense."

"You can?" Emily raised her eyebrows.

"Yeah. I can't remember the last time I've seen Cole this happy. I mean, he's a pleasant guy by nature, and I know he started taking his faith more seriously this past year. But lately, it's like his whole spirit is at peace. And I'm happy for him. He's had a couple of heartaches, so he deserves this."

Emily swallowed a bite of her sub. "What do you mean when you say heartaches?" She wondered if she could get more information about his past than he'd already shared. "You mean his past girlfriends?"

Maria talked around the potato chips in her mouth.

"Oh, those were just bad breakups. Women doing stupid, hurtful stuff. He's so trusting and open and giving, and when the girl he was dating didn't reciprocate, it was painful to watch. But I can tell you're different. And I mean that, Emily. I don't say that to everyone. The first thing he told us about you was how you were paying for that boy's therapy out of pocket. I don't know if he even knew your name at that point, and I could already tell how good of a fit you guys would be."

*Wow.* She'd had no idea how invested Cole had been so early on—she hadn't even been open to the idea of a relationship at the time Cole had been talking her up to his family. It was flattering, if not a little bit scary, but it made her appreciate even more just how patient he'd been with her and how understanding he was about taking things slow. "That's awfully nice of you to think so. I can tell Cole has a great family, especially after meeting you and Tim last night."

Maria bragged about Cole for a few more minutes. Once they were finished with their food, she stacked their trays and stood. "Well, we'd better get moving."

They started their expedition in the main store at the south end of the mall, where Maria tried on half a dozen dresses. Emily loved the very first dress her new friend tried on, but Maria didn't want to settle on anything before she saw more options.

At the third store they visited, Maria held up a full-length, royal blue dress. "You would look amazing in this. You *have* to try it on."

"Oh, that's okay. I'm just here for moral support,

Maria. Not in the market for a dress myself." Except the color was stunning, and she knew the cut would flatter her figure. She'd never wear it anywhere, but just trying it on might be fun.

Maria frowned. "Please? This style is perfect for your body type, and the color would look gorgeous with your hair. Ooh, this one would be great, too." She held up a solid pink dress with sequins covering the top half.

Emily wasn't sure why Maria was so persistent, but she didn't have the kind of budget that allowed her to drop a hundred dollars on something she didn't need. "Thanks, but I don't really want to spend the money on something that will only hang in my closet. I have no occasion to wear something like this."

"Actually, you *do*." Maria's eyes twinkled.

"Uh, no, I really don't." She didn't want to be abrasive, but she wasn't going to let Maria convince her to buy something extravagant and unnecessary.

"Okay, so Cole would kill me if he knew I told you this. But there's this awards ceremony and fundraiser thing next month for people in various therapy professions. Cole was nominated for some random award, like Outstanding Advancement in Pediatric Physical Therapy or something."

Emily raised her eyebrows, surprised this subject had never come up before.

"Yeah. He's too humble to brag about it, but it's kind of a big deal. Anyway, he gets to bring a guest. I know he wants to invite you, but he doesn't think you'd be interested, or you would only agree to go out of obligation, and he doesn't want to put you in an uncomfortable position."

Emily wasn't sure how she felt about what Maria was saying, but she couldn't hide her frown. "I guess I *am* a little guarded. Did he tell you all that?"

"Not in so many words. But the part about him wanting you to go is one hundred percent true. And I wouldn't bring it up, except I know how great you two are together, and how happy it would make him to have you there by his side. It's next month—July twentieth."

Pursing her lips together, Emily stared at the ground. What should she do? A hand touched her arm, and she glanced up at a very sympathetic Maria.

"I know I've put you in an awkward spot, but I'm willing to own it. I can let Cole know I told you, whatever your answer may be, and relay it back to him. Or however you want to play it, really. I'm not trying to interfere or cause trouble. But I really want the best for him. And I can tell you're something special."

Emily swallowed hard. "I don't really know what to say. I mean, of course I want to be there for him. I really care about him, too. Maybe I should be the one to bring it up. Do you think?" While she wasn't much for big to-dos, the idea of dressing up on a fancy date to support a handsome guy she loved was starting to sound like a pretty fun idea.

"Honestly, it's whatever you want."

"Yeah, I'll mention it to him. I appreciate you letting me know about it."

Maria threw her arms around Emily. "You are so great. Thank you for not being upset about it."

Emily swallowed and reciprocated her hug. "Not at

all."

"Then you'll try these on, right?" Maria held up the two dresses she'd picked out. "I promise you, the royal blue one will be a winner for Cole."

After modeling the dresses, Emily had to agree with Maria that the royal blue dress was stunning. "What size shoe do you wear?" Maria asked.

"Uh, an eight. Why?"

"No way! I have the perfect pair of shoes for you to wear with this dress if you want to borrow them."

Apparently, dating Cole brought with it an instant friend in Maria, which was fine by her. She ended up buying the blue dress, turning down Maria's generous offer to pay for it, and made plans to pick up the matching shoes the next day after work, since Maria had no use for them before the banquet.

After buying Emily's dress, they entered every remaining store in the mall with a women's clothing section, where Maria tried on several dozen dresses in total. Maria and Cole weren't joking; when it came to shopping, the woman was a machine.

In the end, they circled back to the very first store and the very first dress—the one Emily had liked best in the first place—and Maria agreed it was the winning choice. *I can't believe I just spent three hours shopping when we could have been done after the very first dressing room experience.* But at the same time, hanging out with Maria had been a lot of fun. She had such a positive personality, an infectious laugh, and stories about Cole that made Emily feel even closer to him. Not to mention the fact that she now had a lovely blue dress of her own, and a banquet date to look forward to once she worked up the courage to let Cole know that she knew about his nomination.

After Maria dropped her off at home, Emily checked her cell phone which had been stashed away in her purse all day and saw she had a text from Cole asking if they were still on for hanging out. She texted back. OF COURSE. JUST GOT HOME FROM THE MALL. WANNA COME OVER?

Cole: YES. SHALL I GRAB US DINNER ON THE WAY?

Emily glanced at the clock. Was it dinner time already? All she'd done since eating lunch with Maria was shop—she sure hoped the entire afternoon wasn't gone. Sure enough, it was almost 5:00. Her stomach growled, though she couldn't believe she was already ready for another meal. SURE. PIZZA?

Cole: YOU READ MY MIND. TOPPINGS?

Emily: YOU CHOOSE. ANYTHING BUT OLIVES.

Cole: BE THERE IN AN HOUR.

Perfect. That gave her just enough time to freshen up.

"DID SOMEONE ORDER AN olive pizza?" Cole asked an hour later, after Emily opened her front door.

She chuckled and leaned over for a quick hug. "Thank you."

He put the pizza and an envelope on the living room coffee table, where Emily had plates and napkins set out.

She got them each something to drink before they sat on the couch and began eating.

After downing a few slices of pizza and chatting about their day, Emily decided it was time to address the banquet. She squeezed her lips together and took a deep breath. "A little birdie tells me you have a pretty big day coming up next month."

Cole's mouth opened and then closed again. He tilted his head. "What day are you referring to?"

Was there more than one big event coming up, or was he just hoping she hadn't found out about the award? "I'm talking about the awards banquet. Congratulations on your nomination, by the way."

His eyes bulged. "How did you know about that?"

Emily stared at him. "Cole. Think. I just spent the entire day with your sister-in-law. Did you know she's a talker?"

His eyes closed as the facts sunk in. After opening them, he gave her a sheepish smile, then stared at the empty pizza box.

"Why didn't you just ask me to go?" She bit her lip, contemplating for the first time that maybe he wasn't as serious about her as he had led her to believe.

He wiped a hand over his face. "I didn't want to put you on the spot. I know we haven't been dating very long, and I know you don't like big, flashy things— neither do I, anymore. Plus, I don't really feel like I deserve to be there. Not compared to people like you, who help kids out for free, going above and beyond."

"Nonsense, Cole. You're excellent at what you do. And maybe a flashy awards banquet isn't my style, but if that's where you're going to be, then I want to support you. I mean, unless you don't *want* me there."

"No way. Of *course* I want you there! I should have just asked you in the first place. It's just that I've known about this thing since right before we met, and I'd already convinced Tim to take off work to go with me. He's going to be so relieved to not have to go, though. And let's face it, you will make a *much* better date." He winked at her. "I never imagined I'd meet someone in this short time who I actually wanted to be there with me. But... I have."

He put his empty plate down on the table and reached over to stroke her back. "Emily, will you please attend the awards banquet with me next month? I can show you the invite with all the details."

"Why, I'd be honored." She put her plate down on the coffee table next to his.

Cole eased back into the couch cushions. "Thanks for being so great about it. Why don't you tell me more about your shopping experience?"

An automatic smile sprang to Emily's face. "Well, I'm beginning to think Maria planned the whole thing for *me* to find a dress for this ceremony thing I didn't even know about until today—and once I did know, I wasn't sure if you were really going to ask me! But she insisted. She even tried to pay for my dress. Can you believe that?"

"I can. Knowing Maria, I believe it."

"Yeah, I have to say, she's pretty great. It was almost like... I don't know, I guess I just felt really loved. And accepted. Which is kind of a new feeling for me."

At that, Cole scooted closer to Emily on the couch and put his arm around her shoulder. Leaning over, he kissed her cheek. "Well, you *are*. Loved, that is." He reached for her hand and interlinked their fingers together.

Emily melted at the gesture and at his words. Her heart beat faster as she rested her head on his shoulder and mentally soaked in the love and affection he'd shown her these last few weeks. Even hanging out with Maria somehow enhanced her attraction toward Cole, given their relation and all the encouraging things Maria had to say about them both.

"Oh, I almost forgot. I have something for you." Cole pulled away from her to reach for an envelope he'd put next to the pizza box and handed it to her.

She opened it to find two pieces of paper. The first was a handwritten note.

Cole cleared his throat. "That's some research I did after you'd shared with me about your Dad and husband. I hadn't found a good time to give it to you, but I didn't want to wait any longer. You don't have to read it now, but I wanted you to have it to refer to someday, when you're ready. Like, when you can't sleep or something. I promise I won't keep asking if you read it, but… don't wait too long." He nudged her with his elbow.

She scanned the first sentence of the note, and she could tell right away it would help. Her eyes began to water, but she didn't want to ruin the moment, so she flipped to the second page. It was a printout from a website showing that Cole had purchased cake decorating classes for two at a local bakery. Her eyes widened as she turned toward him. "You didn't. I can't believe you remembered!"

Cole shrugged. "If you don't have anyone who wants to do it with you, I'll find time in my schedule. I promise."

Emily shoved the papers back into the envelope, dropped it on the arm of the couch, and threw her arms around Cole. "Thank you so much. This was so generous of you."

She leaned her head against his chest, listening to the rhythm of his heart. This man had been doing everything right, and as much as he tried to reassure her, she still felt undeserving. She closed her eyes and sent up a prayer that she would keep the right perspective when it came to their relationship.

They spent the next two hours talking and laughing before Cole stood and stretched. "I'm so glad I got to see you tonight, but I better get going."

He reached for her hand and tugged on it, so she stood and trailed behind as he walked to the door. Turning around in the entryway, he put his hands on her face and leaned down to brush his lips against hers. The brief touch sent a spark through her body.

"Good night, Em. I love you."

She let out a breath. "I love you, too."

After he left, Emily brought their dirty dishes and the envelope he'd given her into the kitchen. She hung the bakery printout on the fridge where she wouldn't lose it and tossed the envelope with his handwritten note on the top of a pile of papers before washing their plates. *God, how can I have this kind of closeness with someone so soon? I know You're in it. Help me to continue trusting You with this relationship.* She only hoped this newfound joy and peace would last forever.

# CHAPTER 30

O N Monday evening, Emily stopped by Maria's house to pick up the shoes for her dress. "Why don't you try them on to make sure they fit?"

Emily put on the beautiful high heels. "They're a bit snug, but I'll be wearing nylons, so I think they'll be perfect."

"Great! Thanks again for shopping with me yesterday. I bet you went home and straight to bed after all that walking."

Emily bit her cheek. "Actually, Cole came over and we hung out."

Maria shrieked. "I should have known! Did you have fun?"

"Oh yeah. You'll never guess what that guy did for me. I had mentioned to him, before we were even dating, how I've always wanted to learn how to decorate cakes. So yesterday, he gave me a certificate for cake decorating classes."

Maria clasped her hands under her chin. "That's awesome! I wish Tim would do something like that for me."

"Hey." A sudden thought struck her. "Would you want to go with me? I mean, I'll totally drag Cole along if not, but he got me two spots in the class knowing I didn't want to go alone. I'd be happy to give the extra spot to you."

"Would I? Absolutely! When is it?"

Emily's mind flashed to the bakery printout on her fridge. "It's Tuesday nights in July, from 7:00 to 9:00. Would that work for you?"

Maria thought for a moment. "Yeah. I'll run it past Tim to be sure, but I'd say you can count me in."

"Wonderful! If you give me your number, I'll text you the details and we can meet there. Sound good?"

"Yes, ma'am. Can't wait!"

After exchanging phone numbers, Emily left Maria's house. As juvenile as it sounded, she was excited to make a new friend. In fact, things were falling into place for her lately. She hadn't felt this happy in years.

The next two weeks brought more of the same for Emily. Her relationship with Cole progressed in ways she could only dream of. After her first cake decorating class, during which she and Maria got to know each other quite a bit more, she stopped by Cole's place on her way home.

"That was so fun!" The words burst from her lips the moment he opened the door. It only took another second to notice he was in shorts and a T-shirt. She had to force herself to focus her attention away from his strong arms and toned body, and onto his face. "I hope you don't mind me stopping by. I didn't want to go straight home. I'm too pumped."

"Of course, I'm always happy to see you. But..." Sudden recognition washed over Cole's face. "Your cake decorating class, right?"

Emily smiled so big it hurt her cheeks.

Cole reached out his arms. "Come here, you." He pulled her close, leaning down to plant a short kiss on her lips then wrapping his arms around her.

After they separated, Emily followed him into the living room and took a seat on the couch. "I can't wait to try out the techniques I learned tonight."

"You *know*... I'd be happy to be your guinea pig in practicing those culinary talents of yours, babe."

Emily laughed. "Aw, aren't you a martyr."

Cole put his arm around her shoulders. "Anything for my girl."

Emily rested her head on him, grateful for their romance and how he constantly managed to sweep her off her feet.

As the first half of July flew by, she continued to experiment with a number of cakes and frostings. The kids in the cancer ward enjoyed being the recipients of her handiwork. She even made a sheet cake for the Mission one Sunday. Cole had convinced her it wasn't selfish to take these classes, and she was happy to see the instant return on his investment.

Before she knew it, it was the Friday of the banquet and Maria had come over to help her get ready. After dousing her updo with a final spritz of hairspray, Maria beamed with pride. "You're gonna knock his socks off, girl."

Emily examined her reflection in the mirror from several angles. With her hair up, her neck appeared longer. And thanks to Maria's makeup application, her skin looked flawless and her blue eyes really popped, picking up a vibrant hue reflected in her gown.

"Thanks so much for all your help and encouragement. I have to admit, I'm kind of nervous." She was comfortable with Cole after six weeks together, but he'd never seen her in this light before. And a fancy banquet wasn't anything she was used to.

"Don't be! Just enjoy yourself. It's not every day you get to dress up to the nines and hang out with the top medical talent in the county."

"Okay, not sure that made me any less nervous, thank you very much."

Maria gave her a hug and wished her luck before heading out. Cole's car pulled into her driveway a few minutes later. When she heard the sound of the car door slam shut, she took a deep breath to calm her nerves. If only she knew how to slow down an excessively rapid heartbeat.

When she opened the door, Cole stood there wearing a black suit and a black tie with royal blue swirls that matched her dress. The cut of the suit emphasized his broad shoulders, and she bit her cheeks to keep her mouth from gaping open. That's when she noticed Cole staring at her, his gaze sweeping her from head to toe. She started to squirm. Was there something wrong with her gown? Was she overdressed for the occasion?

She couldn't stand the silence any longer. "Is everything okay?"

Cole gave a quick shake of his head as if to jolt his thoughts back to the present. "Yeah. Definitely. You just caught me off guard. I mean, I know you're beautiful, but this... *this*... oh man. You are *stunning*, Emily." He flashed that same heart-stopping grin she'd first noticed at the clinic. "And what a gorgeous color. I feel so unworthy right now."

Emily waved her hand to deflect the attention. "Stop it. You're the one who looks amazing tonight in your suit. You're the catch, especially since you're the one up for the award, after all."

Cole lifted her hand to his lips, kissing the top of it while maintaining eye contact with her. Her heart skipped a beat as she grabbed her clutch purse and tried to recompose herself. Then she gestured toward the door. "Shall we?"

"We shall." Cole held out his arm like a gentleman, and Emily slipped her arm through his, feeling like a princess about to attend a royal ball.

In the car on the way, he reached over and squeezed her hand. "Thanks for agreeing to come to this."

Emily glanced over. His eyebrows were pulled together and a vein ticked in his jaw. "You act like we're going to a funeral or something."

"Well, that's not what I meant. But I know this type of thing is not exactly your scene. I would be okay ducking out and going somewhere else with you if you insisted."

"Really?" Sure, she wasn't one for the limelight, but Cole deserved this. He shouldn't even consider ditching his own award ceremony. But that didn't mean she couldn't have a little fun.

"Really."

"So then… do you wanna grab a bite to eat at Antonio's?" She did her best to keep a straight face.

"Absolutely, if that's what you want to do."

Emily jabbed him in the side and smirked. Yeah right. She needed to make sure he was there tonight for the children he'd served so well—she wasn't about to let him weasel out of this. "Lucky for you, I don't. This is a special night for you, and I'm honored to be a part of it."

Cole looked over at her after he stopped at a red light. "Gosh, I love you."

Emily turned to face him and shrugged one shoulder to her chin, holding it there as she batted her eyes. He chuckled until she returned her attention straight ahead at the stoplight. "It's green." Her voice came out sounding fuzzy, at least to her own ears. She was in love with this man, and although the reality was starting to scare her a little less every day, she still found herself overcome with emotion every now and then.

THE TENSION MOUNTED AS the master of ceremonies announced the nominees for the next award—Greatest Achievement in Pediatric Therapy. They had eaten their dinner of roasted chicken, mashed potatoes, glazed carrots and garlic rolls. They had mingled with a few of Cole's coworkers and others in his field who he knew only by name. They had bid for random silent auction items, hoping to score a heated massage pad or a restaurant gift certificate. There had been other awards given out for different medical fields. But now was the moment they had been waiting for all evening.

Cole was one of five professionals in the Kansas City area to be nominated for the award, and Emily reached over to hold his hand under the table when his name was called as a nominee. As the announcer paused before revealing the winner, she squeezed his hand. If anyone deserved this award, it was Cole. She'd seen firsthand all the great things he'd achieved. She held her breath until the name Jeffrey Hounsell came off the speaker's lips, followed by cheers and claps from around the banquet hall.

Emily exchanged glances with Cole as they politely clapped for his colleague. She mouthed, "I'm sorry it wasn't you."

Cole leaned over and whispered in her ear. "I'm kind of relieved. I'm not much for speeches, and I don't really like the spotlight anyway."

Emily hoped his words were truthful. She squeezed his thigh, and he raised his eyebrows at her, followed by a wink.

As Jeffrey gave his winning speech, Cole glanced at his phone with a frown.

"Is everything okay?" she whispered.

Cole shook his head, then showed Emily the text

message. She recognized the number as Maria's. TIM'S BEEN SHOT. KC MED HOSPITAL. PLEASE COME WHEN YOU CAN!

All the blood drained from Emily's face as she re-read the text to be sure she'd seen it right. Tim had been shot? How serious was it? A glimpse at Cole's expression told her he felt the same confusion. He stood, and she followed suit. They excused themselves from their table and walked out to the lobby.

After a moment of speechlessness, she finally formulated words. "I can call a cab if you want to go straight there. I'm so sorry."

"You can come." His response was immediate. "I mean, if you want. Maria's your friend too, and I could use the support. I knew it was always a possibility, but Tim's never gotten hurt on the job before. Not like this."

Emily took a shaky breath. The least she could do was be there for Cole. And for Maria. They needed her support, and her prayers most of all.

"Of course. I'll come with you." Kansas City Med was the hospital where she worked, so she knew exactly where they were headed. On the drive over, the thought crossed her mind that Maria might lose Tim. Just thinking about the pain of that loss made her shudder. She wasn't strong enough to go through another tragedy like that. Perhaps it was better to never love than to risk that kind of pain again. After all, what if it had been Cole? Could her heart survive if she lost him?

*God, please help Tim's injury to not be serious. Help him not to blame me for taking his place at the banquet. And Lord, if my relationship with Cole and his family is doomed, like so many of my other relationships, then please help me to realize it before it's too late.*

# CHAPTER 31

EMILY LEFT COLE IN THE WAITING room and used her passcode to get through the door to the ER. She searched for a familiar face, and Nan appeared a moment later. "Emily? Is that you?" Nan raised her eyebrows while scanning Emily's attire.

"Yes. I'll explain later. Come here." She tugged Nan's arm and pulled her down a hall, away from the chaos of the ER. "What can you tell me about the gunshot victim that just came in? The cop—his name is Tim."

Nan narrowed her eyes. "You know I can't give you that information. Not unless you're family or on the job."

Emily frowned. She was all about following the rules, but now seemed like one of those times when it was okay to break them. "I could just log on myself and find out, you know. Please Nan. Tim is Cole's brother."

Nan covered her mouth with her hand. "How scary for you. I... I wish I could tell you, but—"

"Emily?" She turned on her heels to find a blotchy-faced Maria standing behind her.

Emily enfolded her in a comforting hug. "How is he?"

"He was just admitted into surgery, so now I have to wait out there." She nodded toward the waiting room, and together they made their way through the doors. "The bullet is lodged in his shoulder. He was conscious but lost a lot of blood and was in a ton of pain when he first came in."

Tears stung Emily's eyes. "Oh, Maria. I'm so sorry."

They had joined Cole in the waiting room by then. He stood to give his sister-in-law a hug. "I've been praying for him nonstop. He's gonna pull through."

Maria pulled out of Cole's arms and wiped away a few tears. "The surgery may take a while, so we might as well make ourselves comfortable." She led the way to a cluster of vinyl chairs to wait, and they each took a seat.

Cole leaned his arms on his legs and clasped his hands, his head hanging low. A lump formed in Emily's throat as she saw his worry for his brother. The brother that would have been safe at the banquet if Cole hadn't invited her instead. It was her fault Tim got shot. Her fault that Cole and Maria were suffering right now. No, she didn't have him shot, but she was still to blame. They were better off without her bringing a curse of loss and pain into their lives.

"Your parents are on their way, Cole." Maria was

curled up in a ball in her seat, her arms wrapped around her jean-clad legs. "They were pretty shaken up by the news."

Emily's ears perked up. Although they had progressed in their relationship over the past several weeks, Cole hadn't yet pressured her to meet his parents. This wasn't exactly the circumstances under which she wanted to meet them, either. She suddenly felt sick to her stomach.

She leaned over to whisper to Cole. "I think I'm going to head home after all. This is a time for family, and I'm not sure I should be here." Certainly not now. But maybe never. It was becoming apparent that he deserved a better woman beside him. One that didn't leave pain and sorrow in her wake.

Cole furrowed his brow. "I understand if that's what you want, but please know you're welcome to stay. And I would really appreciate the company."

"I know." Emily watched the door, looking for an older couple to enter at any moment. "But I think it's best I go." She really needed to be alone. The rush of conflicting thoughts swirling around her brain would not be satiated until she was by herself crying out to God for wisdom in what this turn of events meant for her and Cole.

"Okay. I'll drive you."

"No, that's not necessary. I can take the bus. It stops down the street from my house. I'll be fine. You should stay."

Cole shook his head. "No, I insist. Tim'll be in surgery for a while, so no sense in me sitting here helpless while you take the bus this late at night. I'd feel much better taking you home. Since my parents are on their way, Maria won't be alone for long."

He said a few words to his sister-in-law and gave her a hug while Emily paced back and forth in the waiting room. She wasn't looking forward to this car ride one bit.

When they were halfway to her home, Cole put his hand on her knee and broke the silence. "Thanks for being here with me, and not being upset about how things turned out. This isn't how I'd expected our fancy evening to end."

She raised her eyebrows. "How could I be upset? If anything, I feel bad. For *all* of you. I'm just glad it doesn't sound as serious as it could have been." She'd seen her share of gunshot victims at work and pushed back painful images of the bloodshed.

"Yeah, me too. Can I make it up to you? How about we go out tomorrow night?"

Emily closed her eyes in an attempt to clear her head. "I... I'm not sure. I have to work tomorrow, and you'll probably want to see how your brother is doing before making any firm plans. Can I get back to you?"

"Sure." He sounded hesitant. "Yeah, you can just call or text me."

They sat in silence for a few more minutes. "Everything okay?" Cole finally asked.

She had no idea how to answer him. All she wanted was to get inside and let the pent-up tears fall. Why did Cole have to be such an observant, considerate guy? Even with his brother lying in the hospital with a gunshot wound, he cared how she was doing. "Yeah, I'm fine." It was the only thing she could say and still manage to hold it together.

When they arrived at her house, he walked her to her front door. "I'm really sorry things ended this way."

"Don't be." Why was *he* apologizing? "This wasn't your fault. You're not the one who caused this."

Emily looked at him for only a moment, tears brimming in her eyes, then averted her gaze. She wanted him to leave, to return to the hospital where Tim and Maria needed him. But the reality that this might be their last date, her last time being in the presence of someone who loved her without condition, was settling into her mind and heart. These past couple months had been the best she'd known, and she wanted to savor up a few memories to treasure over the lonely years ahead. Did he have a clue of the thoughts raging through her mind?

He held both of her hands and tried to make eye contact again. But she refused to look his way, because then he'd see what she was thinking, and that would make things so much harder.

"I love you, Emily." She blinked back tears upon hearing his reassuring words. Words she'd never realized before meeting Cole that she'd longed to hear for so many years, but ones she'd have to get used to never hearing again.

Emily reached out for a hug. His physical touch. Another element she had come to relish that she'd have to get used to being without. She swallowed the lump in her throat as she clung to his body. Closing her eyes, she reminded herself that it was time to let go—in more ways than one. "Goodbye, Cole."

She took a step back and let herself into her house, shutting the door behind her without giving him another glance. She wasn't going to sleep well tonight. Instead, she would have to use the restless night to plead with God to spare Tim's life and help Cole understand why they couldn't be together anymore.

DRIVING BACK TO THE hospital, Cole kept replaying the short, cold exchange with Emily. They'd been having such a lovely evening until the news came about Tim. Emily didn't seem like the type of person to bail when the going got tough, especially when she dealt with medical trauma every day on her job. So why had she ended things in such a stilted manner and shut him out as quickly as she could? What on earth was going on in that head of hers?

She'd obviously struggled with what to say and how to act around Maria given her own tragic loss, but when she'd deflected his invitation for a date the next night, it was the first time he'd started to feel uneasy. Normally she would jump at the chance to get together, even if it meant hanging out after her shift ended. But she offered up no alternative, showed no interest in figuring something out. And what was it she'd said about it not being his fault? *You're not the one who caused this.* Of course he wasn't—no one was to blame here, other than the shooter himself.

Back at the hospital, a stone-faced Maria sat in a waiting room chair, staring at the floor. She glanced at him, her eyelids drooping from exhaustion and concern. He took a seat next to her. "Any update?"

Maria gave a quick shake of her head.

"And my parents aren't here yet, huh? That's too bad, I'd thought you'd have them for company while I was taking Emily home."

"That's okay. How *is* Emily, by the way?"

Cole sighed. He wasn't sure if he wanted to get into it with Maria—at least not now. At the same time, it might be nice to distract her from thoughts of Tim's surgery. With a shrug, he decided he had nothing to lose. "Honestly? She's... retreating. I'm kind of worried about where things stand right now."

Maria's eyebrows scrunched together. "I'm sure she's just reeling from the craziness of the night. It's not every day your boyfriend's brother gets shot. Not every day my *husband* gets shot." Her voice broke.

Cole sat up straight. Her *husband*. Maybe that was why Emily was acting so weird. Maybe she was flashing back to the accident that took her husband. Had he been insensitive to how she was taking this turn of events? That would explain it. Or some of it anyway. But no, not completely. Something else was going on here. "I hope you're right. I mean, two hours ago we were on cloud nine, but the way she acted when I dropped her off..." His voice trailed off before he shook his head. "No, this is silly. You're right. We have such a good thing going, one stressful event like tonight is not enough to undo all of that."

Maria reached over to rub the top of Cole's back with her palm. He checked his watch, suddenly worried about his parents. It had been well over an hour since Maria had called them. A pit formed in his stomach. Had something happened? After that drunk driver years ago, they'd been extra vigilant when it came to their sons. It wouldn't surprise him if they'd sped here and got into some sort of accident on the way. He'd give it a few more minutes before calling them.

Maria curled up on the waiting room chair while Cole shifted in his seat and loosened his tie, but he couldn't relax in his stiff suit. While he knew it wasn't rational to doubt their relationship based on a night like this, something nagged at him. *This wasn't your fault. You're not the one who caused this.* She was right; this *wasn't* his fault. But it certainly wasn't *hers* either.

They'd already established that she felt responsible for the tragedies her dad and husband experienced. What if she somehow believed she was responsible for Tim's injuries as well? Or was she simply afraid to lose another loved one?

How could he make her see the Truth? When would she understand God wasn't punishing her for her past? Why was she so hesitant to believe these things? He would wonder if she'd read the note he'd given her several weeks ago, except it seemed pretty obvious she hadn't. Not with the way she'd reacted tonight.

*God, show me how to help her move past this faulty theology and into a refreshing relationship with You. Show her that Your grace is sufficient. I can't do this on my own, but I know You can. I'm giving it to You, God. Just like You promised in the Bible—The Lord will fight for you; you need only to be still.*

# CHAPTER 32

"I*T'S ALL YOUR FAULT.*" D*EREK SLAMMED* the front door and stomped into the kitchen before jabbing an accusing finger in her face. A whiff of gasoline permeated her nostrils. Emily's hand shook as she turned down the heat on the burner under the pot of chili she was cooking. What was it this time? She didn't have to wait long.

"All I ask is when you use the car, you check the gas gauge. If it's close to the E, you fill it up." His voice got louder as he spoke.

She narrowed her eyes as she tried to remember when she'd last used the car. Should she respond? Or let him get the rest of his anger out first?

"I was late to my interview because of you. I had to stop for gas and waste time filling the tank so I didn't stall on the side of the road. And do you want to know something?" His red face was only inches from hers now. She turned her head and cowered, looking at him through the corner of her eyes.

*"The pump squirted gasoline on my tie. On. My. Tie!"*

*Emily squeezed her lips together. She felt bad for leaving him with an empty tank, but was he actually blaming her for going to his interview smelling like gasoline? "Derek, I'm—"*

*"No!" He pounded his hand on the counter, and she jumped. "I don't want to hear it. Just another botched interview thanks to you. It's like you're cursed by God, and I'm just in the crossfire." He'd calmed himself down now, but he wasn't done yet. "If only I'd known the truth about you before we got married, then I could have saved myself a lot of trouble."*

*The tears clung to her eyes as she turned back to her pot of chili. Is that really how he felt? Would he not have married her had he known about the fire up front? Such hurtful words. But she probably deserved them for what she'd let happen to her dad. And maybe Derek was right. Maybe she was cursed. Maybe she didn't deserve to be happy, and those she loved would always bear the brunt of her mistakes.*

Emily woke with a start, the glowing face of her clock declaring it was only 3:30 in the morning. Once again, her nightmares had taken an odd twist. How had she gotten from worries about Tim and her uncertain future with Cole to memories of her husband's accusations? Except, he'd been right. Now—like then—was all her fault.

Part of her knew she'd believed flat-out lies. But those lies had more power than she cared to admit, especially when they were spoken over and over by someone she thought she loved.

Some things she simply couldn't un-hear, like Derek saying she was cursed by God and he was caught in the crossfire. And some things she simply couldn't un-see, like her dad's frail body on the gurney outside their burning house or Derek's lifeless body in the car *she* had been driving. She couldn't endure that level of heartache again, which was why it had become apparent she couldn't go any further down this road with someone as wonderful as Cole.

Things weren't any clearer with the eventual dawn of a new day, except for the lingering—troubling—sense that she must end things with Cole. Tim's injury was a wakeup call. What if it was more serious next time? She had lived on her own perfectly fine these past seven years—why, oh why, did she have to mess with a good thing and open herself up to Cole the way she had?

There was no denying it had been a wonderful couple of months, but it had been selfish. She had let her guard down and now her friends were paying the price. It simply wasn't fair to them. God was still not done making her pay for her past, and she loved Cole too much to have him bear the brunt of God's vengeance meant for her alone.

A quick shower did nothing to revive her, so she stopped for a cup of coffee on the way to her 9:00 shift. On the drive, her stomach knotted at the possibility she might run into Cole or his brother at the hospital. Of course, Tim would have been transferred out of the ER by now, but she had no idea how he was doing— whether he'd survived the surgery, if he was in the ICU, or recovering in a different wing of the hospital. While she knew she would have to face Cole in one form or another, she hoped to delay it for a while.

What would she even say? She'd tried to warn him—maybe he would finally believe her now, or even be ready to break it off himself. Wouldn't that be better than having to be the one to end things? Then again, Cole would never think that way. He was too selfless to blame her for this. She dreaded the conversation, but she wasn't going to back down from what she knew had been the right way to handle this in the first place—remaining safely single. She didn't deserve love, not this kind anyway, and she detected a twinge of anger at letting Cole talk her out of that resolve.

After clocking in for work, she logged into the hospital network under the guise of getting up to speed on the current ER patients. But she was really checking on Tim's condition. His file showed that he was in Recovery Room 311. Her shoulders relaxed. He was out of danger, and there was no chance of running into him down here in the ER.

As she went to silence her phone, she noticed a missed text from Cole. TIM'S OUT OF THE ER. THANKS FOR YOUR PRAYERS. I FEEL TERRIBLE FOR HOW OUR DATE ENDED. WHEN CAN I SEE YOU AGAIN? I LOVE YOU.

Ignoring his text, she turned off her phone and began her shift, the decision she'd made still weighing heavily on her mind. Emily closed her eyes and took a deep breath, praying for the strength to remain steadfast in her decision to end things between them. He didn't deserve her life of constant turmoil. Eventually, it would mean tragedy for Cole himself, and she couldn't bear the thought of causing him harm.

WHY WASN'T EMILY ANSWERING his texts? Cole squirmed in the chair beside the hospital bed where his brother dozed. He checked his phone again—he had three bars, so it wasn't the signal, but he'd reached out a few times with no response. After finding out Tim had made it through his surgery, Cole had gone home for a shower and a few hours of sleep before returning to be with Tim and give Maria time to do the same.

He had wanted to call Emily when he found out the good news, but since that was at 2:00 in the morning, he figured they'd catch up today. Instead, she was nonresponsive. Had she slept in? Was she at work already with her phone turned off? If so, that meant she was only two floors away.

When a nurse came and secured a blood pressure cuff around Tim's good arm, Cole cleared his throat. "Excuse me. Are you able to tell me when Emily Jenkins is working today? She's a nurse in the ER."

"I can find out for you as soon as I'm done." The woman took Tim's temperature and keyed in a few numbers on her tablet before leaving the room. Five minutes later, she poked her head back in. "Sir? Emily is working today from 9:00 until 6:00."

He thanked the nurse and then glanced at his brother. Tim had drifted off to sleep again, so now was as good a time as any to go searching for Emily. He prayed for a reasonable explanation for her silence but tried not to get his hopes up.

After making his way down to the emergency department, he waited for someone to open the door and ducked through while they weren't looking. He scanned the area and smiled when he spotted her behind a not-so-private curtain treating an elderly woman wearing an oxygen mask. When she left the woman's bedside to file some paperwork at the nurse's station, he strolled up to her and spoke quietly, trying to act like everything was normal between them. "Hey, beautiful."

Emily spun around and gasped.

"Sorry!" He reached over to touch her arm.

"It's all right." She placed her hand over her heart. "I wasn't expecting you, is all. How did you get back here?"

Cole put his hands in his pockets and rocked back and forth on his heels. "I have my ways. I hope you don't mind me showing up. I'm here at the hospital visiting Tim, but you didn't respond to my texts so I thought I would come see if you were on shift."

Emily pursed her lips. "I'm here. But I… I should really get back to work. I have a couple patients that need me."

Cole's eyes narrowed. He felt like he was being given the cold shoulder, but then again Emily *was* on the clock. He didn't want to get her in trouble for conducting personal business during work hours. "Yeah, of course. But first, I wondered if maybe we could meet up after you get off?"

She looked at him long and hard before turning her gaze to the flecked linoleum. "Um… I have to work really late tonight, so I don't think I can."

Cole's heart dropped. Had this sweet, innocent woman just lied to him? Did he even know her at all? With echoes of Heather and a series of previous cheating girlfriends parading through his mind, he stammered something about calling her the next day.

She wouldn't meet his gaze, but Cole still caught a sheen in her eyes as if she was holding back tears. "I'm sorry, Cole." She turned and walked away without looking back.

Cole fought back tears of his own. Who was this woman acting so cold toward him? Certainly not the Emily he knew. What had changed? And what could he do about it?

# CHAPTER 33

EMILY'S KNEES BUCKLED AFTER HER BRIEF encounter with Cole. She had never told such a blatant lie before—at least not since turning her life to Christ. She had seen the hurt in his eyes but knew this was for the best. It would be hard at first, but once they got through the initial separation, things would all go back to normal. She'd go back to a life filled with work and volunteering. And likewise for Cole—he would bounce back and find someone new. He was quite a catch, and some lucky lady would snatch him up in no time.

A few hours later, she worked on a filing project at the main nurse's station when she saw Cole walking towards her again. Her heart sank. "What are you still doing here?" She hoped her words didn't come off rude. "Is everything okay with Tim?"

"Yeah, he's doing fine. Emily, can we talk? Can you escape for a few minutes?"

"Oh, um… they really frown on that around here. I mean, you never know when someone's going to come in needing immediate attention."

She glanced around, for the first time in months actually *hoping* for an ambulance to pull up. But instead, she caught the eye of her supervisor who strolled over. "I couldn't help but overhear. You can take a few minutes, Emily. We're slow so you might as well take advantage. Just keep your phone on you."

Was she kidding? After all the times Emily had wanted to take a break and hadn't been allowed, *now* her boss pulled through?

Cole raised his eyebrows, no doubt suppressing a smirk at finally catching a break when it came to nailing down her attention. She had no more excuses now.

"Okay." Emily closed her eyes and let out a deflated breath. "You win."

"Is there somewhere private we can talk?"

This was happening. Now. She had to break it off, and not a single part of her looked forward to the conversation. "Follow me." As she led him down a couple different hallways, she took her phone out of her back pocket to give her something to do with her nervous energy. She turned it back on and saw two unread texts from Cole light up the screen before shoving it back into her pocket. They finally arrived at an unused conference room in a different section of the hospital.

She closed the door behind her, then sat down at the table. Cole lowered himself into a seat next to her. "Look." Her words came out at the exact same time Cole said, "So Emily."

They both let out a nervous laugh. "Go ahead." Cole gestured for her to speak.

"Okay." Emily swallowed and offered up a quick prayer for courage. "I'm really glad Tim's going to be okay. But the next time, we might not be so lucky. And I can't have that on my conscience. I can't deal with another loss like that."

"Wait, your conscience?" Cole's eyebrows furrowed. "What do you mean? You didn't shoot him. He's a cop. Every officer knows that's a risk you take on the job."

"I know that." She winced. Didn't he get it? It broke her heart to have to spell it out for him. "But if I wasn't in the picture, he would have been cheering you on at the banquet instead of being gunned down on the job. He may have gotten lucky this time, but it might be worse next time. I can't ignore the fact that everyone I get close to ends up hurt."

"Emily—"

"No, Cole." She slashed her hand through the air. She hated being this firm, but there was no other way to get her point across. "This is exactly why I told you I didn't want to be in a relationship from the start. Every time I find contentment—every time I think my past is behind me—something *bad* happens. To someone I love. I have too many demons lurking inside, and you don't deserve that."

"Emily." Cole slammed the table with his fist, and the sudden sound silenced her. "I don't believe that. I don't believe God punishes us for things in our past, especially after we've turned to Him. Haven't you heard a thing I've been trying to tell you?"

"No. I let you talk me into this in the first place, and now I see what a mistake it was. I can't keep doing this. I have to end it before it gets worse for both of us."

"I don't accept that. This is the first relationship I've been in where I feel like everything is *right*. And I can't lose that. I can't lose *you*. I love you, Emily. Isn't that enough?"

Tears stung her eyes, but Emily remained true to her difficult decision. She shifted her focus to a painting on the wall as she fumbled through her final words. "I'm sorry. I have a responsibility to end this before someone gets hurt. Even worse than Tim." She stood to leave and put one hand on the doorknob before turning back to face him. Her voice cracked. "Goodbye, Cole." She flung the door open and hurried away. This was difficult enough without him seeing the tears streaming down her cheeks.

EMILY OFFERED TO PULL an extra shift on Sunday on top of her regular Monday hours. She hoped it would keep her mind off the mess her life had become, but she found herself on autopilot like a robot at work. She managed to check on Tim's status and discovered he had been released, so she assumed his recovery was going as well as could be expected.

A text from Cole on Monday afternoon confirmed it. TIM IS DOING GREAT. THOUGHT YOU MIGHT WANT TO KNOW.

Can we talk? I miss you.

She pressed her lips together and closed her eyes as she imagined how Cole must feel. If only she'd done a better job explaining her past so he understood. Was it her fault for hiding her husband's temper from him? For shielding him from the details of how bad her dad's drinking had gotten? Had she glossed over too much of the pain for fear of how he'd respond?

As hard as it was to think about never seeing Cole again, she had to move on with her life. Opening her eyes, she deleted his number from her contacts and erased every last text message with a shaky hand. She'd block his number as soon as she got home and could research how. There was no turning back.

On Tuesday night, she decided to go to her final cake decorating class, confident Maria wouldn't be showing up under the circumstances—the last thing she needed was another encounter with anyone related to Cole.

After putting on her apron and washing her hands, she lifted her head to see Maria walk in, and her jaw dropped. Her friend put a hand on Emily's upper arm. "Everything okay?"

Emily swallowed. "Yeah. I just... wasn't expecting you. I thought you might be home taking care of Tim." *Or that you'd taken Cole's side and never wanted to see me again.*

Maria reached over with a hug. "Tim's fine. And I'm not abandoning you, darling."

Her kindness brought a tear to Emily's eye, which she quickly brushed away.

The instructor started class, showing them a new frosting technique, and the women managed to re-focus their attention for the next two hours. When class was over, they cleaned up their station. "Cole really misses you, Em." Maria kept her voice low. "I'm not here to do his bidding, but it's so obvious how much he loves you. I hate to see either one of you hurting."

Emily's heart raced. While she did not want to have this conversation with Maria, she still felt compelled to explain her situation. She sighed. "It's complicated. Everyone I get involved with ends up getting hurt. I had hoped to be past this... this curse, but it continues to haunt me. And I don't want Cole or Tim or *you* to be impacted by *my* mistakes. I can't risk it."

Maria put her hand on Emily's forearm. "No one blames you for the things that happened. Cole told me about it all, and it's ridiculous to think you had anything to do with it. This is coming from me and no one else— you deserve to be happy, to find love. God won't punish you for being in love."

With a sniffle, Emily stared at Maria's comforting hand on her arm. "Maybe if Cole understood everything I've been through, he would know how hard it is to lose someone, how hard it is to watch someone you love go through so much pain, and he'd understand I simply can't go through that again."

"Oh, Emily." Maria's voice was a whisper now. "He *does* understand. Because he *has* lost someone."

Emily's head shot up, her eyes wide. Maria bobbed her head up and down. "He never told you about his little brother, did he?"

"I take it you're not talking about Tim?" Dread pooled in her stomach. What hadn't he told her? Had she jumped to conclusions about Cole?

Maria shook her head. "His name was Roy. He was killed by a drunk driver while riding his bike one day. It was the talk of the neighborhood for some time."

Emily covered her mouth with her hand, swallowing the bile that threatened to come up. Between the two of them, drinking and car accidents were responsible for too much pain in their lives. "That's awful. Why did he never say something to me about this?"

Maria wiped down the counter with a wet cloth, then focused on her friend. "You need to ask *him* that."

Emily's stomach sank. "Thanks for being here with me, Maria. I really appreciate it."

Maria reached out for another hug. "Anytime, my friend. I've had fun. We should hang out again sometime, all right? With or without Cole." She winked.

Emily's eyes glazed over as she tried to make sense of what was happening. But all she felt was confusion and emptiness inside.

# CHAPTER 34

A T WORK ON WEDNESDAY, EMILY STRUGGLED to focus on her patients. Nan eyed her with concern all morning before finally cornering her at the nurse's station after lunch. "What's wrong, hon?"

Emily sighed, lifting her shoulders in a slight shrug. Nan didn't deserve listening to all her baggage. "Just... having a rough time. With Tim being shot, and all."

Nan's eyes narrowed. She wasn't fooled. "You need a dose of truth, my dear. Wait right here."

As her coworker walked toward the break room, Emily bit her lip wondering what she'd meant. Nan returned a moment later and held out a business card. It reminded her of the day Cole handed her his business card, and a fleeting moment of peace washed over her remembering the time on her porch swing that had resulted from that simple gesture.

Nan's voice brought her back to the present. "If you

need someone to talk to, call this woman. She's been a godsend for me over the years. I promise, you'll be glad you did."

Emily looked at the card and recognized the name of their pastor's wife. Would she take Nan's advice? There were so many layers to her story. If only she'd sought professional help when things first started getting bad. As it was, she'd need a month of sessions to unravel the mess. Nah, she'd probably just throw the card away when she got home. But for now, she walked to the break room and slipped it in her purse.

That night, she managed to snag a few hours of sleep before waking up for work on Thursday. A couple hours into her shift, a familiar figure walked toward her, and it took only a second for her to recognize the man as Tim, his injured arm in a sling. To her surprise, a smile came naturally—she was grateful to see him walking around like normal—but at the same time, her heart pounded wondering what the motivation was behind his visit.

"Hey Tim, how are you?" She put her hand on his upper arm—the one not in a sling.

"Never better." He grinned. "I'm actually here for a post-op appointment and thought I'd come over and say hello."

"Well, that was nice of you. I saw Maria the other day, too. If I didn't know any better, I'd say Cole put you both up to it." She tried to sound lighthearted, but she had to wonder if there was any truth to her comment.

"No, no. He has no idea I'm here. I wanted to tell

you firsthand that I in no way blame you for what happened. I heard some silly notion that you felt somehow responsible for this." Emily studied her feet, embarrassed at how word of her insecurities and damaged past was getting around.

"Emily, seriously. I'm a cop. Cops get shot from time to time—and we wear our injuries with pride, I might add. So please don't blame yourself. And please don't make Cole suffer because of some crazy theory of yours. No offense."

*Well that was harsh.* She glanced up to see if he was judging her with his expression, too.

But Tim quickly took a softer approach. "Look, I've never seen Cole as happy as he's been with you. You really seem to bring out the best in him, and I don't want that to end. For both of your sakes."

Emily had to fight back tears at his heartfelt words.

"Well, anyway." He sighed. "I've said my piece. Now I have to get back to desk duty. But promise me you'll think about what I said."

Emily merely smiled and thanked him for coming, which was all she could commit to at that moment.

She stewed about Tim's *crazy theory* comment all day. Were he and Nan right? Did she really need to look for the truth? After all, she knew she'd been told lies in her past. What if she was still believing the wrong things? After her shift, she stopped in the hospital chapel and prayed for a sign. She didn't normally ask for signs—after all, God didn't owe her anything. But her chaotic life suddenly prompted her to cry out to Him in prayer.

A half hour later, her growling stomach put an end to her prayers. She didn't feel like cooking that night and, hoping for a friendly face not at all connected to Cole or Maria, she decided to go to Antonio's. After ordering two tacos, she wandered back to the kitchen. It wasn't very busy; Antonio wouldn't mind the diversion.

"There she is." Emily cracked a smile upon hearing Antonio's voice. He was always happy to see her, which lifted her spirits for the time being. "Where's your fella tonight?"

"You mean Cole?" Emily sighed. She didn't really want to get into it. "I don't know. I just got off work and thought I'd stop by on my own."

"Well, tell him I said hello."

She tilted her head. "You make it sound like you know him." As far as she was aware, they had only seen each other that night she and Cole had come together after grocery shopping a couple months before.

"Hey, I make it a point to get to know my regulars, Em." Antonio put his hands up in defense. "Besides, he's a great tipper."

Confusion set in. "Wait, a regular? What do you mean?"

"He's been coming in once or twice a week for at least a month now, maybe longer. He's a good guy, that Cole. Sure seems smitten with you, by the way."

Emily's jaw dropped. "I had no idea."

"Yeah, tell him thank you for me. I appreciate the business."

Emily said goodbye and returned to her table. Why did this news surprise her? After all, Cole was a good guy and this was totally in his character to do, supporting her friend like this. So why was it so jolting to hear? Probably because it was making her decision not to see him that much harder. Besides, was this the sign she had prayed for only minutes ago? No. It couldn't be. That was one of the reasons she didn't like praying for signs, because the mind could take anything and twist it into a so-called sign from God. Yes, Cole was a nice guy but that didn't mean God was saying she should get back together with him.

Once she was home for the night, she forced herself to focus her thoughts on something other than Cole, and out of nowhere, an image of Tyler came to her mind. It had been a few weeks since she'd seen him, as his physical therapy sessions had recently ended, and she wondered how he was doing. If things were going well, it would be a needed reminder that her good deeds counted for something. Picking up her cell phone, she dialed Barb's number.

"Hi Barb, it's Emily Jenkins. I wanted to call and see how Tyler's doing."

"I'm so glad you called! I've been meaning to give *you* a call. For weeks now, but time keeps passing me by. You know how it is."

"I sure do."

"Anyway, Tyler is doing fantastic. And I wanted to thank you for sending Cole over these past several weeks."

Emily's mind drew a blank. When had she sent Cole over? "Pardon me?"

"You know — Cole. From PT Possibilities?"

"Yeah, I know who Cole is. I'm just not sure what you mean about sending him over."

There was a short pause on the other end of the line. "Oh! I assumed you had something to do with it. I guess not. Well, he's been coming to see Tyler every Friday for a while now, and no joke, it's been life changing for that boy. And I don't just mean his leg. This is the type of role model Tyler has needed all his life."

Emily cleared her throat. "So, he just showed up one day? Out of the blue?"

"Well, he called first, the first time, and ever since we have a sort of standing appointment." Barb's voice held a smile. "He said he wanted to check up on Tyler and hang out for a bit since he missed seeing him on Fridays."

"That's… that's *awesome*." Her heart swelled with this newfound knowledge—could it be God was bringing good out of her circumstances after all? "I'm so glad to hear that."

"Me too. Thanks again for all you've done for Tyler."

"You are very welcome. I'm so glad it all worked out. Tell Tyler I said hello, will you?"

"Absolutely. Have a good night."

"Good night." Emily hung up and put her head in her hands. Everywhere she turned, there was Cole. Doing something good, something she herself would do. And the strangest part was she knew nothing about it when they were together, so he certainly wasn't doing it for show or to win her affection. In fact, he had kept his generosity hidden quite well.

*God, what are You trying to tell me?* Her mind flashed to Nan's comment from earlier. *You need a dose of truth.* Okay... so what was the truth she was missing? Maybe it was time she found out. Retrieving her purse, she pulled out the business card and stared at the lettering. Janice Watson, Christian counselor. She took a deep breath. Was she ready for this? For once in her life, the idea of pouring out her soul sounded inviting. After all, she couldn't keep living this way.

She had been at rock bottom before, and while this wasn't exactly the same, she didn't have much further to go. *God, give me wisdom.*

UNSURE WHO ELSE TO turn to with his frustrations and disillusionment, Cole texted his brother Thursday night. HEY TIM, YOU BUSY?

Tim: NOT REALLY, WHAT'S UP?

Cole sighed. Tim wasn't the most compassionate person he knew, but his brother had a noble heart and a good head on his shoulders. He decided he had nothing to lose. STRUGGLING TO COME TO GRIPS WITH THE FACT THAT THINGS ARE OVER WITH EMILY.

Tim: I FEEL FOR YA, BRO. EVEN I THOUGHT SHE MIGHT BE THE ONE.

Cole closed his eyes. This was the first time he could remember having a relationship end that he truly believed had a chance to last forever. IS IT WRONG THAT I'M ANGRY?

After a pause, his brother's response appeared on the screen. NOT FROM WHERE I SIT. IT SOUNDS LIKE EMILY'S BEING A LITTLE UNFAIR IF YOU ASK ME.

Cole nodded. He had thought the same thing—Emily was justifying her behavior with completely inaccurate beliefs, and he was bearing the brunt of her flawed logic. The events from her past had clearly set her on a faulty path. She had recovered from so much as it was, but there was still a cluster of lies she was holding onto, and he was powerless to convince her otherwise. But he knew Someone who could.

Apparently, his carefully crafted letter hadn't done the trick—he had a sneaking suspicion she hadn't read all the way to the end. Should he have brought up the contents of his letter in person? No, he'd promised he wouldn't, so he'd be true to his word.

Cole: THANKS, I AGREE. SHE'S NOT TAKING MY CALLS THOUGH. SEEMS OPPOSED TO SOUND REASONING. MY HANDS ARE TIED.

Tim: I WISH I COULD FIX IT, MAN. BUT YOU KNOW WHAT MARIA WOULD SAY, RIGHT? PRAY.

Cole smiled despite the heaviness he felt in his heart. This was as sympathetic as Tim had ever gotten, and it was oddly flattering to be the recipient of his brother's kindness.

They said good night, and Cole tried to coax himself to move forward with his life without Emily in it. But how could he stand by and let her live this way? Sure, she had a painful past. But God had turned it into something so beautiful. And yet her heart was held captive by her own fears, by the lies she let herself believe. Wasn't it his responsibility to make her see how unreasonable she was being? How could he, if she refused to even talk to him?

*God, I can't make Emily listen to reason. Please work Your Spirit in her life, even right now, this very night. Show her how different life can be. That she doesn't have to live with guilt or fear the way she's been living. That You loved her before she even turned her life over to You. I know You can, God. And I believe You will.*

# CHAPTER 35

ON Friday morning, Emily awoke with sunlight streaming through her windows. She stood and stretched, realizing that she'd slept better than normal last night. In the kitchen, she saw Janice's card on the table and remembered her anguish the night before. Picking up the card, she had a sudden sense of peace about making the call. Today was the day she would choose to change her life. No more living captive to the lies of her past. It was time to move forward into the life God had for her.

At 8:30, she picked up her phone and took a deep breath. With shaking fingers, she dialed the number and waited. After three rings, she was relieved at the friendly voice that answered.

"Hi, is this Janice?"

"Yes, it is."

"Hi. This is Emily Jenkins. I, uh, I go to your church,

and you might know Nan Johnson as well. She recommended I reach out to you."

"Hi, Emily! Sure, I know who you are. How are you doing?"

Emily swallowed. "I'm all right. I was wondering if you might have an opening to meet with me? About... some issues in my life." How could she even sum it up in one sentence?

"Oh. Well yes, I'd love to set up a time to meet. I know it's a long shot, but I actually had a cancellation this morning if that would be convenient."

A smile crept to her face. It was just like God to make all the pieces fall into place. "Yes, I have off work today, so I'm wide open. What time?"

"Ten o'clock. Would you like to meet at the church? I can bring muffins and make coffee."

Emily let out an audible sigh of relief. "Oh, that would be wonderful. I really appreciate you taking the time to do this."

"It's my pleasure, dear. I'll see you then."

"Thanks, Janice."

A weight was lifted at just the thought of confiding in this woman. Not that one meeting would solve all her problems, but she knew she needed someone to speak truth into her life if she was going to get back on track. She was finally taking a step toward healing.

A ball of nerves coursed through her veins as she drove to the church an hour later. She had always admired Janice from afar, but she'd never sought her out for conversation. She always figured the pastor's wife had bigger things on her plate than chatting with someone like her.

Janice was in the prayer room when she arrived. As promised, there were muffins and coffee on the table where Emily took a seat. "Hi, Janice. Thanks so much for agreeing to meet with me."

"It's my pleasure." Janice reached for a notepad on the table. "Why don't you tell me what's on your mind?"

Emily swallowed hard. She had been reciting her story a number of different ways, knowing Janice deserved to hear it all if she was going to have any chance of steering her on the right path. But spitting it all out was going to be a challenge.

She started with her childhood, how her mom had died of cancer, and how things began unraveling with her dad until that fateful night of the fire. Janice's eyes were full of sympathy, giving Emily the encouragement she needed to continue with her story. She didn't mean to be so long-winded, but there were so many layers to unfold. She explained how she had attempted counseling after the fire, but her rebellious nature and overwhelming guilt made her believe she had to simply bear it alone.

"After high school graduation, I needed a change of scenery—especially since my dad's family blamed me for what happened. They wouldn't even let me visit him in the hospital. Since there was nothing left for me where I grew up, I escaped St. Louis and ended up here in Everly. I met Derek and married him a short time later, even though I still wasn't fully recovered from the fire. I guess subconsciously, I needed to latch on to something or someone that could carry me through."

Janice's forehead displayed concerned wrinkles. She nodded for Emily to continue.

"Unfortunately, Derek was not a very positive influence. I wore my guilt on my sleeve, and he used it to his advantage every time something bad happened to me or to us. Blamed me when he got fired from a job. When he did badly in an interview. And I believed him. Or rather… his words only solidified my own belief that God was punishing me—punishing *us*—for my mistakes."

"Oh, you poor soul." Janice's sympathetic words spurred Emily on to share the story of her car accident. She told her every last detail, including how the new guilt of Derek's death had mingled with the old guilt that had been thrust on her by the aftermath of the fire, as well as guilt for being glad to be free of Derek's continued criticism, making her downright miserable.

"I went to church a few months after the accident for the first time since my mom was alive. After hearing a message on God's love and forgiveness, I responded to an altar call and accepted Jesus into my life. I began living my life to please God, doing all kinds of good deeds for people in need. I even stayed single to show God how serious I was about making up for the sins of my past."

Janice frowned and scribbled something in her notepad as Emily continued. "As you can imagine, the seeds of lies I'd believed my whole life did not immediately disappear. It's like I *knew* they were lies, but they had been spoken so loudly and so often. And to be honest, they made a lot of sense at the time. I just couldn't rid myself of their influence. It was my fault bad things happened. The concept of *grace* didn't make sense—paying for my bad deeds did."

Emily took a deep breath before explaining the latest with Tim and Cole. Then she leaned her elbows on the table. "And that's about where I'm at. Except, now I've hurt a really good friend who didn't deserve to be treated the way I treated him. And I know I need to get right with God. Again."

In the silence that followed, Emily bounced her legs up and down. Had she shared too much? No, Janice had probably heard it all before anyway.

The woman reached over and gently cupped Emily's hands with her own. "Thanks for sharing all that with me. I feel so bad for all you've been through. But can I tell you some good news?"

She could certainly use a dose of that. "Please."

"There is hope for you. You are a wonderful person, but that is not why God loves you. Did you know the Bible says that *while we were still sinners,* Christ died for us? That means He doesn't withhold His grace or forgiveness or love because we did something wrong. He doesn't require us to do good works and clean up our act *before* we come to Him. And nothing you've done, or will do, surprises Him. That's good news, Emily. He loves and forgives you. Exactly. As. You. Are." The last four words were spoken slowly and deliberately.

Emily pursed her lips. "I think my head already knows that. But for some reason, I'm having a hard time with the message sinking into my heart and affecting how I live."

Janice nodded. "I understand. But I still believe His truth can change your life. And if you're willing, I would like to meet with you over the next six weeks or so. I'm thinking we'll spend two hours a week together—so one longer session or two shorter ones per week. And you'll have homework, if you want to call it that, to do on your own. I really think it will help give you an eternal perspective on things and give you the peace everyone longs for and very few find."

It sounded too good to be true, but Janice made it sound within reach. Like God could actually turn her brokenness into something whole again. "I'm willing. I would really appreciate your time. What will it cost?"

Janice chuckled. "Oh, Emily. It's free, hon. You just have to be willing to invest your time and your heart. To totally leave behind your old way of thinking and believe the truths of the Bible instead. So, there will be some reading material, Bible verses to memorize, concerted prayer time. Can you commit to that?"

"Absolutely." Emily knew she was undertaking something huge. But for the first time in a long time, she believed she might be on her way to true freedom, to gaining the joy she'd always dreamt of. And maybe, finally, to a lasting love.

I STILL HAVE YOUR SHOES. Emily texted Maria a week

later. It wasn't going to get any easier to contact Cole's sister-in-law, and it was wrong to hold onto them any longer.

Maria: WANNA MEET UP FOR DINNER TONIGHT?

Emily was surprised at the offer, given that things between her and Cole were still very much over. But true to her word, Maria was keeping Emily's relationship with Cole separate from their friendship.

Emily: SURE. WHEN AND WHERE?

Maria texted the time and place, and Emily was waiting for her in the lobby of the chosen restaurant several hours later. Handing her a box with her shoes in it, Maria grabbed it and reached over for a tight hug. "How are you doing?"

"I'm hanging in there. How are you? How's... how's Cole?" She wasn't sure why she even asked. She'd seen the haunted look in his eyes when he'd tried again to contact her at work the other day. It was a good thing she'd blocked his phone number so she didn't have proof of his pursuit. This was her time to focus on herself.

"I'm fine. And Cole? Well, he's been pretty mopey, to tell you the truth. I don't suppose you could get back together with him just to make Tim's life and mine easier, could you? Could you do that for us? Please?" Maria clasped her hands together and shook them in the air in a pleading motion.

Emily cracked a smile. "Maria, I... " She wasn't sure what to say.

"No, no. I'm teasing. C'mon, let's eat. Their Friday soup is clam chowder, and it's to die for."

A wave of relief washed over Emily. As the hostess walked them to a booth, Emily wondered if she should talk more about Cole or simply try to enjoy dinner out with a friend. She couldn't help but wonder if he was upset with her, even more than being sad about their break-up—she could hardly blame him, the way she left him with no real warning.

It's not like he had done anything wrong, either. In fact, there was nothing "bad" about their relationship at all. It was *she* who needed fixing. Did he understand that? Did he see how wounded her soul was from her past? She prayed he did but decided she would only talk about Cole again if Maria was the one to bring his name up.

After sitting down, they opened their menus. Maria was the first to speak. "Tim says hi, by the way."

"Thanks. How's his shoulder doing?"

"Oh, he's Tim. Meaning he milked it for a while, asked me to do things for him he could do all by himself. But he's fine now, on desk duty for the next few weeks. Do you know what you want to eat?"

"Yes. You?"

"Yeah. I had the longest day at work, and Tim's out with a friend, so I'm ready to eat something greasy and terrible for me and then regret it the rest of the night."

Emily laughed. No one could change subjects like Maria.

After the waitress took their order, Maria sipped her soda and leaned forward with her arms bent on the table. "So seriously, Cole's bummed without you. You really were a bright spot for him, and I'm sad for him that it's over."

Emily's eyes darted down, and she pretended to study her silverware. Her heart ached to hear he was still hurting. "I'm sad, too. And I'd like to think it's not over forever, but I need time to sort through my life. I told him from the start I wasn't in a healthy place, and it turns out I was even more accurate than I realized."

"I'm sorry to hear that, Em. Is there anything I can do?"

She shook her head. "No, not really. But I am taking steps to get better. Meeting with someone regularly." She didn't really want to get into the details of her arrangement with Janice, but at the same time, she wanted Maria to know she was being intentional with her sudden singleness—and that maybe, just maybe, there was still hope for reconciliation. Would Maria report any of this back to Cole? Did she secretly want him to wait for her?

"That's good. I would love to see you and Cole get back together. But I don't want to see him get hurt again. So, if you are bettering yourself, or whatever, just do me a favor and make sure it really fixes the root of the problem before jumping in again."

Emily felt as scolded as when Tim lashed out about her crazy theory. But she appreciated their blunt nature while still speaking the truth in love. Maria wasn't trying to hurt her—she was just being honest. And that was freeing, in a way. She'd already put Cole through enough drama, so she had no intentions of returning to him halfheartedly. "I understand. And I will."

Her friend smiled, shifting the tone of the

conversation. "So, what are your plans for the weekend?"

Maria's personality was a wonder, the way she moved from one topic to another, from serious to jovial, from mother hen to social butterfly, all the while not holding any grudges or being afraid to speak the hard truths.

They talked all through dinner until Emily decided she'd better head home. Though she didn't say so, she had verses to read and homework to complete.

# CHAPTER 36

IT WAS MID-AUGUST—THREE WEEKS SINCE their breakup—and Cole was trying his best not to think about Emily. He had loved her—really loved her. In fact, he *still* loved her. But all his attempts to text and call had been met with cold silence. And when he'd tried to visit her at work again, she'd promptly busied herself with something that pulled her away from him.

He'd even stopped by her house last Friday, in a futile attempt to change her mind, but she hadn't answered—whether she was gone or choosing to ignore him, he wasn't sure. But it was clear he was a thing of her past. And he didn't want to appear desperate or weak, so he decided he'd better take the hint and move on. He only wished he had a better understanding as to why.

Psalm 46:10 had become his life verse through all this, that was for sure. *Be still, and know that I am God; I will be exalted among the nations, I will be exalted in the earth.* He knew that God was in control, that he had to wait on Him and His timing. It didn't make his heartache any easier, but it did give him something to cling to. God would somehow redeem everything that had happened.

While hanging out with Tim and Maria the next night, his sister-in-law gave him a knowing look. "Hey, Cole, I had dinner with Emily last week." He jerked his head in her direction but tried to pretend like he didn't care. No matter—Maria was like a hound dog and couldn't miss his initial reaction.

She had to know her statement would hit a nerve, but he couldn't deny his morbid curiosity. "She feels really bad," Maria said. "But she has some issues to work through. She has too much junk from her past to be in a healthy relationship. I think she's really trying, though. If it's any consolation."

Cole shook his head and sighed. "What kind of issues? I already know about her dad and her husband. And I get those are really hard things, don't get me wrong. But why push away the one person who truly loves her, and helped her get through the nightmares she was having, and was there for her when no one else was? I don't understand shutting me out completely. It's like something snapped and suddenly she wants nothing to do with me." He closed his eyes. And he wanted nothing more than to be able to move on. But the words of his life verse came to mind. *Be still, and know that I am God.*

"I know. And I'm sorry it feels that way." Maria

touched his shoulder. "I wish I could explain it too, but I guess we have to trust she knows herself better than we do. And maybe once she gets through this hurdle, she'll end up right where she's supposed to be."

Cole's eyes narrowed at the word "trust." What Emily did felt like a betrayal. Even though he wanted her back more than anything in the world... how would he ever be able to trust her again? If they *did* end up back together, how would he know she wouldn't bail again when the going got tough? Did he trust God enough to take that leap again?

He excused himself and walked to the restroom, realizing he had to find a way to turn off the incessant thoughts about Emily. The possibility of her coming back to him was completely out of his control, and there was no use guessing how he would respond if she ever did so. The trust they'd shared had diminished when she left him for no good reason, but at the same time, the thought of a life without Emily made his heart ache almost more than he could bear.

While washing his hands, he caught a glimpse of himself in the mirror. Who was that haggard man staring back? He'd paid a steep price for caring for Emily, including a broken heart to go with the bags under his bloodshot eyes. But no matter the cost, he couldn't stop caring. If only she understood the depth of his love.

*I'm trying to be still, Lord, but I just wish I could do something. I'm not good at waiting.*

THROUGHOUT THE SIX WEEKS of counseling with Janice, Emily took her part very seriously. She didn't miss a single verse, a single meeting, or even a single prayer. The time with God did wonders, and she still marveled at the fact that she hadn't thought of immersing herself in His Word like that sooner.

Ever since the accident, and her subsequent turning to God, she had read the Bible here and there, prayed before meals and bedtime, attended church fairly regularly. But digging into His Word with a newfound fascination and hunger for the truths it contained changed her life.

Janice was a blessing as well. Her stern discipline was priceless, but her encouragement was what Emily needed most. It was the perfect combination for someone who knew in her head what she believed and trusted in her heart that God loved her, but who had failed to put those truths into action in her everyday life.

Throughout their time together, Emily was reminded that God's love and grace weren't conditional on her behavior, and He wasn't punishing her for her past sins. No amount of good deeds or random acts of kindness could make her more acceptable or more forgivable, and God wasn't interested in her vain attempts at working for His favor. In fact, if she could have earned His forgiveness on her own, there would have been no need for Jesus' sacrifice.

The more vulnerable Emily had been about the

issues she had struggled with for years, the more Janice armed her with applicable verses and concepts that made her guilt fade away. Janice understood Emily's issues were deep-seated, her feelings were valid, and her pain was real. But she also knew Emily's logic was flawed and her theology was off base—just like Tim had said. Janice had bombarded her with enough truth to combat the lies and as a result, the bondage of her past had fallen away.

On the morning after Labor Day, Emily walked into the church, proud of how far she had come.

Janice greeted her with a hug. "Last day, huh?"

Emily beamed. "It is. And I can't thank you enough. Here." She handed her a potted plant and a card, her meager attempt at thanking Janice for the crucial role she had played in her life. "It's the least I could do."

They spent their time together reviewing the things Emily had learned. Janice took the opportunity to encourage her as well. "You've been set free, Emily. Share that freedom and joy with others, and don't waste any more time dwelling on things you can't change."

A lump formed in Emily's throat upon hearing her mentor's wise words.

"You've made so much progress." Janice wrapped her in a friendly embrace. "I'm so proud of all you've accomplished in such a short period of time. I can tell you really wanted this, and you've truly surrendered your will to God. That's the only way this kind of evident change can occur. Do you believe it?"

"I believe *God* made it happen. But I can't believe I let Him." Tears welled in her eyes at her confession.

"Thank you so much for guiding me down this path. Before, I was so caught up in what I'd done, I failed to realize He was the only one who could put the pieces of my broken heart back together. But the weight of my past has finally been lifted."

She paused to wipe a tear falling down her cheek. "I think I'm ready."

"I think you are, too, dear."

Emily bit her lip and looked down. "I just hope I'm not too late."

That night, she had dinner with Maria, where she was able to admit she was in a better place now. "I'm finally seeing myself the way God sees me. The way Cole saw me. And I understand now why it was so frustrating to watch me spiral in the wrong direction."

Maria propped her elbow on the restaurant table and rested her head in her hand. "I'm so happy for you. Cole would be proud of you."

Emily chewed on her cheek. "And how's he doing? Cole, I mean."

Maria rolled her eyes. "He's still in a bit of a funk, believe it or not."

Using her fork to move the pasta around on her plate, Emily analyzed Maria's confession. "Do you think that means he'll be happy to have me back, or upset by how I treated him and refuse to forgive me because of it?" In her gut, Emily suspected it would be the latter, so she wasn't sure of the best approach to take in reconciling with him.

"Not sure. But the kind of love you guys had, and can have, is totally worth the possibility of rejection.

And he might reject you." Maria lifted one shoulder while tilting her head. "But I think at some point, when he realizes how you feel about him and why you did what you did, he'll come around. Especially if you let him know how much you've changed since then."

They finished eating and hugged before parting ways. What a wonderful friend she had in Maria. She didn't deserve the gift of her friendship—especially given how much she'd hurt her brother-in-law. But they still loved and supported each other. In fact, their relationship was a tangible example of God's grace. She hadn't earned it, didn't deserve it, but accepted it all the same. And she realized with some surprise, she had shown God's grace to kids like Tyler, too. The realization left a warm glow in her stomach.

At work on Wednesday, Emily pulled Nan aside in the break room the first chance she got. "You know how I told you I've been meeting with Janice?"

Nan poured herself a cup of coffee. "Yeah, how's that going?"

Emily's muscles tensed as she revealed her news. "I'm all done! And I'm ready, Nan. Ready to face the future with Cole, no matter what that means. I just hope he's open to talking to me and hearing me out. I have no idea how to approach him."

After blowing on her hot coffee, Nan put her arm on Emily's shoulder. "I've told you before, hon. Just be yourself. And don't find a reason to delay it. It's like pulling off a bandage—it might hurt, but once you expose your heart, you can finally finish the healing process."

Her coworker's logic was sound. If only it was really that simple. Although she believed Cole had sincerely loved her, she also knew how much she had hurt him, and she wasn't sure how accepting he would be of her waltzing back into his life unannounced. Especially since Cole had said he wasn't quick to forgive someone who betrayed him. Did he consider her unexplainable breakup and cold shoulder to be an act of betrayal?

"He would be a fool not to take you back." Nan removed her hand from her shoulder. "I'll be praying for you, Em. Let me know how it all works out, okay?"

Emily blinked and sucked in a deep breath, letting out pent-up stress as she exhaled. "Will do. And thanks for your support."

As Nan walked back to the nurse's station, Emily smiled at the woman's disposition. She hoped once she gathered up the courage and wisdom to approach Cole, she would be empowered to exhibit the same kind of positive attitude.

After work, Emily threw her purse on the kitchen table and saw the overflowing mound of papers on the nearby counter. She sighed. Did she have time to whittle it down? The microwave clock showed it was 6:30. If she tackled it now, she could celebrate with the pint of chocolate ice cream she'd bought the other day. Yeah, it was time to take on the task. The last six weeks were spent cleaning up her heart. The least she could do was devote an hour to cleaning up her kitchen.

As she shuffled through a stack of papers, a piece from the bottom of the pile slid off the counter to the floor. Bending down to pick it up, she noticed Cole's handwriting. When did that get there? Oh yeah, the night he'd given her the cake decorating classes. She'd tossed the note here to read later and had totally forgotten about it. How could she have let that happen? A wave of guilt washed over her for not having cherished his thoughtful note. He'd deserved better than her, but not for the reasons she once thought. No, her past didn't disqualify her for Cole's love, but her insecurities, her self-deprecation, her unwillingness to accept the gifts of grace and love—those had been her stumbling blocks.

It was time now. Time to read the words Cole had lovingly penned for her, even before he knew what a toll her past events would take on their relationship. She sent up a prayer as she unfolded the paper and saw the hand-written note.

*Dear Emily,*

*My heart broke when you shared your story with me, so I spent a couple of nights digging up truths I pray will help heal your wounds. I promise not to nag you to see if you've read through this, but I really hope you do. Because I want you to feel whole again, and I truly believe the only path to that kind of wholeness is through God—His Word and Truth.*

His note went on to list various Bible verses and some of his own commentary. She trailed her finger down the paper as she read his reminders of how God didn't hold grudges, how forgiving He was, how one couldn't earn His love or lose his favor by making mistakes, how God was in control and nothing people did could thwart His plans. Basically, he had listed all the verses and concepts Janice had covered in their six weeks together.

She closed her eyes as she processed the truth of those words. How callous of her for forgetting about his note—especially considering they were the exact words she had needed to hear to turn her life around.

Could reading it sooner have saved him the heartache she had caused, and the six weeks of pain and confusion they had both endured? Was it her fault? Was her disorganization to blame for his broken heart? No, she had to stop thinking that way. Her old self was gone, the new had come, thanks to God's work in her life.

She opened her eyes and continued reading.

*It breaks my heart to know your dad is still alive and you haven't spoken to him for years. I know the last time you tried, your aunt blocked the way and you don't know how to get a hold of him. But I'm willing to bet after all these years, he would be open to reuniting with his daughter. Especially with the way you've turned your life around.*

*I hope this wasn't out of line, but I tracked down your dad by finding your friend Shelly Olivette's family. They told me the cause of the fire, too. I want you to hear it for yourself, Em, but no pressure. When you're ready. That's why I'm telling you in writing instead of putting you on the spot in person. I support you no matter what. Your dad's contact information is below. I love you, Emily Jenkins. Past and all.*

Tears streamed down her cheeks. He'd tracked down her father? He knew the cause of the fire? Her breathing caught in her lungs and then whistled out with a half-sob. How many weeks had he carried this knowledge with him and kept it to himself? Because he assumed she'd read his letter—the free, life-giving gift he'd given her—and had chosen not to discuss it. Not to pursue it. Like she'd rejected all that he'd had to offer her. Just like she'd rejected what God was offering her all those years. What would she have said, what would she have done, if she'd read this while they were still dating? Would it have changed the way their relationship had ended?

Her mind spun as she stared at her father's alleged phone number and address. Was it true? After all these years, would she finally have a chance at reconciling with her father? She couldn't imagine feeling more whole than she'd finally managed to be, thanks to Janice pointing her to the Word. Would seeing her dad cause all that progress she'd made to come unraveled? No, she'd come so far already. She was standing firm on God's promises now. If anything, it might bring her even more closure—closure she never thought she'd have.

# CHAPTER 37

FOR THE FIRST TIME IN YEARS, Emily took a personal day on Thursday. She held in her hands the ability to get in touch with her dad after twelve years, and despite the immense pressure weighing on her as to what this might mean, she had to act and couldn't put it off for even one day. She wouldn't be able to eat until she knew the truth, and she couldn't try to reconcile with Cole without making an attempt to first reconcile with her father. Cole had gone to great lengths to provide that path for her, and it must have felt like a slap in the face that she hadn't taken advantage of his thoughtfulness.

So here she was, 9:00 in the morning on a road trip to her hometown of Olivette, where her dad had apparently been living ever since the fire. Just a couple miles from her childhood home. So, close all these years, and yet completely out of reach.

As she drove, the familiar fears crept in. Would her

aunt still be around and protective of her dad? Would he be open to seeing her? Would he be angry at her for staying out late that night, or for not coming back sooner after all was said and done? And what had started the fire in the first place? Cole's note said he knew. How could he have kept it from her after finding out? It was a lot to grasp, and she had to force herself to take deep, shaky breaths multiple times throughout the three-and-a-half-hour drive.

The sight of her highway exit made her choke back a wave of nostalgia. She hadn't been back to this place since she drove by the empty lot when she was nineteen. Eleven years was a long time to stay away. She swallowed the lump in her throat. It was now or never. No one was guaranteed tomorrow, a fact she knew all too well. If she was going to make things right with her dad, she had to do it today. Too bad her churning stomach didn't agree.

Once she was off the highway, she pulled over on a side street to punch the exact address into her phone's GPS, which proved hard to do given how much her fingers shook. Most people would not be this nervous to see their own father. And a part of her was thrilled at the chance to do just that. But knowing how things had ended—and even how they'd acted towards each other for years prior to the fire—Emily wasn't sure what to expect of their pending reunion.

Should she have called? She had thought about it, but in the end decided not to. She wanted to see his face when she revealed who she was; besides, it was easier to reject someone over the phone. Maybe seeing her face to face would increase his level of sympathy, if he would have any to begin with. If he hadn't changed since she last knew him, there was a very real possibility he would shut her out, slam the door in her face, and return to his six-pack of beer. She had to be prepared to deal with that kind of rejection. But if he had changed? She longed to apologize, to make things right. She prayed he would let her do just that.

Her hands clenched the steering wheel as she turned into her father's neighborhood. It was a quaint subdivision on the east side of Olivette, made up of small ranches and cape cods with tiny yards and no sidewalks. She slowed the car as she saw the number on a mailbox. There it was. She sat in the car with her seatbelt still fastened for a few minutes as she prayed, taking deep breaths in an attempt to calm her racing heartbeat. If she was still dating Cole, would he have offered to come with her? Would she have wanted the moral support? No sense in wondering that now. Here she was, alone, and she wasn't leaving until she at least knocked on the door.

At last, she unbuckled her seatbelt and opened the car door. As she walked up the driveway, she imagined what she might find on the other side of the front door. In only a few moments, she would find out.

The paint on the house was faded and crumbling but appeared to be in the same condition as the others on the block. Her insides tightened as she approached the front stoop. This was it. No turning back now.

A handwritten note advised that the doorbell was broken, so she raised her fist to knock on the door. She pounded out five firm, quick knocks, then shoved her hand into her pants pocket. Suddenly, she found herself hoping he wouldn't be home. But deep down, she knew she had to face him. And she wanted to—she *needed* to. She didn't come this far only to back out.

Just as she raised her fist to knock again, the front door opened and her breath caught. In an instant, a familiar face came into view. His hair was greyer, his appearance more worn down than she recalled, and the skin on his cheeks had obvious burn scars that almost made her wince when she thought of their source. But it was clearly him. Her father.

The flat, cordial expression on his face made her suspect that he didn't recognize her. It had been so long, why would he presume that his prodigal daughter had decided to return on this of all days? She resisted the urge to throw her arms around him. She had long since forgiven her father for the way he'd treated her as a teenager, but she had wondered if her old feelings of anger would resurface upon seeing his face. Her shoulders relaxed at the realization that the anger was gone for good. She sensed an immense need to apologize for her part in the tragedy he'd endured. Tears clung to her eyes, and before the small lump forming in her throat became big enough to restrict her from speaking, she finally managed to get a word out. "Dad?"

Her voice was thin, frail, much like her father's frame. The word caused something in her father's face to shift. For a moment, it appeared his knees had given out on him and he started to collapse in the doorway, but he quickly grabbed the side of the door to catch himself, regaining his composure. He brought a shaky hand to his mouth as his eyes glossed over. "Emily?"

Her heart leapt at his response to the crucial moment of recognition. If nothing else, she'd caught him off guard. But was that a good thing? Then, without warning, he reached over and wrapped his arms around her so tight it almost sucked the breath out of her. In all their years living in the same house together, they'd never hugged this way before. As they embraced, she felt her father's whole body shaking. The tears in her eyes rolled freely down her cheeks.

A moment later, he pulled away and a smile formed on his tear-stained face. Then he quickly took a step backward and looked at his surroundings. "C'mon in, dear. I have so much to tell you."

Her dad turned around and strolled slowly into the living room with his back to her. Emily bit her lip. The last time she'd tried to see her dad, her aunt had blocked the way and made it clear Emily was no longer welcome in their home, their family. Would her presence cause any problems? She took a tentative step into the entryway, then decided it was best to come out and ask. "Dad, is... is Aunt Nora here?"

Her dad turned back around and closed his eyes for a moment. "Your aunt passed last year. I wish I could have told you, but I had no idea how to get a hold of you. I tried a few times, but you must have changed your name."

Emily nodded, sad for her aunt's death but also grateful she wouldn't be facing her wrath and accusations—at least all signs pointed to her dad not holding a strong grudge. He cleared a stack of newspapers from the couch and put them in a pile in the corner. "Please. Sit." He took a seat on an armchair, and Emily sat on the end of the couch next to the chair.

Her dad sat on his hands and leaned forward. "So. Tell me what you've been up to all these years. And what brings you here after all this time?"

Emily sighed. Where to start? It was a miracle her dad was being so friendly, so receptive to her presence. How could she catch him up on the last twelve years of her life? "Well," she finally began. "I did change my name. I actually got married shortly after leaving town."

Her dad raised his eyebrows. "You're married? Am I a grandpa?"

Emily chuckled despite the seriousness of their conversation. "No, I'm afraid not. And I'm not married anymore, either. My husband died in a car accident seven years ago. Long story." One she knew made no sense to get into at the moment. "But after that, after all I suffered with the fire and the accident, I sort of gave up on love—romantic love anyway—and turned to God instead."

Her dad nodded, his brow furrowed. "I'm glad. I turned to God, too, sweetheart. He really helped me see the error of my ways. I owe you one heck of an apology." He lowered his head then, pinching the bridge of his nose with his thumb and forefinger before his whole body began shaking.

"Dad, I'm the one who needs to apologize. I'm the one who disobeyed curfew that night. I was awful to you. I know you were harsh, and you drank way too much. Things were rough all around, we both know that. But you didn't deserve that level of disrespect. And I want you to know I tried to make amends a lot sooner, but..." She didn't wish to speak ill of the dead, but he had to know. "Aunt Nora wouldn't have it. I came back to see you a year after the fire, but she pushed me away, told me to never come back. I shouldn't have listened, Dad, but I was so lost. Can you ever forgive me?"

He looked up and caught her gaze, tears streaming down his cheeks. "Oh, Em. I was never angry about that. It was my behavior that drove you away in the first place. I only have myself to blame. Besides, the fire..." His voice trailed off.

What had he been about to say? "What about the fire, Dad?"

He closed his eyes, letting out a tired sigh. When he opened them, his complexion seemed paler somehow. "I fell asleep, Em. My cigarette fell to the ground where my drink had spilled, which only helped the fire spread. It was all my fault. Losing our house, losing my dignity, nearly losing my life. And worst of all, losing *you*. My fault. All of it. And I've lived with that fact to this very day. I tried to contact you, but I was in rehab for a while, and by the time I was home and adjusted, you must have already changed your name." He closed his eyes again, lowering his head in shame.

Emily's breath caught in her throat. The guilt she'd born for the fire all these years was the exact same guilt her father had taken upon himself. And neither of them was justified in doing so. God allowed things to happen for a reason, she knew that now more than ever. And here she was, in the place to offer her dad the same grace she'd only recently learned to fully embrace herself. "Dad… I don't blame you. And I forgive you for how we treated each other back then. Please don't waste another minute feeling guilty. You can't live in the past. It'll only rob you of being used by God *today*."

He nodded as he stared at the floor. "I know. I finally came to that conclusion, turned my life around. But seeing you is making the memories flood back."

Emily squeezed her eyes shut. "I'm sorry."

"No, don't be. Your knock on my door is the best thing that has happened to me since the fire. Well, other than giving my life to Jesus. He saved me from the awful thing I'd let my life become, but now He's brought you back into my life and I couldn't be happier."

The sincerity of his voice made her open her eyes. She drank in the love and truth shining in his gaze. He leaned over, throwing his arms around her for another hug. She reciprocated, tears welling up once again.

"How did you finally find me?" he asked after pulling away from their embrace.

An image of Cole crossed her mind, and the hole in her heart rose to the surface. "Well, I finally met someone I felt safe enough to share my story with. And he… he found the Olivettes, I guess, who passed on your whereabouts. He wanted to help me heal, to move on."

He nodded. "Sounds like a keeper, that fellow. Will you tell him thank you for me?"

Emily's shoulders slumped. "I sort of messed things up with him. But I will pass on the message if he'll have me back."

"Oh, honey. Just be honest with him. If it's meant to be, he'll forgive you."

A hopeful smile sprang to her lips. For some strange reason, when her dad said it that way, the notion sounded within reach. "Thanks, Dad."

"No, thank you, dear. For the first time in years I feel like I finally have something to look forward to here on earth again. Emily, I love you. I always have, just didn't know how to show it before. But I'm so, so grateful you've given me another chance."

Emily wiped away a trail of tears from her cheek, realizing that while she wished she could take back every bad thing that had happened in her life, it had all ultimately led her here, to her dad's doorstep, as if part of a bigger plan. "Well, I'm the one who's thankful for second chances. And I love you too, Dad." It was the first time she could remember saying those words to him since her mom passed away. And it was wonderful.

# CHAPTER 38

O N FRIDAY, EMILY WAITED AS PATIENTLY as she could in her car, having put her intended plan into action. All of the confidence she'd had the past few days with Janice's inspiring words ringing in her ear, Nan's reassuring words of encouragement, Maria's gentle prodding—even her own father's support—was starting to dissipate at the thought of actually seeing Cole again.

She had thought about him on numerous occasions over the past six weeks, but physically seeing someone was a lot different than a mental image. Her palms began to sweat in anticipation of catching her first glimpse of him.

As she peered at the house, she thought back to the phone call she'd made the day before when she'd asked Barb if Cole still came to see Tyler on Fridays. She knew it was a long shot, but after Barb confirmed it, she hoped catching him with the very person who had ultimately brought them together in the first place might soften his heart and open him up to the idea of reconciliation. She was ready to commit wholeheartedly to their relationship at last. The big unknown was whether or not Cole still cared after all this time. She'd thought about texting him, but she'd deleted his number. Of course, Maria would have given it to her if she'd asked, but this was best done in person anyway.

Similar to what happened whenever she waited outside the hospital until an incoming ambulance arrived, Emily's heart beat a little faster upon seeing the front door of Tyler's house open. She got out of her car and walked to the front of it, leaning against the hood as she took calming, shaky breaths. Sure enough, the outline of a man appeared, and Emily could tell it was Cole.

He didn't see her at first, his eyes focused on his keyring to unlock his car. But he was parked right in front of Emily on the street, so there was no way he could miss her once he looked up.

When their eyes met from a distance, Cole's pace immediately slowed. His eyebrows pulled together, and he opened his mouth but then closed it again without uttering a sound. Emily didn't know what to make of his actions. She flashed him a smile, but he simply stared at her before stopping on the sidewalk a few feet from where she stood.

"Hi." It was a simple word to break the silence.

"Hi." Cole's voice didn't give a hint as to what he was thinking.

"I was, uh… I was hoping we could talk." Her voice

sounded nervous even to her own ears. She didn't like the uncertainty of not knowing where his head was at, but she was powering through in hopes that Maria, Nan, and Janice were all right about how this conversation would go.

Cole's eyes narrowed, confusion peeking through his otherwise guarded face. Emily knew without a doubt he was masking his hurt, and it killed her to know that as hard as this was for her, it was probably ten times worse for him.

It seemed like hours before Cole cleared his throat. His voice was strained and cold when he did finally speak. "I'm listening."

Emily lowered her eyes. "I'm sorry." Even as she said it, she realized how overused that word was, and how it didn't do justice to what she wanted to say. "For hurting you. For being such a mess when we were together. I thought I hid it well the first few weeks, but you have to understand, my state of mind was—" Just then, a loud dump truck drove by, breaking her concentration. "Do you think we could go somewhere else to talk? Somewhere more private?"

She wasn't expecting him to pause at the question. She had hoped it would be a no-brainer. A few moments later, without changing his expression one bit, he nodded and headed toward his car. "Follow me."

THEY ENTERED HIS FRONT door in silence, and Emily

knew by their lack of eye contact that she still had her work cut out for her. After sitting down on opposite sides of the living room, she finally spoke. "I'm ashamed to say I finally read this only two days ago." She pulled Cole's letter out of her purse and held it up for him to see.

Cole glanced her way, expressionless but nodding, as if giving her permission to continue.

"That was a bold move, tracking down my dad. I'm pretty surprised you did that."

Cole sat up straight. "I cared about you. I wanted you both to have a chance to make amends."

Emily nodded. But why had Cole used the past tense—he *cared* about her? Did he still care? "Well, thanks to you, we did. And it was incredible, for both of us. So, thank you." His cavalier attitude made her look down at the tear-blurred vision of his note in her hands. She gripped it tightly before finally looking up and taking a deep breath. "I want you to know I've been doing a lot of thinking and reading and praying these past six weeks. I've also been meeting with my pastor's wife for counseling. Twice a week, every week." It was humbling to admit, but she wanted him to know the full truth. It was the only way to make him realize she was serious about having changed—serious about being ready to move forward with him, if he would have her.

"I had a lot to work through, Cole. A *lot*." Her eyes widened for emphasis as she searched his face for a reaction that would give her hope as she laid her heart bare before him. "And it really helped. You should know that my ex, he... he said things to me. Lots of things. Stuff I never shared with you but things that made me doubt my worth like crazy. And I know that was years ago, and I know I should have been wise enough and mature enough to realize my worth comes from God and who He made me to be. But living through the things I have, with the constant demeaning influences I had, and then isolating myself from anyone who might speak truth into my life, well… I guess I let those seeds of doubt grow into something wild."

She paused, hoping that Cole would give her an indication as to whether anything she said was softening his heart. No such luck. He was listening, that she could tell, but his face remained stoic.

"I know I was being completely unfair to you. To us. And I don't expect you to give me another chance. I mean, I know I don't deserve that, and it would be a big risk for you to take, given my history. And given *your* history." She paused again, this time to pray for the courage to spit out the words she really came to say.

"But I wouldn't be able to leave here without telling you that I miss you. And that I still love you. And… I really want you back in my life, if you'll have me."

She quickly focused her gaze downward upon revealing that truth, her face growing warm, tears welling up in her eyes. "I just wanted you to know that." She choked on her words.

Not wanting him to see her cry, she covered her lowered face with her hands. She hadn't planned on being so emotional—she hadn't even been entirely sure what she was going to say until the words came spilling out. But sharing her feelings had drawn her pent-up emotions to the surface, and she couldn't stuff them down anymore.

The silence was hard to take. Glancing up, she noticed Cole seemed genuinely conflicted. Apparently unsure of how to respond, he looked away, quickly wiping a tear away from his own eye. She tried to remember if she had ever seen him cry before. The image was humbling.

Despite his display of emotion, it had been a good minute or two since any words had been spoken, and he was clearly not about to make a move. She wasn't sure if he would eventually say something the longer she stayed, but she realized with sad clarity she was quickly becoming an unwelcome guest in his home.

If he planned to take her back as a result of her plea, he would have said something by now. The next move was hers to make, so she stood. "Well, I guess I should go. I know we've been apart for as long as we were together in the first place, but I really need you to know that I still love you. And I'm not in the same place I was before. When I first told you I wasn't in the position to be in a healthy relationship? Well, for what it's worth, I don't think that's the case anymore."

Cole's expression still revealed nothing, so with that, she walked to the front door before turning to face him with one final plea.

"I know this is a lot to take in. So, after it sinks in, if you're interested, I'll… I'll be at the coffee shop by your work around 8:00 tonight. I'd love it if you met me there."

It was the same invitation she had received from

him months ago. She hadn't taken him up on the offer back then, but now that the roles were reversed, she prayed he wouldn't make the same decision she had that particular night.

"Goodbye, Cole." She closed the door behind her.

Once outside, Emily let the tears fall more freely. Her worst fear had been realized. The way her heartfelt testimony had been received couldn't have gone any worse. Did he really not have a soft spot for her somewhere in his heart? Might Maria have been wrong when she said that although Cole might initially reject her, he would come around after a while? She wasn't sure what to think, but she spent the car ride home praying for God to intervene like only He could.

# CHAPTER 39

A FTER EMILY LEFT, COLE LEANED BACK in his chair and let out a big sigh. It was hard to believe all that had transpired. He had almost done a double take when he first saw her outside of Tyler's house, so casually leaning against her car like it was no big deal to show up where she must have known he would be. And how had she known, anyway? Had she followed him? Did she have Maria somehow find out his schedule? The moment he'd realized it was her, a wave of conflicting emotions flooded his soul. His very first thought had been how much he wanted to wrap his arms around her. But his next thought had been to demand that she leave.

He had been a wreck these past several weeks, and he was finally starting to come to terms with the way things had ended and move on with his life. Realizing he had to carry on without Emily in the picture took a lot longer than it had taken to fall in love with her in the first place. Seeing her again, out of the blue, brought back quite the array of emotions.

Despite the short duration of their relationship, he had never been more confident about someone in his entire life. And to have had it end so abruptly, without warning, without reason, had been hard to take, to say the least.

And now she was finally coming to her senses? Talking to him like it was just another day? When she'd first started speaking to him outside Tyler's house, he had barely registered the meaning of her words, with how fast his mind was racing trying to make sense of the whole situation.

He still wasn't sure how he felt about her reappearance in his life—it almost felt like an intrusion. But at the same time, his heart had raced upon seeing her, and he had been curious to hear what she had to say. After only a moment's hesitation, he'd agreed, and everything she told him moments earlier in his living room had pierced his soul.

She'd said she was ready for a relationship now. That she'd spent the past six weeks improving herself, getting closer to God, being counseled on a regular basis. Could it be true? Was her past no longer holding her hostage? Had she really gotten over the issues that had caused her to leave him in the first place? Could he trust her, or would he be setting himself up to get hurt again, like he'd done so many times in the past with his other girlfriends?

The answers evaded him, but he prayed for clarity as he debated whether he should show up at the coffee shop that night. In his heart, he wanted nothing more than to reunite with the woman he loved. But his mind told him it wasn't wise to go down that road again. He truly didn't know which path to take. Why was it so hard to know the right thing to do?

EMILY ORDERED A FRAPPE to soothe the raw, aching feeling in her throat and sat on the black leather couch in the far corner of the coffee shop. It was almost 8:00, and her heart raced. She was under no illusion that Cole would show up, but she'd done what Nan had told her to do—she'd been herself, and the rest was up to God. Was her sudden reappearance too much for him to take in all at once, or had he already resolved not to give their relationship another chance?

As the seconds ticked by, Emily tried to distract herself from her view of the entrance door. It was like waiting for water to boil, except at least when boiling water, she knew the end result would eventually be realized. Here, there was no guarantee. She opened her Bible app and read various passages as she anxiously awaited her fate.

Even if he *did* show up, he may not be there to take her back. He could have finally decided he wanted to give her a piece of his mind or seek closure as to why she had left him in the first place. No, Cole showing up was only the first step. So, when she saw him walk through the door a few minutes later, she rose to her feet and tried not to get her hopes up. His eyes met hers, but his facial expression did not reveal his state of mind. He walked in her direction with an unhurried, steady pace and stopped a few feet in front of her.

"I'm glad you came. Would you like to sit?" She gestured toward the couch.

Nodding, Cole took a seat on the far-right cushion while Emily sunk into the opposite end. It was nerve wracking not knowing what his intentions were—should she say something? Or let him get the first word in?

Finally, after a few more moments of silence, Cole spoke. "Did you really mean everything you said at my house today?"

Her breathing was shaky, but she hoped he didn't notice. "I did. I'm really in a better place now, Cole. And it's due in large part to you. In case I never told you, I want to say thank you. For everything."

Cole nodded. "And you still... you still love me?"

Hope sprung to Emily's chest at Cole's question. "I do. With all my heart. I never meant to hurt you."

He stared at the floor, as if mustering up the courage to say what was on his mind. "Well, I still love you too, Emily. I tried to let you go, but I couldn't figure out how to stop loving someone as wonderful as you. I mean, this has been the longest six weeks of my life. But every time I tried to move on, God kept telling me to just wait and be still."

Emily let out a sigh of relief, then scooted closer to Cole on the couch. "I'm so glad He did. And that you listened." She placed her hand on his knee. "I promise to never again let something like this get in the way of what we have, if you'll take me back."

Cole turned to face her. He gently stroked her cheek and kept his hand on her face as he pressed his forehead against hers. With a sideways glance around the coffee shop to make sure there weren't customers staring, he stole a quick, soft kiss from her lips.

Emily could hardly believe what was happening, and she had a sudden urge to pinch herself. Instead, she let a smile creep to her face as she gazed into Cole's gorgeous eyes. "Is that a *yes*, you'll take me back?"

Cole's eyes and mouth were as serious as she'd seen them. "Without a doubt."

"That makes me so happy," she whispered.

He put his other hand on her other cheek. "*You* make me so happy. Do you want to get out of here?"

"Yes, please." She stood and reached for her melted frappe, holding it up to inspect its consistency. "Well, that was a waste."

"Let me see that." Cole took the cup in his hand and smiled. "No, trust me. This was worth every penny."

Back at Cole's house, they sat next to each other on the couch for several minutes, a comfortable silence allowing them to soak in the wonder of the evening. Emily laid her head on his shoulder, his cheek resting on the top of her hair. After enjoying the moment, a question sprang to Emily's mind. "Cole, why did you never tell me about your little brother?"

He raised his head, causing Emily to do the same. "Maria," she said, responding to the confusion in his eyes. "Will you tell me about him? I was so wrapped up in my own secrets and demons, I never even dreamed there was something you may be holding onto. I guess I'm not as selfless as you seemed to think, huh?"

"No, you are. You had no reason to think there was something I was hiding. I mean, it's not something I talk about a lot anyway. But as I got to know you, I guess I didn't tell you because I didn't want to minimize *your* pain or detract from your healing process. I mean, Roy's death was tragic and senseless, but I didn't have the guilt you did. So, if I brought him up to try to identify with what you were going through, I didn't want you to think I was making light of your experiences."

"Oh, Cole. I wouldn't have thought that. I'm so sorry I didn't leave room for your pain to be shared." She paused. "I'm listening now, though."

Cole kissed her forehead and smiled. "I was fifteen the summer Roy was killed. He was ten. He loved the local baseball team and the color royal blue, so we sometimes extended his name to call him Royal. He started to really play it up, wearing royal blue everywhere he went—he was even wearing his favorite blue jersey when the car hit him. He was on his way home from a friend's house one night. It was starting to get dark, and it wasn't a busy street, but… wrong place, wrong time, I guess."

"I'm so sorry. Did you find out who the driver was?"

"Yeah. He did some time in jail, but he's out now. He sought reconciliation with my parents several years ago, and they forgave him."

Cole paused, so Emily reached for his hand. "How

did that make you feel?"

He didn't immediately respond, but his face grew serious as he gazed down at their clasped hands. "It was hard, but the truth is we all make mistakes. And just like you had to learn to forgive yourself for what happened in your past before you could be set free, so to speak, we also had to forgive this man, y'know? Holding onto that anger, we were only hurting ourselves, and I know Roy wouldn't have wanted us to live our lives with so much bitterness in our hearts."

His story got Emily thinking. "So, I take it that's why Maria suggested I wear that royal blue dress to your awards banquet?"

A smile crept to Cole's face. "Yeah, I figured she had something to do with that. To me, it was like a silent tribute to my brother. Only you didn't know it."

Wiping a tear from her eye, Emily reached over and hugged Cole. "I love you," she whispered. "Thank you for taking me back."

"Thanks for *coming* back. But Emily, bad things are going to happen. That's part of—"

"I know," Emily interrupted. "And I promise to stick by you through it all. I see how wrong my thinking was now, and I know how fortunate I've been to find you. I promise I'm not letting go. No matter what."

Cole turned to look her in the eyes, the sincerity of his gaze causing warmth and love to permeate her body. "I'm glad. Because I'm not letting go either."

# EPILOGUE

A COOL NOVEMBER BREEZE BLEW THROUGH Emily's down jacket as she walked up Cole's front sidewalk. In her hands was a pumpkin spice cake decorated for fall. She'd spent a long time perfecting the golden leaves on the frosting, but the way it had turned out made it worth the investment.

She knocked on the front door, but hearing the commotion from inside, she decided to just walk right in. Scattered throughout the house were her dad, all of Cole's family, and several of their closest friends. This was the Thanksgiving gathering she'd always dreamed of as a kid. After greeting everyone in the living room, she made her way into the kitchen and placed her cake on the table.

Cole and his mom, Diane, were preparing dinner. He was in front of the stove turning the heat up on a pot of chopped potatoes. A memory of them making mashed potatoes at the Mission that summer came to her mind, and she smiled. "Hey, babe." She stepped on her tip toes to plant a kiss on his cheek.

Then she put her hand on Diane's shoulder, who was standing at the counter sprinkling paprika on top of a tray of deviled eggs. "Hi, Diane. I feel so bad that I had to work and couldn't be here to help with the meal." The ER nurses rotated holidays, and this year was her turn to work Thanksgiving.

Cole's mom stopped what she was doing and turned to give her a hug. "Oh, darling, it's no trouble. I love cooking for a crowd. And this is my favorite kind of cooking—a good old-fashioned feast with all the fixins."

At the word *fixins*, Emily jerked her head toward Cole. He caught her eye, and they exchanged smiles. Diane then cleared her throat. "Well, I'm going to leave you two alone for a bit." Her stare was deliberate as she walked by her son, as if she was telling him something with her eyes.

Once she was gone, Emily wrapped her arms around Cole and leaned into his chest. "Even though I had to work, this day is what I've always dreamed of. It's absolutely perfect, don't you think?" She couldn't imagine not spending the rest of her life with the man she loved.

"Oh, I don't know. I can think of one thing that would make it even better."

Emily raised her head from his chest, surprised by his words. "You can? What's that?"

Cole pulled away from her and reached into his pocket. Pulling out a small box, he dropped to one knee in the middle of his kitchen. He opened the box to reveal a gorgeous diamond ring. "What would make this the perfect day is if you agreed to spend the rest of your life with me. Emily Jenkins, will you marry me?"

Her jaw unhinged as she covered her open mouth with one hand. "I... I don't know what to say. I mean, of course! Yes! Yes, I'll marry you."

Cole stood, his face beaming as he slipped the ring on her finger. She exploded into his arms. She still couldn't believe he'd done it—convinced her to give love a chance, to move past her guilt, and to allow God's grace to change her. But he had. He had captured her heart, and now she had the rest of her life to show him that same kind of love in return. As far as she was concerned, their wedding day couldn't come soon enough.

# ABOUT THE AUTHOR

KATY EETEN is married to her husband, Jason, and they have two school-age boys. She lives with her family in southeast Wisconsin, despite her dislike of cold weather. She works full-time in the business world, but her true passion is writing. In addition to *A Heart Held Captive*, she is the author of Christian romances *Blast from Her Past* and *Christmas in Meadow Creek*. When she's not working or writing, she enjoys taking walks or bike rides, baking, and spending time with her family.

Learn more about Katy at her website—
https://katyeeten.wordpress.com/

Made in the USA
Columbia, SC
06 July 2020

12702456R00202